JUST KEEP BREATHING

A DI Benjamin Kidd Thriller

GS Rhodes

Dark Ship Crime

Copyright © 2021 GS Rhodes

All rights reserved

The characters and events portrayed in this book are fictitious. Any similarity to real persons, living or dead, is coincidental and not intended by the author.

No part of this book may be reproduced, or stored in a retrieval system, or transmitted in any form or by any means, electronic, mechanical, photocopying, recording, or otherwise, without express written permission of the publisher.

Published Worldwide by Dark Ship Crime

Cover design by Meg Jolly

Also by GS Rhodes

The DI Benjamin Kidd Thrillers

When You're Smiling

Just Keep Breathing

Your Best Shot (Coming Soon)

CHAPTER ONE

Sarah Harper's voice was hoarse from all the yelling, all the screaming. That's all her life seemed to have been for the past couple of days, a series of arguments with people that she thought were supposed to be on her side. All because of some stupid bloody pictures.

Well. A lot of stupid bloody pictures, come to think of it.

They'd all bought it though. They'd seen them fighting, seen them yelling at one another and crowded around like she'd expected them to. Some were filming it on their phones, others were taking pictures, they were all talking about her.

It was the only way to deal with it.

Her phone buzzed in her pocket. She took it out and couldn't help but smile at the message, before pocketing her phone and carrying on her walk.

She was avoiding going home. She knew

that once she got there, her mum would be all over her wanting to know if she was okay, maybe even wanting to get some shots in for her own Instagram account. There were days when Sarah wondered if her life was a fashion accessory to her mother's "brand."

She shuddered.

The fact that her mother had a brand.

She walked through Kingston town with her hands in her pockets, her jacket, the one Dexter let her borrow at the start of their relationship, wrapped tightly around her, her legs exposed to the elements in her school uniform, not knowing where exactly to turn. If only all those people who'd enjoyed watching her downfall at school could see her now, it would certainly give them something to laugh about. To laugh at.

Sarah Harper with the perfect life.

Sarah Harper with the perfect boyfriend.

Sarah Harper with the perfect grades.

Perfect everything.

They had no idea. Not really.

She caught her reflection in the front of the Bentall Centre, her blonde hair being blown about by the wind, her cheeks a little flushed from the cold. To an outside eye, her perfect life was in tatters around her and she had no one else to turn to. And that was true to an extent. There were maybe two people she could call at a time like this. But she knew she shouldn't.

Sarah took out her phone and took shelter beneath the awning outside the front of the shopping centre. The stark white lights from inside leaked out and made her squint a little.

She rounded her shoulders, not wanting to be seen. It was so unlike her. She started scrolling through her friends, former friends, not finding a single name she could click on, a single person she could message. They'd all turned on her, every last one and—

"Sarah?"

The voice pulled her focus to a face that she recognised, maybe from a past life. She couldn't remember the last time she'd heard that voice.

"Hi," she said.

"What are you doing out here? You must be freezing."

She swallowed. "I am," she said. "Just got nowhere left to go, do I?'

A raise of an eyebrow. The shake of a head. "We both know that's not true."

And they walked. They walked blissfully unaware, into the beginning of a nightmare.

CHAPTER TWO

For the past hour or so, DI Benjamin Kidd had not been a detective for the London Metropolitan Police, he hadn't been in charge of a team of four people tasked with bringing criminals to justice. The only things he'd been in charge of for the past hour were his niece and nephew. He was the storyteller, the climbing frame, the punching bag, you name it, he was it and he didn't mind at all.

"Alright, alright, it's bedtime!"

This elicited a groan from Tilly, the eldest, and just a series of babbles from Tim who didn't really know what was going on. But for Tilly, it was the voice of doom. Ben's sister, Liz, trudged into the living room, a tea towel slung over her shoulder. She looked at Kidd who was holding Tim, his six-month-old nephew, and three-year-old Tilly was hanging off his arm. "Thanks for watching them."

"Thanks for cooking dinner," Kidd replied

with a smirk. They were one of the shining points of his life. He loved coming around to see them and spending time with Liz. The kids loved him and he loved them. The best part being, when the night was over, he got to go home to a quiet house and not be disturbed by them at all hours of the night.

Between them, they put Tim and Tilly to bed, returning downstairs to find the house smelling so wonderful, Kidd's stomach growled involuntarily.

"Oh, sorry about that," he said. "Been a long day."

"You're not skipping meals are you?" Liz asked as she walked back to the kitchen.

"No, *Mum*, I'm not skipping meals," Kidd said. "Just been a busy time at work and when it's busy, I don't get the chance to breathe, let alone eat."

"Big case?" she asked.

"Not yet," he replied. There had been a lot of paperwork after the last case and he had a feeling that something else was around the corner. The scumbags of the world didn't like to give them a break if they could help it. Kidd had barely been back at work a month after being signed off with stress, and the case they'd brought him back to work, should have been enough to have him signed off all over again.

The Grinning Murders were a series of murders that had occurred fifteen years ago, when

Kidd had first stopped being a uniformed officer and become a DC. When a body like that had shown up on the borough again, Detective Chief Inspector Patrick Weaver had wasted no time bringing him back. The copycat had been nothing more than a poor imitation, but it was still enough to give Kidd and his team the runaround.

They'd gotten news of the conviction today, a life sentence for what Tony Warrington did to Jennifer Berry. It was the outcome that they'd hoped for but didn't dare expect. It wasn't every day that you got a good result like that, so they basked in the win, allowing themselves to relax for the afternoon. But it would only be a matter of time before something else came along, sending them all over town trying to track down some nutcase who was running riot. Whatever it was, he hoped it didn't come too soon.

"Anything juicy?" Liz asked, opening the oven to check on the roast. The smell that wafted out almost had Kidd clutching his stomach. It certainly had his mouth watering.

"You're killing me here, Liz," he said with a smile. "It smells great."

She turned to him and raised an eyebrow. "I take that to mean you're not telling me a damn thing."

Kidd sighed. "I'm trying to get better at not talking about work all the time," he said. "I got obsessed. I need to be less like that, for my own sanity."

"Plus, you have someone else to occupy your time now," she said, a knowing look in her eye. "Do I get to meet him properly anytime soon or do I just have to suffer you making goo-goo eyes at your phone whenever he messages you?"

She was talking about John. John McAdams. Kidd had met him at a bar about two weeks ago, and deciding that maybe he didn't want to be alone for the rest of his life, had tentatively dipped his toe into the dating pool. He was still getting over the disappearance of Craig Peyton nearly two years ago, so it was baby steps, but things were looking up.

"You'll meet him at some point," Kidd said, heading to the fridge. "You want a drink?"

"You really are dodging everything I throw at you tonight, aren't you?" Liz said with a laugh. "I'm zero for two."

"Try harder," Kidd said, pulling a bottle of wine and a bottle of cider out. He moved to the cupboard to get glasses.

"So, your school reunion is this week, isn't it?"

Kidd made an involuntary shudder. "It is. I'm…I'm thinking of skipping it."

Liz mock gasped, her hand flying to her chest. "No, you missing a social event, it couldn't possibly be true!" She rolled her eyes and walked over to the cupboard where the glasses were, pulling out three wine glasses and a pint glass for his cider. "You should go."

"Do I have to?"

"No," she said. "But you never go out."

"I go out," he protested. "Why do we keep having this conversation?"

"Because you don't go out," she retorted. "You go out with John, you sometimes go out with your team, but this is meant to be fun. You can go there and you can flaunt your DI status to all the people who bullied you at school."

"And they can ask me for free legal advice?" he offered. "Or they won't tell me anything because they'll think I'm going to cuff them there and then."

"Kinky."

"LIZ!"

"I'm kidding," she groaned. "Stop being so dry all the time."

She lifted the lid off the veggies that were bubbling away on the stove, giving them a quick stab with a knife to check if they were done. She opened her mouth to speak again, probably to start another onslaught of harassment about him going out, when the doorbell rang.

"Saved by the bell," he said with a waggle of his eyebrows. "I'll get it."

He headed out of the kitchen and down the hall, opening the door to see DS Zoe Sanchez on the porch looking like a walking icicle. The breeze that came in with her drove its way right down into Kidd's bones. It really was fresh tonight.

She looked up at him and smiled. She'd let down her brown curls that she usually kept away from her face during the workday and had changed from her work get up into a pair of jeans and a sheer, black blouse. She'd even put on a little bit of makeup for the occasion.

"You look nice," Kidd said with a smile.

DS Sanchez's brow furrowed. "Implying that I don't usually?" she asked.

"Ha ha." Kidd rolled his eyes. "Come on in, I'm sorting drinks. Wine or cider?"

"Cider for me," she said, shrugging off her jacket and hanging it on the hooks by the door. "Sorry it took so long to get here. Got caught talking to Owen on my way out."

"Christ, poor thing," Kidd replied.

"He started talking about the case, the conviction and such, and then about going for a drink." Zoe walked into the kitchen. Her face brightened when she saw Liz. "Liz, you're looking well. It's been ages."

"Way too long!" Liz replied, hurrying over to wrap Zoe in a hug. She pulled out of the hug. "Okay, don't mind me, I'm just about to dish up, you guys keep talking."

"What did you say?" Kidd asked.

"I told him I was coming here, and he said maybe some other time, and then I left because it was so awkward!" She opened her bottle of cider and poured it into the glass. "Do I want to be dating someone? Probably. Do I want it to be Owen Campbell? Absolutely not!"

"What's wrong with DC Campbell?" Liz asked. It was a question that only someone who didn't work with DC Campbell would ask.

"He's just..."

"He's DC Campbell," Zoe finished. "But we're talking about work and that's boring. What were you talking about before I got here?"

Liz eyed Zoe gleefully, knowing that she would have someone on her side in this and Kidd felt his stomach drop.

"I'm trying to convince Ben to go to his school reunion this week," Liz said. "He's saying he doesn't want to go but not giving a real reason, so..." Liz shrugged and gestured to the two of them. "Discuss." She went back to serving up dinner, Kidd sending daggers into the back of her head.

"Come on then," Zoe said, turning back to him, taking a victorious sip of her cider before she carried on speaking. "What's the reason you're not going?"

"I...I don't have the best memories of that school," Kidd said. "I think, as a night, it will be dull and I don't really want to use up a whole evening that I could be spending with Liz or you or John, hanging out with a bunch of people from my high school that I don't even talk to anymore."

Zoe eyed him carefully, seeming to process this for a moment. She eventually shrugged. "That's actually a pretty fair reason," she said. "All I'm saying, though, is that it could be fun. You could go with John, make an evening of it, just show off your life a little bit and go home. It might not be all that bad."

The phone started ringing, a shrill chime that seemed to rip through the whole kitchen. Liz called out an apology and said that she'd get it. Zoe's laser focus was still on Kidd.

"Thoughts?"

Kidd shrugged. "I don't know, that's not a bad idea."

"Really?"

"It might not be horrible if I go with someone," he said. "I mean, honestly, the worst part about going would be that I would be there by myself and it would be a terrible throwback to being fourteen and so awkward."

"What's the difference now?" Zoe said with a laugh.

"The difference now is that I'm awkward, but have a badge and a duty to pretend that I'm not."

Zoe lifted her glass to cheers him. "I will drink to that."

"To what?" Kidd asked. "Faking our way through our careers?"

Zoe nodded. "Exactly that."

They clinked their glasses together, the

two of them taking long gulps from their drinks. Kidd had been working with Zoe for the past ten years or so. They'd been put on a team together and they just happened to click. Zoe didn't take any nonsense from anybody, and that included Kidd. Even though he was technically her boss, it didn't feel like that half the time. She'd put it best when he'd come back from leave a couple of weeks ago—they were friends first, colleagues second.

Liz reappeared in the kitchen, clutching the phone in her hand. She looked like she'd had the wind knocked out of her sails. Kidd's mind immediately went to the worst-case scenario, wondering who it could have been on the phone.

"That was Greg," Liz said. She looked up at them. She didn't have tears in her eyes, so maybe it wasn't all that bad, but she still looked pretty hurt by whatever had been said. "He's not coming home for dinner, apparently something at work came up."

Kidd let out a heavy breath. He'd expected worse than that.

"No problem," Kidd said. "We can save some food for him, it will be fine."

"Yeah," she said. "Sorry, we just argued about it. I've barely seen him for the past couple of weeks. Miss my husband, you know?"

Zoe put her glass down and hurried over to Liz, wrapping her in a hug. Kidd followed suit and did the same. He hated seeing his sister hurting. Greg was a good guy most of the time, Kidd didn't want to think the worst of him, but he certainly didn't want anyone making his sister feel like that.

Liz pulled herself out of the hug and took a deep breath.

"Okay," she said. "Wow, didn't expect to be almost crying tonight." She shook herself a little, fixing the smile back onto her face. "He's just working a lot, and it's obviously getting to me more than I thought. Whew. Okay. Let's get to the table or this is going to go cold. Ben, you want to grab the wine?"

Zoe took Liz into the dining room while Kidd headed back to the kitchen and grabbed the bottle of wine. He was unable to shake the feeling that something wasn't quite right. He shook it from his head, sure that he was overthinking it.

CHAPTER THREE

Dinner was delicious. Once they'd sat down and started eating, it was as if the conversation Liz had with Greg never happened, something Kidd was certainly glad about. He didn't like seeing his younger sister upset.

They worked their way through the roast talking about the school reunion still. Kidd decided somewhere along the way that he would ask John if he wanted to go with him. Maybe it would be fun. But at least if it wasn't, he would be able to get out of there pretty swiftly.

They worked their way through the rest of the meal, Kidd and Zoe clearing up while Liz checked on the kids, the three of them drinking coffee and chatting until Liz could barely keep her eyes open.

"I'm sorry," she said through a yawn. "It's barely nine o'clock and I'm yawning like I've pulled a full shift."

"You have pulled a full shift," Kidd said.

"Those kids are a handful."

"You're not wrong," Liz replied, downing the last of her coffee.

There was a sound from the front door, all three of them freezing and turning in the direction of the hallway. Someone struggled to get their keys in the door and then quickly opened it, shivering as they stepped inside. Greg was home.

They heard him kick his shoes off and head down the corridor towards the kitchen. When he turned into the dining room and saw them all sitting there, his face dropped a little. He'd obviously forgotten that tonight was happening, and Liz had decided not to remind him about it over the phone.

Greg was a fine-looking man, tall, broad-shouldered, his dark hair cropped close to his head, a little stubble around his jawline. He was in a shirt and a pair of smart trousers, his collar open, his tie hanging out of his pocket. Kidd knew that look. Someone who had been on shift all day and it had been so hard and tiring that you find yourself half undressed before you've even made it to the car. He looked absolutely beat. But there was something else, something in his face that Kidd couldn't quite place...

"Evening," he said, his voice a little gruff. "I didn't know we had company tonight."

"We planned it a couple of weeks ago," Liz said quietly. "Remember? Just a little dinner party with Ben and Zoe, this is Zoe, DS Sanchez, they work together in the Met."

Zoe said her hellos, Kidd waved from where he was sitting. You couldn't cut the tension in the room with a knife, you'd need something a heck of a lot sharper. A saw perhaps. Liz wasn't happy, that much Kidd could see and he didn't want to get in the way of anything.

"Well," Kidd said, standing from the table. "It's getting late."

"Yeah," Zoe said, quickly following his lead. "We've got to be in the office early tomorrow. Thanks so much for dinner, Liz."

Liz looked up and plastered a smile on her face, but Kidd could tell that she was playing the happy housewife. That Greg coming home had put a damper on what had been a very lovely evening.

"Thank you so much for coming," she said. "We'll have to do it again sometime."

They said their goodbyes, Kidd promising that he'd be in touch with Liz later on in the week to check-in, Zoe promising they won't leave it so long next time, and then they were out in the cold.

Kidd wrapped his coat around himself, shoving his hands deep into the pockets. It was glacial. It was February, and it felt like this winter had gone on forever. If there was one thing Benjamin Kidd hated, it was the cold.

"That was uncomfortable," Zoe said as

they walked towards her car. "Very uncomfortable."

Kidd nodded. "They're obviously going through some stuff," he said. "I think we did the right thing by getting out of there."

"I'll say," Zoe said. "So, I didn't get a chance to ask, we managed to avoid the topic for the whole of dinner. How are things with you and John?"

"Me and John?"

"Yes, Ben, you and John," Zoe said. "Don't repeat things back at me to save time. What the heck is that?"

Kidd laughed as they walked. "Things are good," he said. "It's early days and we're not about to go booking a venue, but it's nice. I'm happy." He checked his phone. "He was at the Druid's Head tonight with some friends. I might see if he's still around."

Zoe widened her eyes at him. "Detective Inspector Benjamin Kidd staying out late on a school night," she said. "People will talk."

"And I expect you to shut them up."

"Sure thing, boss," she said with a wink. "It's good to see you happy and before you say that you were happy before." She'd obviously seen Kidd opening his mouth to retort. "I know you were, but now I'm seeing you happier and it's nice."

"Thanks," Kidd said.

He walked Zoe to her car, bidding her

goodnight before he started walking towards the middle of town and the Druid's Head, the usual haunt for the team at Kingston Police Station. He wouldn't stay for long, maybe stopping for one before heading home. He didn't want to get in the way of John's night.

He got there in pretty good time, making his way to the front door to see John was stood in the window, laughing with a few of his friends. He was wearing a blue checked shirt, his hair, usually in a perfectly placed quiff had fallen a little bit forward, but he brushed it out of his face, still grinning at whatever had just been said.

He looked like he was having a good time. A good enough time that Ben decided that maybe he would leave it for tonight and talk to him tomorrow. That was, until John saw him through the window. He smiled and beckoned Kidd inside. He shook his head.

John made his way outside, not bothering to grab his jacket so the second he stepped into the cold, his hands made their way under his armpits for warmth. He tottered over to Kidd, all smiles, eyes sparkling even though it was dark. How did he do that?

"I was hoping I'd see you," John said, still smiling.

"Were you?" Kidd replied. "That's…that's nice. I'm glad I came then."

"Are you coming in? As much as I'm enjoying standing out here talking to you, I'm freezing," he said. "You can meet the gang if you want?"

"The gang?" Kidd replied. "You sure you're ready for me to meet the gang."

John shrugged. "If you want to."

Kidd smiled and looked back at the window at the people who were now staring out at him, the guy who'd dragged their friend away. He instantly felt guilty.

"I actually came to invite you out tomorrow night," Kidd said, stuffing his fingers down into his pockets, trying to ignore the sweat on his palms. "I've got a school reunion that I don't want to go to, and I thought maybe we could go together. Well, it was DS Sanchez's suggestion, she thought…" he trailed off. "And I agreed that…" He shook his head. "Do you want to come?"

John was still smiling. He looked like a slightly more frozen version of the John McAdams that Kidd was enjoying getting to know, but he still looked incredibly handsome when he smiled. And that smile was all for Ben.

"Sure thing," he replied. "Lunch *and* an embarrassingly cringe school reunion, I am blessed."

"You don't have to if you don't—"

"I'm coming," he said. "Now are you coming back inside with me?"

Kidd looked around John again, the people in the window quickly readjusting themselves to go back to whatever it was they were now fake-talking about. He tried not to laugh.

"I'll leave you to it," Kidd said. "I'll see you tomorrow for lunch, yeah?"

"I'm working from home so I can take lunch pretty much whenever," John replied. "So just let me know."

They stood there for a few seconds, a strange amount of distance between them that John eventually closed, planting a kiss on Ben's cheek.

"See you tomorrow," he said quietly before turning back to the Druid's and walking inside.

Not wanting to see the reaction of his friends when John made it back to the table, DI Benjamin Kidd quickly walked away, starting back towards his house.

He made his way out of Kingston's Market Square, taking a shortcut down to the riverside. It was the long way around to get home, sure, but he wanted the walk to take in the night. It may have been glacial, but this was his favourite spot in the whole town, and even though there were the sounds of restaurants in the background, happy couples walking by, groups of friends heading out for drinks, he liked it here.

His phone buzzed in his pocket and he took it out, seeing he had a couple of missed calls from DCI Weaver and a message from John. He went to that first.

JOHN: Hope you had a lovely evening, was nice to see you, however briefly. I'm looking forward to lunch tomorrow. And the reunion. Xx

KIDD: Nice to see you too. One o'clock suit you? Xx

The message came back through almost immediately, which made Kidd smile.

JOHN: Perfect. I'll see you then. Sleep tight. Xx

You too xx

Kidd found himself hesitating before listening to the messages from DCI Weaver. He was off duty now. He was trying to get better at the whole work-life balance thing, learning to switch off so he didn't end up staying up half the night thinking about it.

He'd been terrible at that before he ended up getting signed off with stress. But Weaver wouldn't call unless it was urgent. It was almost like a change in the air around him. Something had happened, and he'd called Kidd because why? Because he needed someone to talk it over with? If he listened, he knew he wouldn't sleep tonight.

Before he could stop himself, he moved to switch off his phone when another message came through. One from a name he hadn't seen in a very long time.

    Andrea Peyton.

CHAPTER FOUR

*H*ello Ben,

Long time no speak. I'm sorry it took me such a long time to get back to you. I wasn't entirely sure what to say. The topic of Craig in our family is still a bit of a sore subject but you asking about him brought it all back.

Kidd's heart was in his mouth as he read it, every word running through his head at a hundred miles an hour.

I hope you're doing well. I know things must have been really difficult for you over the past two years as well. The family hasn't had an easy time of it. I think a lot of them, my parents included, have just found it easier to assume that Craig is dead and won't be coming back. I prefer not to think that way. I want my brother to still be out there.

Kidd practically ran the rest of the way home. He wasn't able to message back as clearly as he had wanted to, his thumbs absolutely frozen so he couldn't get the words down.

I want to know where he is too. More than anything in the world but I'm afraid with me you're a little bit out of luck. I've kept looking when I can, but I keep coming up with dead ends no matter how hard I try.

I thought I was getting somewhere not too long ago, someone on a forum somewhere claimed to have seen him when I posted his picture but it all came to nothing. Someone was even using his old photos from Facebook on a dating app, can you believe it? Why do people do that?

He could barely get his keys in the door, his hands trembling as he tried to get them in the lock. When he managed it, he swung the door open with such force it crashed into the wall of the landing. He'd end up with a dent there, but he didn't care.

He locked the door behind him, kicking off his shoes, and barrelling upstairs. He turned on his laptop and opened up his messages, reading it all through one last time.

But I do have one thing that I can share with you. It's not a lot, and it might not be right, but it might help. I think it will. If nothing else, it will give you hope.

All love,

Andrea x

Kidd scrolled down to the bottom of the message, to the attachment that Andrea had attached to the message. He opened it up and there it was as clear as day. Well, not nearly as clear as he would have liked but he would recognise that person in a crowd of thousands. He was so sure it was him.

Craig Peyton was on a train station platform. It looked like Waterloo, but it could have been any of the London terminals. He couldn't quite place it. But he was there on the platform.

He looked down at the date of the CCTV. It was dated just shy of a year ago.

Kidd sat back on the bed and stared off into the distance, his breath catching in his chest.

He looked at the picture again, trying to make out details, features, anything that might give the person away as being Craig but it was so blurry. But it had to be him, hadn't it? His sister had sent the picture over, so she must have thought the same.

Craig Peyton was alive.
Maybe.
Possibly.
He had to be.

He looked at the picture again, very quickly losing his resolve. It could be anyone. He could feel the disappointment filling his chest like a balloon. For a moment, it had felt so certain. At first glance he was sure it was him and maybe it was, but he couldn't be sure.

He opened a reply to Andrea.

Dear Andrea,

Thank you so much for getting in touch I'm—

Kidd's phone started ringing and he answered it without looking.

"Hello?"

"Kidd!" DCI Weaver barked, his Scottish accent coming through hard enough to make Kidd nearly jump out of his skin.

Shit, he thought. *I should have checked who was calling first.*

"Yes, boss?" he replied, running a hand through his hair. How could he have been so stupid?

"I've been trying to get you all night, where have you been?"

"I was having dinner at my sister's tonight," Kidd replied. He could see his boss's face in his mind, the brick of a man breathing heavy, absolutely panting about it. "Is something the matter?"

"You could say that," DCI Weaver said.

"Have you checked my messages?

"No, sir," Kidd said. "I was going to check them in the morning, or when I got to work perhaps."

Kidd could hear DCI Weaver nodding down the phone. He was pacing, he could hear the swishing of whatever material he was wearing. He took a heavy breath, distorting the receiver.

"Well, I'll talk to you about it tomorrow then," DCI Weaver said.

DI Kidd stood up, joining DCI Weaver in pacing. "Sir, you've got me now, tell me what's going on."

DCI Weaver let out a heavy sigh again. Whatever it was, there was no way that it could be worse than dealing with *The Grinning Murders* again. At least that's what DI Kidd told himself. It couldn't be, could it?

CHAPTER FIVE

Kingston Police Station looked ominous that morning. Clouds were circling overhead, and Kidd didn't want to walk inside, knowing exactly what it was that awaited him. It might not have felt as bad as The Grinning Murders, though when it came to crime there wasn't really a sliding scale, but this time someone's life was on the line. And having that weighing on your conscience is always quite a cross to bear.

After talking to DCI Weaver, Ben had finished his message to Andrea before trying to get some shut-eye. It hadn't come easy. His brain had been awake, already trying to figure out what he needed to do the following morning to get a jump on this. He'd even tried running that morning, down through town, along the riverside, attempting to clear his head as he pounded the pavement but it didn't happen. There were two images in his head. Craig Peyton and the girl who had gone missing.

"Good morning, DI Kidd," Diane chirped from behind the front desk. Her eyes twinkled at him as she smiled, her dark hair pulled into a tight bun, everything about her welcoming him as she had done for pretty much every day of his career, an endlessly joyful human who was always there to help anybody in their time of need. "How was your evening?"

Kidd laughed a little. "Something of a rollercoaster," he said. "Never a dull moment. How about you?"

"Fine, fine, fine," she said. "Nothing out of the ordinary!"

"Ha!" Kidd barked. "Diane, you're making me jealous."

"Hardly, dear!"

"Oh, Diane, I would kill for a bit of ordinary," Kidd said.

She tutted at him and shook her head. "You wouldn't have a clue what to do with yourself."

Kidd buzzed himself through the door and started down the same maze of familiar corridors he'd walked for most of his life. When he stepped inside the Incident Room, he was quickly greeted by three pairs of eyes before they switched back to what they'd been doing when he'd entered.

DC Simon Powell was sitting on DC Janya Ravel's desk, the two of them talking animatedly about something as Kidd approached. DC Powell was a child, at least as far as Kidd was concerned, fair-skinned, fair-haired, and a little chubby. He was also sinfully clumsy and Kidd was counting down the days before it cost them something in a case. DC Ravel was quite the opposite of Powell. She was self-assured, pretty straight-laced, and knew exactly what she was doing most of the time, which made Kidd's life a heck of a lot easier.

"Morning,"

"Morning, boss," they chorused.

"We've got a case, I want you ready for briefing in—" He looked at the two of them, quickly realising he was missing something. "Where's DC Campbell?"

"Out, sir," DC Ravel said. "Went to get breakfast."

"Christ," Kidd replied. "Do you know when he'll be back?"

DC Ravel checked her watch. "Shouldn't be too long, sir, but you know what he's like."

Ben knew exactly what he was like, so he left them to it. He would brief them when he got back. Apart from this, Weaver wasn't there yet with the information. So long as Campbell was back in time, he might save himself a bollocking from the boss.

DS Sanchez was at her chaotic desk, papers piled up left and right, enough coffee cups to cover half of Brighton Beach. She nodded at Kidd as he walked past, but something in him caught her eye that morning, maybe it was the expression on his face, or the bags weighing heavily under his eyes. Whatever it was, it made her rise from her desk and follow Kidd over to his.

"What's up?" she asked, concern spreading across her face. "What the hell happened after I left you? You didn't get beaten up by some thug again, did you?"

"No, nothing like that," Kidd said sitting down in his chair and leaning back.

"Then what?" Zoe asked, entirely puzzled. She pulled the chair over from her own desk and sat down. "Come on, you're killing me here."

He didn't know where to start. He didn't know whether to brief her on the case or tell her about what Andrea had sent him last night. Given how things had been going with John, he didn't know how impressed she would be with him dredging up the past. But he hadn't expected Andrea to be in touch. It had been over a month since he'd messaged her after all.

"I—" But Kidd didn't get a chance to finish, the door to the Incident Room flew open and DCI Weaver barrelled in like a charging bull. The door crashed against the desk behind the door and all eyes suddenly moved to him, a well-built man in a pristine blue suit, his temper as fiery red as his hair. He looked around at each of them, probably trying to land on DI Kidd. When they did, he pointed a meaty finger at him.

"You ready?"

Kidd got to his feet. "Not briefed them yet, sir," he said. "Was waiting for Campbell, and yourself, of course, to show up."

"Fine, fine, fine," Weaver grumbled, looking around the room again. "And where is Campbell?"

"Went to get breakfast," DC Powell said through a mouthful of croissant. "Think he was heading to Pret, sir, he shouldn't long."

"He should already be here," DCI Weaver growled.

"No harm starting without him, sir," DI Kidd said. "He's a few steps behind the rest of us at the best of times, might as well start as we mean to go on."

DCI Weaver clearly didn't know whether DI Kidd was joking or not, his mouth twitching at the corners like he was unsure whether or not to smile, laugh, or verbally smack Kidd in the face. He shook it off and turned to address the whole room.

"I had a case file land on my desk last night," he said, holding a thin, yellowing folder in his beefy hand. "It's a bit of a doozy and requires your full attention immediately. I briefed DI Kidd last night, but there have been more details since, so gather around please."

They did as they were told, following DCI Weaver to the front of the room and the empty Evidence Board. They perched on the edges of desks, sat on wayward chairs, their eyes fixed on him as he addressed them like a general would his troops.

"We have a teenage girl missing on the borough," he said.

"Oh," DC Powell said, involuntarily because he quickly clapped a hand over his mouth. "Sorry, sir."

"Oh?" Weaver asked. "What do you mean oh?"

"Nothing, sir, I just thought it was going to be more…serious…" DC Powell looked like he wanted the ground to swallow him up. Kidd wanted it to as well.

"Well," Weaver said through gritted teeth, his face getting redder by the second. "It might not sound like a lot, but the parents are known in the community, Dad works for a local building firm, lots of houses around the place, Mum is some kind of Instagram influencer, something to do with cleaning I think."

"Cleaning?" DS Sanchez echoed, incredulous. "Really?"

Weaver waved the folder. "I've got pictures of her feed to prove it. It's…harrowing," he said. "They post everything about their lives online, and that includes the disappearance of their daughter Sarah Harper. She went missing four days ago, no one has seen her, no one has heard from her, apparently her phone has been switched off all this time so the parents are losing their minds. Understandably, of course, but it means they're breathing down my neck and so are a lot of their followers."

"How do you mean, sir?" DC Ravel asked.

"Social media," he said. "It's a scourge on our society, means everyone is in everyone's business. So we've got all of their followers bombarding Twitter and Facebook with posts wanting to know where she is, wondering why we haven't done anything yet."

"And why haven't we?" Simon asked.

Big mistake. Weaver rounded on him.

Has he been taking notes from Campbell? Jesus, Kidd thought.

"They reported her missing yesterday," Weaver snapped. "She has a boyfriend, they thought she might have been staying with him, an awful lot of friends that she could have been staying with too, so when she didn't show up all weekend, they just assumed she was with them."

"Hardly seems responsible," DS Sanchez remarked.

"I did think that," Weaver said. "But they obviously trust her enough to go off and do her own thing most of the time, give her that freedom. Just so happens that this time it's backfired majorly, because they can't get a hold of her. No one can. Her phone is off and everything."

He handed the folder to DI Kidd, who took it gingerly and opened it up, looking at the photographs of Sarah. She was sixteen years old, blonde, beautiful, filtered to high heaven in the selfies that they'd tracked down of her. She had a lot of friends too, or at least the pictures made it seem that way. She was popular. Perfect. That didn't sit right. Kidd feared the worst.

"She didn't show up to school on Monday and the school rang her mum to find out what was going on," Weaver said. "She had no idea where she was and started ringing around the parents of the friends, of the boyfriend, and they hadn't seen her since the previous week."

"Jesus Christ," Kidd muttered, looking through more of the pictures. There were more photos of her with friends, a lot of friends. All of them looked somewhat similar, striking the same poses, faces fully made up, fingers in a peace sign, legs bent. Not one of them had any contact with her? He found it hard to believe that she'd just disappeared off the face of the earth.

"There are a lot of people looking at us for this one," Weaver said. "She's high profile. Media is already breathing down our necks and want a press conference arranged ASAP. Superintendent Charles wants one as soon as this afternoon, if we can manage it."

"This afternoon?" Kidd echoed. "That's not enough time. What will we have to say? They'll gut us."

"We'll tell them we're looking into it, hope it calms down the crazies gunning for us online." Weaver sighed, running a hand over his face. "You on this, Kidd?"

"Yes, boss," Kidd replied, turning to his team. "We need to set up a timeline. Find out who last saw her and when, try and figure out where she could have gone. I assume we've got a trace on the phone? If it gets switched on, I want to know about it. We'll check CCTV around the school, check social media profiles, all that." He turned to DC Powell, handing him the folder. "Pop these on the board, would you DC Powell?"

"Sure thing, sir," he said, getting up from his seat and immediately tripping over his own feet. The folder spilled out across the floor, photographs, documents, the small amount of evidence that had been handed to DCI Weaver late last night.

DI Kidd looked at his boss, who was currently in the process of rolling his eyes at DC Powell for his clumsiness. He looked tired. He probably hadn't slept. DI Kidd could relate.

He got down and started picking up the wayward photographs with DC Powell, whose face was burning red, muttering to himself about being stupid. DI Kidd cursed himself for thinking it.

"You're alright, Simon," he said quietly. "Easy now."

DC Powell looked over at him and smiled. "Thank you, sir. Sorry, sir."

"It's fine, it—"

But something caught Kidd's eye, something that made him stop dead in his tracks. He picked up a photograph of the family together, one he hadn't come to himself while he was inspecting the folder.

"This the parents, sir?" he asked, holding up the photo to show DCI Weaver.

DCI Weaver squinted at the photo before nodding. "Yes, apparently they came in to report it themselves, then went live on Instagram to talk about it, asking anybody with information to come forward if they knew anything. This is going to be a doozy, Kidd, the mother is a total nightmare. Why do you ask?"

He looked down at the picture one more time. There was a woman who looked very similar to Sarah, now that he thought about it. She was slender, peroxide blonde, striking a similar pose to the one that her daughter struck. She looked deliriously happy, one of those photographs where either the photographer had told a joke beforehand or they'd just decided to make it look as natural as possible by laughing through it. As he looked closer at her, really took in her face, it dawned on him.

"This is Laura Martins," he said.

"Laura *Harper*," DCI Weaver corrected.

"Right, right, but that's not what I knew her as," DI Kidd said, staring down at the photo in disbelief. He shook his head. "I went to school with her."

CHAPTER SIX

He remembered her so well now. She'd always been one of the popular girls at school, surrounded by friends, going out on Friday nights and always having stories running around the school about her that she vehemently denied. She was a star. It was hardly surprising that she'd managed to transform that real-world stardom into some kind of internet fame.

He recognised the husband as well, though less so. Christopher Harper had been a student at his school too, and they were in the same year, but he was one of the sports guys, someone who Kidd had tried to avoid if he could manage it. It was exactly the kind of person he would have expected Laura Martins to end up with.

DC Powell got to work setting up an Evidence Board. He put the photos of Sarah on one side and the photos of the parents on the other, under the heading of suspects. You could never be too careful with things like this, and as with most missing persons cases, you would have to rule out the parents first. Most people would be surprised to know how many times it had turned out to be the parents all along. He hoped that wasn't the case this time.

DC Ravel got to work looking at Sarah's social media, tracking down the names of the people she was photographed with most often. They'd be the people they would need to speak with first at the school, they would be the ones who would help them figure out a timeline.

DC Campbell appeared shortly after DCI Weaver had vanished. *Bloody convenient timing*, DI Kidd had thought. Kidd had filled him in and then sent him straight back out to gather coffee and pastries for the team.

Ben returned to his desk, flicking through the evidence they had so far—which wasn't a lot—and scrolling through Laura's Instagram. The fact they had gone to school together still floored him. He hadn't thought about her for the past twenty-five years or so and here she was, cleaning on the internet for hundreds of thousands of people.

DS Sanchez appeared at his side.

"So, that certainly puts the whole school reunion thing in perspective, huh?" she said, pulling up a chair to sit beside his desk. "I take it you're definitely going now."

"For sure," DI Kidd said, not looking away

from the screen. She seemed to still hang around with people they'd gone to school with. There were people whose faces he recognised in a vague sort of way, but couldn't for the life of him remember what their names were. It was like she hadn't moved on from those days, hanging out with the same people, probably talking about the same things they had always talked about, reminiscing about old stories.

The comments section on the post where she announced that Sarah was missing—with a photograph of the two of them standing next to one another, looking gorgeous in the same outfit, same poses, the lot—was flooded with people wishing them the best, wishing for her safety, saying they were sending up hopes and prayers. Kidd's mind boggled at these strangers being so invested in the lives of someone they didn't even know.

"I can—" The door swung open again, DI Kidd half-expected it to be DCI Weaver storming in again with new information or to give Simon the bollocking he had avoided earlier on. But instead, DC Campbell stood in the doorway, several cups of coffee in a carrier, a paper bag bursting with pastries.

His grin was wide like he had just found the girl out on the street, his fake tan still as orangey-brown as ever, making his teeth seem all the whiter. He wasn't a bad guy, Kidd knew that. He just had a tendency to say the wrong thing at the wrong time, or make light of a situation that really didn't need to be made light of.

After the last case where he'd been battered by the guy who ended up being their murderer, he'd toned down some. But that only seemed to last as long as he had a bruise on his forehead. It had faded, and so had any sense of him being a decent human being.

"The cavalry has arrived!" DC Campbell proclaimed, handing coffee to DC Ravel, a mint tea to DC Powell—DI Kidd tried not to rip into him for it—and two more coffees to Kidd and Zoe. He took an almond croissant for good measure. He was bloody starving.

"What do you want me to do, boss?" Campbell asked, mock saluting and throwing a pain aux raisins across the room. "Oops."

"First of all, I want you to pick that up," DI Kidd said, suppressing an eye roll. "Then, I want you to get in touch with the parents, Laura and Chris Harper. I'd love to get an interview done today if possible. I can go to them. It's probably easier. Have they sent a Missing Persons Officer?"

"They requested it," DS Sanchez said. "Been run off their feet apparently."

"Of course they did," DI Kidd replied. He wouldn't be surprised if a photo of them showed up on Laura's Instagram page sooner rather than later, or a full review of how they were performing. "Okay, Campbell, if you could get on with that for me, that will be great."

DI Kidd returned his gaze to the screen and Laura Harper's social media. It was fascinating the number of people who were invested in her life, in how she cleaned her living room, in where her family were going on trips. When he clicked on Sarah's profile, he saw that she had a lot of followers too, many of whom had probably come from her mother.

They were presenting themselves as this perfect family, the perfect house, the perfect life, everything so squeaky clean. But nothing was ever that cut and dry, DI Kidd knew that. They probably wanted Sarah found so quickly because it made things look bad. How can you be the perfect parents if you don't even know where your child has gotten to?

DS Sanchez was still at his side. DI Kidd turned to her.

"What's up, Zoe?" he asked.

"You were going to tell me something before DCI Weaver came in," she said. "I'm not trying to push you or anything, but it seemed like it was going to be important."

He looked at her for a moment, the image that might be of Craig flashing up in his mind again. Did he even want to tell her? She was his friend, but would she think less of him for still looking for Craig while starting things up with John? He wasn't sure he wanted to tell her. Maybe he was making something out of nothing, a mountain out of a molehill, a sighting out of a blurred CCTV still.

"No," he said. "I was just going to tell you about the case, that's all. DCI Weaver just beat me to it." His focus needed to be on the case right now. He couldn't get distracted by yet another wild goose chase looking for Craig Peyton. It hadn't worked when he'd had his time off and went gallivanting across Europe, it certainly wasn't going to work now. It would only really succeed in making him more miserable. He needed to accept that Craig was gone.

"Oh," DS Sanchez replied. "Never mind then, I thought it was going to be something serious." She moved to walk away.

"Oh, actually," DI Kidd said after her. She turned around. "You want to come to this school reunion with me?"

She eyed him curiously. "Sure, I can if you want," she replied. "I thought you were going to take John."

"I was," Kidd said. "But things have changed a little in the last hour. I wonder if it might be good for us both to be there. And if I go with John, I'm not going to be focussing on the case and..." he trailed off and took a moment. "You never know what's going to come up. If Laura and Chris are going to be there, maybe something new will come to light."

Zoe nodded. "Okay," she said. "Sure. You don't think John will mind?"

DI Kidd hesitated. "I don't think so," he

said. "I'm sure he'll understand."

But he had that creeping feeling in his stomach that he was putting work before his personal life again, that thing he'd told himself that he needed to stop doing. But it wasn't a big deal, was it? John would understand. It was a work thing. It would be fine.

As DI Kidd turned back to his computer, staring at the perfection of Laura Harper's life. He wasn't so sure.

CHAPTER SEVEN

With everyone on task, DI Kidd and DS Sanchez left Kingston Police Station to make their way to Sarah Harper's school. It wasn't lost on Kidd that it was the same school he had attended over twenty years ago. Although it had since been transformed into an Academy, he wasn't thrilled at the prospect of going back.

"We could send someone else," DS Sanchez said as they walked out into the car park. Zoe took a set of keys out of her pocket and clicked them, her favoured blue Focus in the corner lighting up as they approached. "Campbell could do this questioning if you want."

"I don't know if notes about one of Sarah's teachers being attractive is going to help us here," Kidd parried.

"He's not that bad," she replied, rolling her eyes. "You just don't seem keen."

"No, no," Kidd said. "You know me, Zoe,

scene of the crime and all that. I just want to get started."

He didn't want to go but he knew that he had to, that he needed to start where Sarah was last seen. He needed to get on top of this and he needed to get on top of it fast, if DCI Weaver's attitude was anything to go by.

"I wonder if any of the same teachers are there," he said as he climbed into the passenger seat. "Last time I went back was…I don't know, ten, fifteen years ago? And it still looked exactly the same as it had done before."

"Schools have a habit of doing that," Zoe said. "I remember going back to get a reference for this job at my old secondary school and it still smelled the same. It was grim, brought back way too many memories."

"You're not exactly encouraging me here, Zoe."

She shrugged, starting the engine. "You started it!"

The drive didn't take all that long, following the one-way system out towards Richmond, pulling into a set of very familiar gates (though with a seemingly fresh lick of paint) and an all too familiar car park. Kidd looked up at the school. It still managed to look imposing, even after all these years. Across the front of the main school building were a lot of windows and you could see students milling about inside, but every pair of windows was like a pair of eyes, staring at you, taking you in. You never quite knew who was watching. To say it was unnerving would be an understatement.

"Shake it off, Kidd," Zoe said as she shut off the engine, leaning back in her seat. "What's the game plan here?"

Kidd took a moment, getting his thoughts in order. "Game plan is to go in there and get as much information as we can about Sarah. Everything on her social media channels is showing nothing but a perfect life, nothing at all going on that seems in any way out of the ordinary."

"That's social media though," Zoe said with a shrug. "It's a highlight reel, no one is ever really telling the truth, are they?"

Kidd considered this. "I suppose not," he said. "But we need to try and establish what was really going on, figure out some kind of timeline so we know what she was doing, really get inside her head."

"You think this is the place to do it?"

"Well, she spends more time here than she does anywhere else," Kidd said. "Even more time here than at home really. Nine until three, Monday to Friday, that's a whole lot of life. There will be people here that know things. Her friends will know things, they have to."

He wasn't certain of a lot of things in this case, but he was certain that there would be at least one friend that knew what was going on with her.

Zoe nodded. "Let's get going then."

They got out of the car and started towards the front doors and the reception area. It was a path that Kidd had walked many times before, throwing him right back to when he was in his youth and showing up late after oversleeping or an argument with his parents, having to sign in at the front office instead of going to his form class, being threatened with detentions and demerits every other day.

The hardest part was that Liz hadn't gone to the same school. It might have been easier, or maybe he would have had happier memories if he'd been able to share the experience with a sibling. But Liz had been way too clever for this school. She'd ended up at a grammar school in Richmond. It took her an age to get there and back, but she excelled, their parents were obsessed with her for it.

Kidd opened the reception doors and was hit with a blast of warm air as he stepped inside, and then that same smell that would probably stay with him for the rest of his life. It was a combination of carpet cleaner, furniture polish, and some kind of air freshener that was probably the cheapest that could be found in bulk. There was also the lingering smell of sweat, something that most schools probably struggled to hide most of the time.

He walked to the glass window, a portal to some of the teacher's offices within. There were people in there tapping away at computers, drinking coffee, chatting to one another. No one noticed his presence until he cleared his throat.

"Sorry about that!" A woman cooed as she tottered over. She was wearing a name badge that marked her out as Ms Lu, her black and white streaked hair pulled back into a tight ponytail, her glasses on a chain around her neck. Kidd couldn't age her. She was simultaneously a child and a grandmother. "What can I do for you? Are you signing in?"

"No," Kidd replied. "We're—"

"Is this a visit?" Ms Lu chirped excitedly. "Are you looking at this school for your child?"

DS Sanchez choked on the air while Kidd struggled to keep a straight face.

"No, not at all," Kidd replied. He reached into his pocket and pulled out his warrant card, pressing it against the window so that Ms Lu could see it was definitely him. "I'm DI Benjamin Kidd, this is DS Zoe Sanchez." She'd managed to get her breath back and waved at Ms Lu. "We're here to talk to the headteacher, and then some students if possible. It's about the disappearance of Sarah Harper."

All the excitement she had greeted them with fell from her face. She looked suddenly unspeakably sad. "Gosh, yes, horrible business that," she said softly. "Such a sweet girl, never had a bad word to say about anyone, can't imagine why…" She trailed off and sniffed. Was she crying? "To take her away? Who would do such a thing?"

Kidd cleared his throat. "It really is an awful business, Ms Lu, but we're here to figure out her movements prior to her disappearance, try and find her if we can," he said. He wasn't in the business of making anybody false promises, but he would certainly do his best to bring her back in one piece. It seemed to placate her a little because she offered him a small smile.

"If you would like to take a seat," she said, gesturing across to a pair of blue chairs. "I'll go and grab Ms Chowdhury, she's the headteacher, wonderful woman, and she will take you through to her office. Won't be a moment."

Ms Lu scurried away, leaving DI Kidd and DS Sanchez to sit on the blue cushioned chairs in the reception area. There was a TV screen up in the corner displaying students' work, a couple of school news items, and reminders for students of the school rules. It felt like a little bit much, and definitely felt out of place in an office that had stagnated over time.

"Can't believe she thought we were a couple," DS Sanchez whispered.

"I know," Kidd grumbled. "I'd rather not think about it if I'm honest."

"Rude."

"Excuse me?" He looked at her, incredulous.

"Well, what's so wrong with the two of us

being a couple?" she asked, a twinkle in her eye that told him immediately that she was messing with him. He wasn't really in the mood to be messed with.

"DI Kidd, DS Sanchez." The voice caused them to turn their heads towards the door where an Indian woman was standing in a maroon, Hilary Clinton-esque power suit. Her hands her folded neatly in front of her and she was fixing them both with a sweet smile, though it didn't quite make its way to her eyes. "Sorry to keep you waiting, would you like to come with me?"

She was soft spoken, not the kind of person DI Kidd thought would be a headteacher. The headteachers he had encountered over his years in school were 1) usually men and 2) gruff types who were in positions of power and determined to scare the living daylights out of you with a single, withering stare. Ms Chowdhury seemed the exact opposite of that.

She led them through a door that Ms Lu had to buzz them through, guiding them through a labyrinth of desks to a large, secluded office. There was one window off to the side, large, letting in a huge amount of light. The walls were painted sky blue, relaxing but cold. She gestured to the two seats opposite her desk and took a seat herself, leaning back slightly in front of a wall covered in books, a couple of trophies, and framed certificates. It looked like she was setting up for a photo-op rather than a discussion.

Kidd took a seat in one of the chairs, immediately sinking down into it. She was seated higher than he was, which he didn't like, the squashy chair he was in making it almost impossible to get comfortable.

"Ms Lu tells me that you're here to talk about Sarah Harper?" Her inflection went up at the end like a question, but she knew exactly why they were there. She had to have been expecting them.

"Yes, Ms Chowdhury," DI Kidd said, struggling to the edge of his seat so he could get somewhat comfortable. He still wasn't, but at least now his knees weren't positioned by his ears. "It was reported to us last night that she was missing—"

"Yes, she caused quite a stir when she didn't show up for school yesterday," Ms Chowdhury said, stopping short of rolling her eyes, which Kidd found more than a little off-putting. One of her students is missing and she doesn't seem to care. "I imagine she will show up in a day or two."

Ben blinked. *What is she talking about?*

"Do you?" DS Sanchez asked, filling in for Ben's silence. "What makes you say that?"

Ms Chowdhury smiled, leaning forward in her chair to lock eyes with DS Sanchez. "This isn't my first rodeo, DS Sanchez," she said. "And it certainly isn't Sarah's."

"She's disappeared before?" DI Kidd asked, taking out a notebook and quickly jotting that down.

"This is one in a series of disappearing acts made by Sarah Harper over her years at this school," Ms Chowdhury said, placing her hand delicately on her mouse and clicking a few times on her desktop. "It happened when she was in Year 9, twice in Year 10, and in Autumn term of Year 11 she had already managed three."

"She'd vanished three times?"

Someone should have bloody mentioned that, Kidd thought. They were starting to look like amateurs here.

"Like I said, DI Kidd, it's a habit of hers," Ms Chowdhury said. "When something happens at school that she doesn't agree with or she doesn't get her way, she takes it upon herself to make a dramatic exit and show everyone who's boss. It's about control."

"Is it?" DS Sanchez asked.

"Absolutely," the headteacher said firmly. "She disappears for a day then returns as if nothing has even happened, her friends fawning over her, any problem she was having miraculously solved."

"But then, why is this the first time she's been reported missing?" DI Kidd asked. It didn't make sense. If Sarah had a habit of vanishing into thin air, why would her parents not have reported it before? "What's different?"

"That's what you're trying to figure out, isn't it DI Kidd?"

It was a verbal slap that Ben wasn't expecting. He took a moment to right himself. He hadn't expected to be battling with the bloody headteacher to get information about Sarah. Though, Ben supposed, she was giving away perhaps a lot more than she thought. It just wasn't about Sarah.

"Something like that," he said, holding her gaze. She had intense eyes, a sort of burnt hazel colour that she was probably used to using to unnerve her students. Maybe she didn't need to raise her voice when she could fix them with a stare like that. Kidd, however, was not about to crack.

Ms Chowdhury broke off first and turned back to her computer screen. "Normally, Sarah would go missing midweek and reappear a day or two later," she said. "I imagine that doesn't quite line up this time?"

"Sarah Harper has been missing for somewhere around four days," DI Kidd said, irritated at how nonchalant the headteacher was being. Seeing someone in a position of power barely batting an eye at one of their charges vanishing was unnerving, to say the least. "She last made contact with her parents on Friday morning. She came to school and after that nothing. Do you know what might have led her to do a 'disappearing act' as you called it?"

She turned to him sharply and raised a perfectly drawn-on eyebrow. She wasn't used to people talking back. But Kidd refused to be intimidated by her.

"Sarah Harper was dramatic," Ms Chowdhury said.

"You mentioned," DS Sanchez interjected with a poisonous smile.

"Well, as such, the drama followed her around," she said. "There was always something happening, whether it would be at home or with her friends or with her boyfriend." She started tapping away on her computer, not saying another word for a minute or so. Kidd was starting to wonder if they had been dismissed without him realising, until she took hold of the screen and turned it toward them. "I think this might have been what sparked it."

"Jesus Christ," Kidd blurted.

CHAPTER EIGHT

On the screen in front of them was something that looked like a gossip website. It was a screenshot from a webpage with several pictures of Sarah on it. She was kissing a boy in one of the photos, caressing his face in another, the boy's hand squeezing her bum in another. Whoever had taken that photo had really zoomed in for it. It was grim.

Across the top of the page read: EXPOSED! SARAH'S CHEATING WAYS ON DISPLAY FOR THE WORLD TO SEE! NOT SO SWEET NOW!

Ms Chowdhury pulled the screen back towards her, tutted, and clicked to remove it from her desktop.

"That appeared on Thursday, the day before Sarah vanished," Ms Chowdhury said. "We know that there were several arguments that broke out between Sarah and her friends, also with her boyfriend, though we are yet to find the identity of the person who posted these things about her."

"We're going to need a link to that website —"

"It's been taken down," Ms Chowdhury interrupted.

"Then any screenshots you have will be useful," DI Kidd said. "And we're going to need the names of anyone who knew Sarah. We would like to talk to them today."

"They're in classes—"

"That wasn't a request."

"They have lessons—"

"There is a teenage girl missing, Ms Chowdhury," DI Kidd said plainly, struggling to believe that he was having to spell this out to an educator, to a headteacher of all people. "We don't know where she is, and yes, this may not be out of the ordinary for her to do for a day or so, but Sarah has been missing for the past four days. She has had no contact with her family whatsoever, so we need to know if there is anyone here who has made contact with her."

There was a silence that fell on the room, Ms Chowdhury staring at DI Kidd with an open mouth, not really knowing what to say. So DI Kidd took up the mantle once again.

"If you could find us a room somewhere so that we could talk to the students, that would be wonderful," he said. "If you would prefer there be a member of staff present as well, that's fine, but we would like to get this investigation moving. Any holdups that we have here could hinder our efforts to find Sarah, do you understand?"

A silence pushed its way between them, Kidd eyeballing Ms Chowdhury as she sat there stony-faced. She certainly wasn't used to being spoken to like that but Kidd was ready to explode. How could she not care?

Ms Chowdhury nodded, backing down. "I will set up one of the spare offices for you and have Ms Lu go and collect the children from their classes one at a time." She pressed a few buttons on her computer, the printer behind her desk spitting out a copy of the website she had shown them a few moments ago.

Kidd folded it and put it in his pocket, waiting for Ms Chowdhury to finish whatever it was she was tapping out on the computer. Eventually, she got up from behind her desk, DI Kidd and DS Sanchez following suit, and without another word, led them out of her office and into the office next door.

It was almost identical to Ms Chowdhury's but for the lack of books and certificates on the walls. It would have looked like an interview room down at the station were it not for the brightly coloured blue walls and the large window. The interview rooms at the station had a tendency to get quite claustrophobic. No chance of that here.

"Thank you, Ms Chowdhury," DI Kidd said as she scurried out of the room. When she'd closed the door behind her, DS Sanchez rounded on him, her face alight. She looked like she wanted to drag Ms Chowdhury back in here for round two.

"Well, that was certainly a battle," she said.

"I know."

"Did she even care?" she said. "What's that about?"

"It just wasn't getting through to her," he said, looking at the door as if she were about to walk back in. "Even when we mentioned Sarah had been missing, she was batting away questions, batting away anything that would actually help us."

"It was odd," DS Sanchez said. "It's not beyond the realm of possibility that she had something to do with it, you know."

"You mean if Sarah isn't being dramatic and flouncing off for a couple of days," DI Kidd said with a raise of his eyebrow. "You're not wrong. She didn't seem to like her much."

"Which is odd when Ms Lu was practically in tears at the very mention of Sarah's name."

"I know," DI Kidd said, staring out the window and looking at the car park. He hadn't expected that kind of reaction from Ms Chowdhury. But, he supposed, he hadn't expected Sarah to have done disappearing acts on a regular basis. Though it was certainly possible that her parents didn't know about them, or had her staying off sick at home or something. The interview with the parents was certainly going to help them in all this.

"What about that website?" DS Sanchez said. "Whoever posted that obviously has it out for Sarah."

"It's one thing to have a healthy dislike for someone, but to post about it? To go out and look for evidence—"

"I think the kids call them receipts."

"Receipts, then," DI Kidd said. "That's vicious. There's something in that for sure, we just need to find out exactly who it was that did it."

"But the website has been deleted."

Kidd shrugged. "The tech bods will have a way to figure it out

They waited a little while longer, DS Sanchez fielding a lengthy call from DC Campbell—where he almost certainly asked her out again given the number of times DS Sanchez said, "No, no, for the last bloody time Campbell, no!"—during which he gave them the address for Sarah Harper's parents. She told him they would make it there by early afternoon.

DI Kidd's phone pinged in his pocket. A message from John.

JOHN: We still on for 1?

DI Kidd checked the time on his phone. It was already getting on for eleven. Given the amount of time this was going to take, and if they were going to be at Sarah's parents' house for the early afternoon, it wasn't looking likely.

> How about 3pm?
> I know it's late but something has happened at work.
> I can explain.

Kidd waited as the three dots appeared on the screen, seeing that John was typing. He held his breath.

JOHN: 3 is fine. I'll meet you at the station.

> Great. See you then.

Kidd turned back to DS Sanchez who was watching him carefully.

"You okay?" she asked.

"Just rearranging lunch with John."

"Ah," she said. "Sweet."

"Not really," Kidd said. "I don't want him to think I'm blowing him off or anything."

"Well, Ben, I think he'd want to know if—"

The door opened to interrupt her, Ms Lu walking in ushering a young dark-skinned girl, her hair curly and free around her head. She fixed both of them with a nervous look before turning back to Ms Lu.

"What's this about, Miss?" she asked, looking from Ms Lu back to Kidd and Zoe. "I've not done anything."

"Nothing to worry about," Zoe said, painting a smile on her face. This was what Zoe was good at. Kidd had a tendency to be a little abrasive in interviews, even though this wasn't officially an interview, while Zoe always managed to be on the cooler side. "We just have a few questions about Sarah Harper we wanted to ask you. It won't take long, then you'll be free to go."

The girl eyed them both warily.

"I'm not under arrest, am I?" She looked nervous. She crossed her arms and backed towards the door.

"Not at all," Kidd said, trying to soften what was probably quite a hardened look on his face. "We're just trying to track Sarah down and we thought you might be able to help us."

Kidd walked over to the table and took a seat on one side. DS Sanchez joined him. The girl still looked nervous.

"Can I ask you what your name is?" Zoe said softly.

"Taylor," she muttered. "Taylor Grant."

"Taylor, we just have a few questions," Zoe said, again keeping her tone as measured as possible. "It won't take long."

Taylor nodded and walked over to the chair on the opposite side of the table. She pulled her blazer tightly around herself as she sat and crossed one leg over the other, her body not quite facing the two detectives. She looked as if she would make a break for the door at any second.

"Taylor," Kidd said. "I wondered if you'd be able to take us through the last time you saw Sarah Harper."

"The last time I saw her?"

"Yes, please," Kidd said. "I understand some…information was revealed that she didn't really want out in the open. Can you tell us about that?"

Taylor tutted. "She was sneaking around with Jonno when she was actually with Dexter." At the look Kidd gave her, she amended, "Dexter Black. Her boyfriend. She was stupid and got caught. Well, someone caught her. They should be worried about their life when they find out who it was."

"Why's that?"

"Well, Dex isn't exactly happy about it," Taylor said. "He's not the nicest guy. Neither's Jonno, come to think of it. Don't know why we hang out with them."

"You're friends with them both?"

"They're in our friendship group," Taylor said. "That doesn't mean we're friends. Dexter and Jonno are tight though. Well, they *were* tight. After it happened, Dexter and Jonno got into a fight. Had to get Mr Warren and Mr Deans to pull them apart."

"Who are they?"

"PE teachers," Taylor said, laughing. "They were probably just happy to be doing something useful."

Kidd took all this down, noting the names of other people they would need to speak with, if not today, then at some point in the future. There were a lot of names. The net for who might not like Sarah was getting cast wider and wider.

"So, how well do you know Sarah?" DS Sanchez asked.

"We've known each other since we started here," Taylor said. "We were really good friends for a few years, but then boys started getting involved and then came the drama, and with the drama came…well…Sarah liked the drama, so the more of it that came, the more of it she wanted and it became sort of vicious."

"Right."

"And then she'd vanish for a couple of days and…" Taylor trailed off and shook her head.

"What?" Kidd said, leaning forward in his chair. "Finish that thought, Taylor, what were you going to say?"

"No, because if I finish that thought, you're going to arrest me like I've done it or something."

"Done what?"

"I don't know, kidnapped her, killed her, how should I know?"

The room fell silent and Taylor slumped back in her chair. That nervous look settled across her face again like she'd just realised she was talking to two detectives, not two people on the playground.

"I didn't do anything," she said quietly, her voice shaking a little. "Sarah and I were friends for the most part. But whenever things were getting dramatic, I always took a step back. And the times when she would vanish, were the times when I would get a chance to figure out my own shit, you know? I'd get to...be myself. And not worry about what Sarah was doing. I needed that."

DI Kidd looked at Taylor, a scared young girl who was just telling them how she felt. Even from just her online presence, it was pretty clear that Sarah was a big personality. If she was anything like her mum, she could fill a whole room with just her presence. If you're trying to be her friend, that had to be suffocating at times. Taylor was just looking for a chance to breathe. She hadn't wanted it to be like this.

"Thanks for everything, Taylor," DI Kidd said. "Is there anything else you want to add? Anything you think can help us find Sarah?"

Taylor took a breath. "There was a fight on Friday," she said. "Everybody was there. I mean, it wouldn't be surprising if you couldn't hear it all the way from town. Basically, the whole school saw it."

"What happened?" DS Sanchez asked.

"No one got beaten up or anything like

that," Taylor said. "It was just a lot of yelling."

"Who was yelling?"

"Dexter," Taylor said. "Dexter was yelling at Sarah."

CHAPTER NINE

"Their relationship was weird," Taylor said.

"Weird how?"

"Well, he did that a lot."

"Did what?"

"Yelled," Taylor said. "He and Sarah would get into fights quite often. They were supposed to be this golden couple and if you only saw them in the halls or saw them on Instagram, you would definitely think that, but Dex is darker than that. He has problems."

"What kind of problems?" DI Kidd asked. DS Sanchez was furiously scribbling notes next to him.

"Anger," Taylor said flatly. "He would flip out at the weirdest things and go off on her about them. And she'd yell back, because she's Sarah and she never goes down without a fight, but that didn't make it right. Their relationship was weird, like I said."

DI Kidd looked over at DS Sanchez. She was still writing when he looked, and he saw her write DEXTER BLACK in block letters, underlining it a few times. If there was one person they needed to speak to in all this, it was Dexter.

"You keep saying that," DS Sanchez said. "What do you mean?"

"They try to seem like they're this perfect couple," she said. "But if you know them, it doesn't really fit. They're like, best friends, but they wouldn't hang out all the time. Or there were times when I'd think they were together because I couldn't get hold of her and then I'd see Dex on his own. Or the other way around."

There seemed to be a lot more going on than even Taylor could say. She had a front-row seat to the inner workings of their relationship but she still had questions that had gone unanswered.

"Can I go?" Taylor asked suddenly. "I'm still not in trouble, am I?"

"No," Zoe said with a smile. "This has been great. If you think of anything else come see us at the station, or just phone."

"What, 999?"

"Erm, no," Kidd said, reaching into his jacket pocket he pulled out a crumpled card. "This number, here. You can text or leave a message if you think of anything else."

"Thanks," Taylor said, putting the card in her pocket. "I...uh...I know I made it seem like

I don't like her all that much," she added. "But she's still my friend, you know? I hope she's alright."

She walked to the door without another word and headed back to her classes. Ben got to his feet and went to the door after her, looking for Ms Lu.

"Ms Lu," he called when he caught sight of her. She had been hovering by the photocopier, probably listening to report back to Ms Chowdhury. He wouldn't put it past her. "I don't suppose we could talk to Dexter Black next."

Ms Lu walked over to him, her head bowed a little low, the people at the other desks in the office watching her closely. Kidd didn't like being part of a media circus and this was quickly becoming that with all the people listening in. He shouldn't have raised his voice.

"Dexter hasn't actually been in school since last week," she said.

"What's that now?"

"He was last in on Friday," she said. "Didn't show up for school yesterday or today. His parents called in sick for him."

Kidd looked at her closely. She shrugged apologetically and left the office, probably off to get them the next one of Sarah's friends to talk to. Kidd returned to the office, closing the door behind him.

"He's not here," Kidd said, walking back over to the desk and taking a seat on the edge of it.

"Dexter?"

Kidd nodded. "Also hasn't been here since Friday, so since Sarah was last seen."

DS Sanchez narrowed her eyes at him. "That seems a little too easy," she said.

"What do you mean?"

"You're suggesting that the fucked up, anger problems boyfriend who has a weird relationship with Sarah is the one who has her," she said. "It seems a little bit too simple to me."

Kidd shrugged. "What else do we have right now? We at least need to talk to him in order to rule it out."

"Maybe a house call after we see Sarah's parents?"

"Might be a good idea," Kidd said as the door opened once again, Ms Lu ushering in a boy. Kidd recognised him immediately from the photo that Ms Chowdhury had shown them on her computer. This had to be Jonno.

He was about as tall as DI Kidd, but he was slouching which made him look a little shorter than he was. His light brown hair was buzzed close to his head, and when he looked up, Kidd saw the most piercing green eyes he'd ever seen. They were really quite something.

"Jonno, is it?" Kidd said.

Jonno looked confused. "Yeah," he said. "How did you know that?"

Kidd smiled. "Lucky guess. Have a seat."

Jonno did as he was told, slumping down in the seat opposite them as Taylor had done a few moments ago. They found out his name was Jonathan Edwards but everyone, even the teachers, called him Jonno. He recited pretty much the same story that Taylor had, but with a little more detail. He and Sarah had been sneaking around with one another for the past three months because apparently, Dexter had been doing the same and Sarah was out for some kind of revenge.

Kidd's mind boggled at the lives of these teenagers. When he was sixteen, he would sneak out and drink with his buddies in the park, but he hadn't had nearly as much drama as all this. Maybe it was amplified because it all came out on social media. Maybe all of his friends had things like this happen to them and he just hadn't been a part of it because he'd known he was gay from such a young age.

"What about the fight on Friday?" Kidd asked.

"What about it?" Jonno replied, locking eyes with Kidd and staring him down.

"In your own words, can you describe what happened?"

Jonno watched Kidd carefully and straightened up in his chair.

"Everything about me and Sarah came out on Thursday so there was a lot of tension around," he started. "Dexter got into it with me, we got into a scuffle, punches were thrown, words were too, it wasn't pretty, but it didn't feel...I don't know, it didn't feel serious. Dex is my bro." He coughed and wiped his mouth on his sleeve. "Then on Friday, Dex finally grew a pair of balls and decided to talk to Sarah about it. And by talk, I mean chase her through the school shouting abuse at her when she decided she didn't want to listen to him anymore."

"What do you mean by that?"

"Well, it started out as a little chat by their lockers. Sarah calmly explaining what was going on—"

"And where were you when this happened?"

"I was watching," Jonno said. "We all were. The whole group was there just watching them talk."

"Why?" DS Sanchez asked.

"Because we'd taken bets on how long it would take for Dexter to blow up at her."

Kidd managed to hide the grimace, DS Sanchez did not.

"What? We did it all the time!" Jonno said, actually grinning. DS Sanchez went back to taking notes, but she was gripping the pen with increased ferocity.

"What happened after that?"

"Well, she wasn't having any of his shit," Jonno said. "She's Sarah, she doesn't really do apologies, and she refused to feel bad about it so off she went. And he followed her and he just wouldn't stop shouting." Jonno's attitude changed. "It was scary really. Like, I didn't know what he was going to do. And I've known Dex for years. I've never seen him get like that."

DI Kidd nodded as Jonno trailed off, looking at the ground, probably reliving it all in his head. They'd had enough out of him, enough that they knew that the person they needed to speak to was Dexter Black. And Kidd had a sneaking suspicion he was going to be hard to track down.

"Thank you, Jonno," Kidd said. "Ms Lu will take you back to your class."

Jonno left the room without another word, looking a little deflated. He stopped when he reached the door and turned back to them.

"What's going to happen to Sarah?" he asked.

"What do you mean?" Zoe asked.

"Well, you don't know where she is right now," he said. "Do you know…?" He hesitated. "I don't mean this in a bad way. Do you know anything?"

Kidd nearly had to stop himself from laughing because, at this stage, they really didn't know anything. They were right at the beginning of an investigation. Who knew where it would lead them.

"At this stage, we're just trying to figure out her movements on Friday," Kidd said.

"Everything that you've said has been really helpful."

Jonno nodded. "I'd just like it if you brought her back," Jonno said. "I know she could be difficult or a bit of a bitch to some people but..." He shrugged. "I like her. I don't want her to be in trouble."

DS Sanchez met his eyes and offered him a soothing smile. "I get that," she said. "We're going to do our best. If you think of anything else, don't hesitate to get in touch."

DI Kidd managed to scrounge up another crumpled card and hand it to Jonno before he left. It wasn't long before Ms Lu was back at the door, awaiting instructions.

"Do you know who you want to talk to next?" she said. "Or should I just bring another of Sarah's friends down?"

"If you could, that would be useful," Kidd said.

And their morning ticked by like that. Interview after interview, teenager after teenager, all of them reciting the same story, often with their own spin, their own flair. They all confirmed that Dexter blew up at her. A couple even mentioned the weirdness of Sarah and Dexter's relationship, how there was something off about it. And maybe that was his anger. Or something else. Kidd couldn't place it.

By the time they were finished, they had a pretty good idea of Sarah's last moments at the school. It was something to go on, and all signs pointed to Dexter. It may have seemed easy, but they needed to start somewhere. The anger issues boyfriend seemed like a good place to go.

"I think we're done here," Kidd said when Ms Lu returned one final time. "I think we know who we need to talk to. Can you get us Dexter Black's address?"

CHAPTER TEN

Ms Lu obliged, scribbling down a contact number and an address for Dexter Black's family. He didn't live all that far from Sarah's house, something that set off alarm bells in Kidd's head. Could she really be right around the corner? If she was, he hoped she was at least safe.

They thanked her, dropping into Ms Chowdhury's office to let her know that they were leaving, and started out of the reception once again.

"What do you think of the headteacher?" DS Sanchez asked as they walked.

Kidd shrugged. "I'm going to keep an eye on her, that's for sure," he said. "I half expected my old headmaster to be there, but he must be long dead by now."

"Wow, cheery stuff, Ben," she said. "Tell another one."

"She was weird," he said, thinking back to the conversation they'd had just an hour or so ago. "Didn't seem to care about Sarah or her welfare at all. Even when we told her she'd been missing for longer than perhaps normal, sure she gave us what we wanted, but beyond that, she wasn't a lot of help."

"I'll keep tabs on her," DS Sanchez said. "We'll put her on the board, if it comes to it we'll figure out what her movements were over the past few days. Maybe have someone look into it anyway, just to be sure."

"Sounds good."

As they started towards DS Sanchez's car, Kidd's phone started ringing. DCI Weaver's name was emblazoned across his screen and he really wanted to pretend he was still in interview and ignore it.

"What?" Zoe asked.

He showed her the screen and she grimaced.

He took a deep breath and answered. "Hello."

"DI Kidd," Weaver said. No pleasantries. No time for that apparently. "We've got the media hounding us for information, do you have anything?"

Kidd did his best not to sigh down the phone. "Nothing yet sir, but we're on our way to see Sarah's parents now, get what we can from them. Chatting with the students was enlightening, I think—"

"Glad you're having a good time, Kidd,

but a teenager is missing and the Inspector is breathing down my neck to get this done ASAP," he growled. Kidd could see Weaver's face in his mind's eye, cheeks puffing, eyes bulging, ready to explode at a moment's notice.

"Doing my best, boss," Kidd said.

"Do better," Weaver snapped. "We've got a press conference here this afternoon."

"What time?"

"Whatever time you get here," he snapped. "So don't dawdle."

Weaver hung up before Kidd could properly respond, leaving him staring at the phone screen as they walked to the car.

"So?" Zoe said.

"Press conference," he said.

"When?"

"Whenever we get there," Kidd grumbled, pocketing his phone.

"Kidd." A different voice this time, though still one that DI Kidd recognised. He looked up to see a boy with curly brown hair leaning on the hood of DS Sanchez's car, just as he had done the first time they'd met him just over a month ago. He looked scruffy, another thing that Ben expected from him.

"Joe Warrington," DI Kidd said, walking towards him. "Get off the car."

"Oh, yeah, sorry." Joe got to his feet, his hand wrapped tightly around his phone. He looked up into the looming figure of DI Kidd.

Joe Warrington was the brother of Tony Warrington, the guy they'd caught for the copycat killing of The Grinning Murders. There had been a time when Kidd had been convinced that it was Joe who had done it, but that had proved to be false. Joe had just been covering the news story as best he could for his social media channels, which had brought him into pretty sharp focus.

"Do I really need to ask what brings you here?" Kidd asked. "You chasing this story too?"

"I used to go to this school," he said. "So I still follow socials, they use me as a success story every now and again so I'm still in the loop with stuff."

"So you have an in?" Kidd said. "You getting an exclusive on it?"

"Hardly," Joe said, rolling his eyes. "Her parents have dominated the major news cycles. Laura Harper posting all sorts of things to her Instagram basically makes me pointless."

Kidd raised an eyebrow at Joe Warrington. There was no way that Joe would be covering this story if he didn't think he could get some kind of exclusive on it and there was no way he would be here if he thought it was pointless. There was definitely something more going on here. He folded his arms and waited.

"So what are you talking to us for?"

"Because I think I have something that might help you," Joe said. "And I don't just want to put it out there when I think it could actually help find Sarah."

It was the last thing that DI Kidd had been expecting. When Joe had been posting things about The Grinning Murders, Kidd had assumed Joe was just an obnoxious young man who was hungry for a viral moment. He tried to get all sorts of information out of Kidd and just ended up rubbing him up the wrong way. But now he seemed to want to help.

"What have you got?" Kidd asked. "And what do you want in return?"

Joe wrapped his arms around himself. "A ride back to Uni would be great."

◆ ◆ ◆

"Go on then," Kidd said from the front seat. It was no bother driving him back to the University, especially when he was going to give them information.

"What do you know so far?" Joe asked.

Kidd sighed. "Are you recording this? Are you after information from us?"

Joe rolled his eyes. "I have pretty much everything, I just want to know what you know."

They locked eyes in the rearview mirror, Joe eventually giving up and pulling out his phone. Kidd didn't want to give him too much. Even though he was only in his twenties, Joe was technically still press. He shouldn't even be telling him anything but, and this was something he had figured out during the last case, he seemed to know a lot. And if he'd gone to the same school, there was every possibility he could help them out.

"Website exposing the fact Sarah was cheating, fight on Friday afternoon, Sarah hasn't been seen since," Joe said, all of it matter of fact, not a lick of emotion. "You got all that?"

"Yep."

"Good, because I think I know who it was who set up the website," Joe said with a grin.

"You're joking," Kidd said. He pulled the piece of paper Ms Chowdhury had printed for them out of his pocket and showed it to Joe. "This is all we got. Headteacher said it had been deleted."

"It was, but I was all over it before the guy responsible could take it down," Joe said. "The thing about having a website is, there's an IP address, and it doesn't take a genius to track down who owns a domain. So I've got the name of the guy, and confirmation that he was in Sarah's year at school."

"Well, who is he?"

"Nicholas Ayre," Joe replied. "I know the name won't mean much to you, but he's all over social media so you'll track him down soon enough. He's not in their crowd or anything, sort of an outsider from what I can tell, but he has a vendetta against her. Could be something."

"You got anything else?"

"Only that Sarah's social media presence isn't all it seems," Joe said. "From what I've got from people who knew her and people who knew *of* her, it all sounds very Mean Girls/Gossip Girl/tired teen drama. She was the queen bee and there were a lot of people who wanted to see her fall from grace. And when I say a lot, I mean a lot."

"I got the impression from her friend, Taylor, that she wasn't all that keen on having Sarah around all the time."

"She's not, none of them are, really," Joe said. "It's a little bit sad, I've got to admit. But everybody I know at that school has it in for her."

Kidd turned his attention back to the road, DS Sanchez was pulling onto Penrhyn Road, getting ready to turn into the University car park. He felt a little bit sorry for Sarah. He knew from the news that kids were using social media too much, using it to the point that they were causing themselves damage, faking that they were happy when they weren't, but this was ridiculous. Sarah's social media was full of her friends, or people she thought were her friends, all of them doing things together and having fun, and all of that was fake?

"You okay?" DS Sanchez asked quietly, shutting off the engine as she parked off.

"Yeah, yeah, good," he said, turning back to Joe. "You got anything else for us?"

Joe shook his head. "That's all I had. I didn't know you guys were going to be there today. Just a stroke of luck on my part." Joe said, shuffling across the back seat towards the door. "Nice to see you both again—"

"Joe," DI Kidd interrupted. "Just wanted to check, everything alright with you?"

Joe eyed him curiously. "How do you mean?"

"I just mean at home, given everything that happened."

"Given you arrested my crazy ass brother?" Joe said, a twinkle in his eye. But there was something else, something Kidd couldn't quite place. "My dad has been pretty cut up about it. Mum too, but for different reasons. But they're fine."

"What about you?" Kidd asked. Joe had been there the night they'd finally caught up with Tony and arrested him. He'd ended up with a knife to his neck. One false move and Joe might not even have been here to talk to them about all this.

Joe took a breath. "I'm fine," he said. "It's a weird thing for people to know me for. I certainly get some stick for it. But I'm okay. Just looking after myself, my family too."

Kidd smiled at him. "Good. And if you come up with anything else—"

"I'll give you the exclusive," Joe said with a wink before shuffling out of the car and heading off towards the reception of the University.

DS Sanchez turned to Kidd. "What are you thinking?"

"A lot of things."

"Give me specifics," she said.

"I'm thinking that there are probably more suspects in this than we first thought," he said. "I know we need to go and talk to the parents and see if they're involved in any way, but the more I hear about these kids that hate her, this headteacher who doesn't give a shit about her, the more concerned I am for her safety."

"So the kids at school hate her," Zoe said. "That doesn't mean that they're capable of kidnapping her and holding her hostage."

Kidd looked over at Zoe. She locked eyes with him and it was like she read his mind. They both knew better than that. They'd seen enough to know that anyone was capable of absolutely anything under extreme circumstances.

She turned the engine on and drove away.

CHAPTER ELEVEN

Sarah Harper's family home was exactly the kind of house that DI Kidd expected Laura Martins to have moved into after finishing school. It was at least three times the size of Kidd's place and looked like it belonged in a magazine rather than on the outskirts of Kingston town. It was just across from Fairfield Park, a stone's throw from the middle of town, and Kidd was fairly sure that they had bought two houses and knocked through to build one, giant house because it definitely looked out of place.

"Who the hell needs a house this big?" DS Sanchez asked as they stepped out of the car. "Honestly, who needs this many rooms? Do they ever see each other?"

Kidd shrugged. "Maybe they don't." It certainly looked like the kind of house that you could spend an entire day in without bumping into another single soul. There were probably more bathrooms than Kidd had rooms in his house.

He walked up to the front door and knocked, stepping back from the huge, black double doors with DS Sanchez, neither one of them knowing which one was going to open.

It creaked open, just the tiniest crack. A small woman that DI Kidd instantly recognised as Sarah's mother appearing in the gap.

"Can I help you?" she asked. This was not the woman that DI Kidd had seen online. Laura's online presence had her fully glam at all times, always done up, always with a smile on her face, and a filter to go with it. The only exception to that was the video where she told her fans that Sarah was missing, but even in that video, everything seemed perfectly placed. Seeing her now, a little bit off guard, she seemed smaller.

"My name is DI Kidd, this is DS Sanchez," Kidd said. "We're investigating Sarah's disappearance, someone should have called ahead from the station. Is this a bad time?"

Laura opened the door a little further, drawing up to her full height and painting a smile onto her face. And now Kidd saw something more of the woman he had seen on Instagram, the smile, the high cheekbones, the perfect blonde hair. How had she managed to do that in just a few shifts of her body?

"Lovely to meet you both," she said, her voice steady, her eyes glistening a little. Had she been crying recently? Kidd couldn't tell. "Do come in, you must be freezing."

She opened the door a little wider, the two of them stepping inside and taking in the gigantic hallway. This place had definitely been gutted and put back together again, there was no way a house on this street could look this modern without that. The high ceilings meant that every movement they made was echoing around them, the windows above the door letting in so much natural light there wasn't really any need for anything artificial.

"Come through to the kitchen, I'm sure we'll all be more comfortable there," she said with a smile.

"I'm sorry, do you mind if I use your bathroom?" DI Kidd asked. "I wouldn't normally ask but we've been out of the station all morning."

Laura smiled at him. "Of course not, it's just up the stairs, second door on your left," she said, but then she stopped suddenly and took a step back from him. She narrowed her eyes, like she was seeing him much clearer in the light of the hallway than she had done when he was outside in the bright winter sun. "Do I know you from somewhere?"

Kidd laughed a little nervously. He hadn't really anticipated saying anything so soon but perhaps he hadn't changed as much as he thought over the past twenty or so years. He was older, a little more wrinkled and grey, but no less himself. "Yes, actually, we were at school together," he said. "Secondary school. I didn't know whether or not you—"

"Little Benji Kidd," she said, her face lighting up. "I can't believe it's you, you look so different."

Kidd shrugged. "Well, it's been twenty years."

"And you're a detective inspector now, that's very impressive! How long have you been a policeman?"

"For about twenty years or so," he said. "But we'll have more time to catch up in a second," he added, gesturing towards the stairs. "Or at the reunion, you're coming to the reunion, aren't you?"

Laura opened her mouth to respond but faltered. "We weren't sure whether or not we were going to go," she said. "With everything happening with Sarah, I didn't want anybody looking at us and thinking we were off having a good time while our daughter is missing. We may show our faces, for old time's sake, because in a way it would be weirder to not go, we'd be expected to go. But it's so good to see you. We really do have some catching up to do."

She turned on her heel and marched off down the hallway. Zoe looked up at Kidd, her face screwed up in confusion. Kidd gestured for her to follow Laura, which she did.

Kidd started up the stairs, suddenly very aware of his quite unclean boots on her very clean hardwood floors. Then again, it would probably give her something to make a video about. He looked back to make sure he wasn't traipsing mud through her house, relieved when he couldn't see footprints behind him.

There were photos hung on the wall by the stairs, photographs of Sarah at various ages in school uniforms, seeming to get older as he ascended. All the photos were posed, perfect, professional photographs, or at least made to look like that. There were some photos from what Kidd assumed was Laura and Michael's wedding. Though it looked new, so maybe it was a vow renewal. Or just a party where Laura decided to wear a big, white dress. She looked beautiful. Sarah was made in her image.

He made it to the top of the stairs and turned left as he'd been instructed, immediately heading towards the open door to what would likely be the most opulent bathroom he'd ever been in. But he stopped at another open door on the way.

Had it not already been open, practically begging him to come inside, he wouldn't have looked. At least, that's what he told himself. He looked left and right, making sure there was no one hiding behind any corners, watching him in case it was some kind of trap, before he pushed the door open a little further and stepped inside.

He was almost certain that the room belonged to Sarah, the only clues that really gave that away being a few photographs attached haphazardly to a cork board and the fact that it didn't look like the kind of master bedroom Laura Martins would have.

It was nothing like the rest of the house. Compared to everything else in the house, it looked like it had been ransacked. While, what he'd seen of the house and Laura's online presence had shown her to be the queen of clean, this was precisely the opposite. Perhaps she hadn't been able to bring herself to touch it after they'd come in here for the search. Maybe it was too much for her.

The room would already have been searched last night, looking for a suicide note or anything that might show her to be high risk. They also would have been looking for body parts or signs that the parents were responsible. Kidd knew the drill. But they'd not found anything. Kidd couldn't help but wonder if they'd missed something. There was more going on here than he could tell right away. He listened for the sounds of anyone coming up the stairs or coming down the corridor. He knew he shouldn't be in here, but he couldn't resist.

He didn't even really know what he was looking for. Something to help him find her, absolutely anything. He started over towards her desk. There was a computer on it, a few notebooks that were leaning over as if one of them were missing, either the ones she'd taken to school with her on Friday or ones they had seized.

He picked one of them up at random.

He opened it to find beautiful drawings in it. Sarah was artistic, it seemed. The pages were dotted, but she'd filled them with hand-drawn calendars and daily jottings. He found himself skimming over a couple, the names Dexter and Taylor coming up more than a few times. Jonno coming up a lot too, though not really with any reference to their relationship. She was even hiding it from her diaries too.

He put the notebook down and opened one of the desk drawers. It was full of makeup, lip glosses, mascaras, eye shadow palettes, the whole drawer practically overflowing when he opened it. He closed it and opened the next one, this time there was stationary. He rummaged a little, past the pens, the pencils, the sharpies, his heart pounding faster because the more time he spent in here, the more likely it would be that someone downstairs would wonder where he was.

Then his eye landed on something interesting.

It wasn't much. An Apple logo. But he found himself moving quicker, grabbing it and pulling it out from beneath the piles of pens. It was the same as the handset he had, a year or two out of date. Kidd couldn't imagine this family going without when it came to new tech. The parents had said she'd taken her phone with her, and the last ping on the phone had been near her school, so it all checked out. This had to be an old phone.

He wondered if there was anything on it, anything that might be able to help.

He pressed the on button, greeted with the Apple icon before the phone opened up before him. He opened the photos, selfie after selfie of Sarah. He checked the dates and saw that it was from just over six months ago, nothing new since then. At least it confirmed in his mind that it was an old handset.

He opened the internet browser, immediately clicking on the history. There was one place she visited more than most. *ThisIsMyHeaven.* It was a Tumblr, whatever the hell that was, stark white with pale grey writing on it. He saw the initial D and J in a block of text that seemed to go on forever.

Then the screen went black.

He tried to switch it on again, now greeted with an empty battery icon.

"Shit," he muttered.

"Can I help you?"

DI Kidd froze. Busted.

CHAPTER TWELVE

He closed the desk drawer, slipping the phone up the sleeve in his jacket out of sight. He turned around slowly to see PC Clara McCulloch stood in the door frame. They had worked together on a previous missing persons case some years ago. She was tall, dark-skinned, fairly well built, and staring daggers at DI Kidd. Her jacket was still zipped up like she'd just come in from the cold. Perhaps she had and Kidd had been too distracted to hear the door open and shut in the hall, to hear her footsteps on the stairs.

"Afternoon, Clara," he said, straightening up and looking her square in the eye. The only way he was going to get through this was with some blind confidence, maybe a little blagging. "I didn't know you were on this case, how have you been?"

"I've been better," she said flatly. "You here for—?"

"To discuss Sarah with her parents, yes," he said.

She eyed him carefully. "And what were you doing in Sarah's bedroom?" she asked.

"Looking for the bathroom," DI Kidd said, keeping his voice level, staying cool. He knew he'd been caught out here. They would have had a warrant for the search last night, but that didn't mean he could just wander into rooms in the house and start rummaging through drawers. This was the kind of mistake that could get him in trouble if he didn't play this right. "What about you?"

"Was coming to the bathroom myself. I just got here," Claire said, flashing him a smile. "Just a quick visit to make sure Mrs Harper is doing okay."

"I don't think she is."

"Neither do I," Claire replied. "But she certainly manages to put a brave face on it most of the time, don't you think?"

"I've only just met her," Kidd said. "Well, I knew her about twenty years ago, but I hardly think that counts."

"No," she said. "Did they sign another search book?" she added quickly.

"Not exactly," Kidd said. "Like I said, I was looking for the bathroom."

She stepped out of the doorframe and pointed down the hallway to where Kidd already knew the bathroom was. "It's just there."

"You're more than welcome to go first," Kidd said.

"You were looking," she said. "I don't want you to get any more lost than you already are." She knew what he'd been doing, snooping, looking for answers to questions he hadn't had the opportunity to ask. But she wasn't about to call him out on it.

"Thank you," he said. "You're very kind."

He walked out of Sarah's bedroom, sliding past PC McCulloch and towards the open door of the bathroom.

"They've already done a search of the room," PC McCulloch said quietly. "It's the first thing they do, you know that."

"They didn't find anything," Kidd said. "Looks like they ransacked the place."

"And did you?"

"Did I what?"

"Find anything," PC McCulloch asked.

DI Kidd smiled at her. He turned and pointed to the bathroom. "I found exactly what I was looking for."

He stepped inside, closing the door behind him before PC McCulloch could ask him any more questions. He took the phone from his sleeve and put it in his jacket pocket. He'd been looking, but as far as she knew, he'd not taken anything. She couldn't prove it. The only thing now was that there was an old phone burning a hole in his pocket and he wanted to fire it up and see what was on it.

He relieved himself, washed his hands, and left the room to find PC McCulloch still waiting for him to appear. No chance he was getting back into Sarah's room just now. Little did she know he might have already found what he was looking for. He nodded at her on the way past and headed downstairs once again, snapping pictures of the photos on the stairs as he passed, just in case there was anything in them that they could use.

DI Kidd walked down the hallway towards where the sound of clinking could be heard. DS Sanchez was sitting at the breakfast bar in the kitchen, the cold, white light from the garden making everything looking a little washed out. She eyed him carefully as he walked in. Laura was on her feet, shuffling around, getting mugs out of the cupboard while the kettle boiled on the stove.

Kidd did a double-take. She was using a vintage-looking metal kettle on the stove.

Each to their own, he thought.

"Sorry," Kidd said as he reappeared. "Took me a minute to find it."

Laura turned around from the cupboard, three pastel pink mugs balanced on the ends of her fingers. She was smiling, though it seemed a little strained. "No problem," she said. "DS Sanchez and I were just talking. Did you bump into PC McCulloch on your way down?"

"Yes," DI Kidd said. "She gave me quite a fright. Wasn't expecting to see another one of ours here today."

Laura laughed. "She's been awfully good to us," she said. "Always making sure everything is alright, asking if we've had any contact with Sarah, if we remember anything that might have…" she trailed off. "I suppose we'll come to that in a moment, won't we?"

The kettle whistled aggressively behind her. She poured the tea and brought it over to the breakfast bar, sitting across from them. She wrapped her hands around the mug, her nails a little chipped, the only thing about her that maybe wasn't quite as put together as the rest of the house. Her knuckles were white with the ferocity with which she held the cup, like it was a lifeline. He could tell that she'd already prepared herself for the worst. Maybe she was already grieving in her head.

"So," she said softly. "Where do you want to start?"

Kidd cleared his throat. "Is your husband here at all?" he asked. "It would be useful if—"

"He's at work," Laura interrupted. "The world hasn't stopped for him like it has for me. He still gets up every day at five o'clock, heads down to the office, does his day's work, and returns sometime around seven." She looked up at the two of them, her eyes looking a little misty. "Not that I mind, of course, it's keeping a roof over our heads."

"Maybe that's just his way of coping with it," Zoe said. "Everyone deals with things like this differently."

"Very true," Laura whispered, taking a sip of her tea. She winced at how hot it was, chuckling a little before returning her mug to the breakfast bar. "What do you want to ask me?"

"It really would be great if we could talk to your husband at some point," Kidd said. "I know he's a busy man but—"

"Well, he's trying to keep the business afloat," Laura said, nodding. "But I can give you the number of the office and I am sure he would be more than happy to set something up. He wants her found as much as I do."

"Has the business been struggling?" Kidd asked.

"There were layoffs," Laura said. "He had to make some very difficult decisions, stop some of the properties he was building mid-build, fire people who we were close to."

"Are you not close with them anymore?"

She blinked. "What's that?"

"You said 'were', Mrs Harper," Kidd said. "Have your relationships changed?"

"I don't see what that has to do with anything."

"I'm only thinking out loud, Mrs Harper—"

"Call me Laura."

"Laura, then," Kidd said. "I'm only thinking out loud. If your husband has made layoffs recently, upset people, it is possible there could be a connection to Sarah's disappearance."

"Like revenge?" she whispered.

Kidd had seen it happen many times before. People get low, people get desperate, and it makes them do desperate things. Of course, at this stage there likely would have been a ransom note, some demands that needed to be met, so it was pretty low on his expectation list but he wanted to cover as many bases as possible here.

"It's possible, Laura," DI Kidd said. "I'm not trying to upset you, I'm just trying to build a picture." She nodded, so he continued. "Could you give us a list of those people? It might be useful and it would give us places to look, just in case."

She nodded again. "I can ask Chris when he comes home. Chris, that's my husband," she added quickly. "Anything else?"

"What was Sarah's mental state like last week. It might give us some clue as to what might have happened."

"You think she might have run away rather than been kidnapped?" Laura asked, perking up suddenly. "Why would she do something like that?"

"We're keeping our options open," Kidd said.

"Well you just asked me about enemies, I thought that—"

"Her headteacher mentioned that Sarah would often do little disappearing acts from school," Kidd interrupted. "Wouldn't show up for a day or two at a time, usually when something happened in her personal life or at school."

"She got sick sometimes," Laura said, sitting up a little taller, affronted at the suggestion that Sarah was faking it. "The school worried about her attendance but if my daughter says that she's sick, then I'm not about to send her to school to infect other people or so that she's there feeling terrible for the whole day. What kind of parent would that make me?"

Laura returned to her cup, her hands shaking a little.

"We're not judging you, Mrs Harper," DS Sanchez said. "We're just trying to get an idea as to what Sarah might have been going through up to her disappearance."

"She seemed perfectly normal," Laura said. "No more upset than she normally was. We saw her on Friday morning, just like we usually do, and then we just...we didn't see her again. I thought she would be with a friend, she did that sometimes, but even checking her social media she hadn't been anywhere that we could see. Nothing had been updated."

"You check her social media?"

Laura nodded. "Of course," she said. "We know all of her accounts just so we can check up on her if we need to. And sometimes her messages." She looked at DI Kidd and DS Sanchez, doubling down as she caught whatever look was on their faces. "It's not spying," she insisted. Kidd got the impression she'd had this conversation before. "It's just parenting. With all these new social media outlets, we have to be more aware of what our children are up to than ever before. That's why."

DI Kidd wondered if it was also because Laura herself had a brand that she needed to uphold. If people were following both of them, surely anything Sarah did or said would reflect on her mother. Which might explain the website on the phone, giving her a place where she could express things she couldn't express publicly.

"So, Mrs Harper," DS Sanchez started. "It would appear that Sarah was having a bit of a tough week at school. Some secrets that she had were plastered all over the internet and shared around."

"What are you talking about?"

"From what we can gather, Sarah was cheating on her boyfriend Dexter with a different boy, Jonno," she continued, though DI Kidd noticed the face that Laura made when Zoe mentioned Dexter. A flash of disgust. "And someone took photos and posted them online."

"Why would someone do something like that?"

"That, we don't know yet," Zoe replied.

"But with everything that was happening at school for Sarah last week, did she show any indication that she was upset?"

Laura shook her head, tears filling her eyes. It barely took a moment before they were furiously cascading down her face. But she wasn't sobbing, she was just letting them fall, like she had simply turned on a tap.

"So you think it's more likely she's run away?" Laura replied. "Or could it be worse than that?" She choked on the last few words, her hand flying to her mouth as she tried to hold back the flood of emotions roiling just under the surface. "Could she have...? You don't think she's...?" She took a breath, composing herself, locking eyes with Kidd as she asked. "Do you think she might have taken her own life?"

"There's no indication of that," DI Kidd said flatly. "Sarah might have been in a fragile state of mind, but at the moment there's nothing to suggest that's what happened. We just want to find her. And we're doing our best, Laura, it just might take some time."

"She has to be okay, Ben," Laura said, her voice catching on practically every word. "She just has to be, I don't know what I'd do without her." And that was what it took for her to break down, sobs coming in heaving waves.

PC McCulloch, who'd been watching from the door, approached and started speaking softly to Laura, reassuring her that things were going to be alright, calming her down. Kidd wondered just how many times she'd had to do this since she got here.

"One last question, and then we'll be on our way," Kidd said. PC McCulloch looked up at him sharply. She didn't want him to ask any more questions, but he needed to know. "What were your feelings about Dexter Black?"

The sniffing stopped almost immediately, the crying quickly giving way to a stern expression that caught Kidd a little bit off guard.

"I didn't like him," she said bluntly.

"Why?"

"Why?" she repeated. "You're the investigating officer, DI Kidd, you don't need me to tell you what a terrible influence that boy is."

"I think I do," DI Kidd replied. "If nothing else, I'd like to hear your opinion."

Laura Harper took a few steadying breaths, brushing PC McCulloch away. She was staring daggers at Kidd again. Maybe this was a topic they'd already covered.

"I think he is a bad influence," she said flatly. "I think if anyone is responsible for her running away or for leading her astray, it's that boy. She drops everything for him, always with him if she can be," she said. "Though, maybe she was with that other boy, I don't know. Have you interviewed Dexter? Have you? Have you arrested him yet?"

"Mrs Harper, please calm down," PC

McCulloch said. "There's no use getting yourself all upset."

"Don't tell me to calm down," Laura barked. "That boy is a menace. And if you really gave a shit about finding my daughter you'd be talking to him, not coming here and upsetting me, her mother, a woman who fucking misses her daughter, alright?" And that was the last thing she said before she broke down in tears, putting her head on the breakfast bar and sobbing.

DS Sanchez turned to DI Kidd, moving her eyes towards the door. She was right. They'd probably gotten all they could out of Mrs Harper at this stage, and besides that, Kidd had a website in his pocket that he was desperate to look at, desperate to share with Zoe.

He took his phone out of his pocket and found a string of angry messages peppered with a lot of colourful language from DCI Weaver asking him where he was. They would have to visit Dexter Black later. It looked like it was time for the press conference, where Kidd would say what? They were looking into it? He hated this part. Feeding the vultures.

"Mrs Harper, we'd best be going," Kidd said, quickly downing his cup of tea before getting to his feet. "You've been very helpful and we will keep you updated as this develops."

"Just bring her back to me," Laura said, looking up at Kidd, tears running down her face, pulling her mascara with it so that black rivers ran to her jawline. "Please. I know I shouldn't beg, I know, but I am begging you, please bring her back to me."

"We're doing our best, Mrs Harper," DS Sanchez said, joining Kidd in standing. "We'll see ourselves out."

"Thank you, Laura. PC McCulloch." DI Kidd nodded to the PC before he started towards the front door, DS Sanchez on his tail. He opened the door and stepped out onto the driveway, practically marching away from the situation. DS Sanchez jogged a little to catch up.

"Someone's in a hurry," Zoe said. "What's happening?"

"Just hoping that PC McCulloch isn't following us, that's all," he said.

DS Sanchez took a heavy breath. "Why? What have you done?"

As they turned the corner, DI Kidd reached into his pocket and pulled out the phone. DS Sanchez jaw hit the floor.

CHAPTER THIRTEEN

"You must be out of your mind," DS Sanchez growled as they got back into the car. Kidd had explained going into Sarah's room, looking through her things, finding the phone, and then the website. And PC McCulloch catching him. "Do you know how much trouble you could get in for doing that?"

"Yes," he said. "But the door was open and I couldn't help myself."

"You absolutely could have helped yourself, Ben." Sanchez groaned. "You could have helped yourself from going in there and contaminating evidence."

"I didn't contaminate a damn thing," he said, pulling on his seatbelt. "They ransacked the room last night looking for something and found fuck all. I went in there and found something and if this ends up helping our investigation—"

"Then you acquired it illegally and you've

completely fucked it," she barked.

"It looked like a whole private blog, Zoe. I only read a little bit of it but it's in code. Enough code that a google search isn't going to make it pop up in the results. This could give us information on how she was feeling, what she was thinking, maybe even details on where she could be hiding. It could be the key to everything."

"Or it could get you fired."

Kidd sighed and leaned back in his seat. "Always going straight to the negative."

Zoe turned on the engine. "I'm trying to keep you grounded," she said. "You can't just go around doing whatever you like and thinking you're going to get away with it. You're not untouchable."

Kidd let the silence hang between them. He knew that he shouldn't have done it, even as he'd plucked the phone from the drawer and tried to switch it on he'd known it was a mistake. The fact it hadn't been found in the first place wasn't entirely surprising. They would have been looking for a suicide note or something of that ilk. And why would they look for a phone when the parents said she had it with her.

He took his phone out of his pocket, another message from DCI Weaver asking where he was.

"We need to go back to the station," Kidd said.

DS Sanchez turned to him. "Why? What

about Dexter?"

"He's going to have to wait." Kidd sighed. "The vultures have arrived."

"Feeding time on the Serengeti, how wonderful," she said, pulling out of her parking space. "What's on the menu for today?"

"Me," he replied. "Christ." He looked out the window before he eventually said, "I do not think I'm untouchable."

"Don't you?" Zoe asked. "Because I certainly wonder sometimes."

◆ ◆ ◆

They didn't say much else on their way back to the station, and Kidd didn't dare get the phone out in case it caused Zoe to go off at him again, but he was itching to see what Sarah had written. If her parents didn't know about it, it could be anything and maybe, just maybe, it would lead them to find her all the quicker. Even if Zoe wasn't impressed with the means, if it got them an outcome then she could hardly complain.

They made it back to the station, the car park a little fuller than it had been when they'd left, and made their way inside.

The Incident Room was humming with activity. The evidence board was full of social media pictures, names connected to faces of Sarah's friends and acquaintances. It looked busy, and busy meant that they might be getting somewhere.

"DC Ravel," Kidd said as he crossed the room to her desk. "I need you to do a search for a Nicholas…" he trailed off, turning to DS Sanchez. "Nicholas?"

"Nicholas Ayre," Zoe shouted.

"Thank you, DS Sanchez," he replied. "Nicholas Ayre. Also, anything you can get me on Dexter Black and Jonno Edwards, they also seem like they're going to be pretty important in all of this." He turned to see DC Powell over by the evidence board. "DC Powell, those are two names you'll need for the evidence board. Dexter Black. Jonno Edwards."

"Yes, sir," he said, heading over to his desk.

"What's happened then, sir?" DC Campbell asked, somehow still nursing a pain aux raisins, or maybe he'd been out to buy another. "Any updates?"

Kidd cleared his throat before he told them everything that had happened that morning, the discussion with Sarah's parents, with Sarah's headteacher, and how Dexter Black is nowhere to be found. It was that last thing that filled him with the most worry. He'd seen what young people were capable of in his time on the force, and angry young men made up a lot of them too. He hoped he was wrong about Dexter, but until he could speak to him he couldn't be sure.

"What's the plan then, boss?" DC Campbell asked.

"I've got a few things I need to look at first," he said. "If we can get the evidence board in order then we'll figure out our next move." He moved to walk over to his desk when the door to the Incident Room flew open, DCI Weaver standing in the frame.

"Did you get my messages, Kidd?" he barked across the room. Kidd took his phone out of his pocket, reminded of the string of missed calls he'd had outside the Harpers' house.

"Sorry, sir, was a little busy," he replied.

"You got my messages, why didn't you come to find me?" Weaver said. "Press conference. Outside. Now."

"Shit."

CHAPTER FOURTEEN

DI Kidd followed DCI Weaver back to his office, explaining to him on the way everything that they had so far, which in Weaver's eyes at least, wasn't a whole lot. He didn't mention the phone, if he mentioned the phone he would get a proper bollocking and he needed to make sure it had been worth taking before he set himself up for that.

"They're leads," Kidd said. "We didn't have leads this morning, at least now, we have people to talk to, people to track down, this morning —"

"This morning you had nothing, this afternoon you have a little bit more than nothing," Weaver interrupted. "It's not going to be enough."

"Then why call a press conference?"

"I had the superintendent breathing down my neck to get *something* out there," he barked.

"So, you gave me four hours to get something?" Kidd snapped. "Hardly seems fair."

"I don't give a shit about fair, Kidd. I give a shit about getting the job done," he parried, leaning on his desk. "The fact is, we have the nation's press outside and we need to tell them something."

Kidd eyed him from across the table, once again seeing the exhaustion in his face, the heavy bags under his eyes. It wasn't usual for their team to be going after a missing person but this was high profile. If the superintendent was breathing down his neck, if the nation's media was waiting outside for something to be said, he would have to say something. He hated talking to the press.

"Are they ready?" Kidd asked.

"Do you want to brief me on what you're going to say?" Weaver grumbled.

"We don't have time for that," Kidd replied, getting to his feet. "Not if you want them gone as soon as possible."

"I do want them gone, bloody vultures, scourge of the earth."

"Save it for the cameras, boss. I'm sure they'd love that." That made a smile twitch at the corners of Weaver's mouth. It wasn't a lot, but at least it was something. "I'll tell them where we are, but tell them the leads we have are promising, and then I'll answer a few questions. Unless they piss me off then I won't answer any at all."

They made their way down the corridor and towards the front of the station. Sure enough, there were cameras set up out the front, the major news stations emblazoned on the sides of them or on the microphones of the presenters waiting to quiz him on the investigation. If it had been tomorrow, maybe he would have had a little more, but it wasn't, it was now. And he needed to give them something.

"You're up, Kidd," Weaver said, clapping him on the shoulder. "Don't do anything I wouldn't do."

"So don't yell at them?" Kidd said with a raise of his eyebrow. "Thanks for the heads up, sir."

He headed outside and winced a little at the surge, as they all tried to jostle their way closer, pushing against the PCs that had been stationed there to keep them back. They were a vicious bunch, Kidd knew that all too well. One wrong foot and they'd sink you for it.

He took a breath, cleared his throat and stood tall in front of them.

"Hello, my name is Detective Inspector Benjamin Kidd," he said. "I'm the investigating officer on the disappearance of Sarah Harper. I'm here to give you an update on the investigation so far, and to answer some questions if you happen to have any." He didn't add, "I'm sure you do," even though it was tempting.

"We started our investigation last night

when Sarah Harper was reported missing and have since been tracking her movements, trying to fit together a timeline of the last time she was seen. She wasn't reported missing until Monday afternoon, so we have a little bit of catching up to do in that regard," Kidd stated. "We've conducted some interviews already, collecting all the information that we can and we are slowly seeing some leads beginning to emerge. There's still a lot of work to do on the investigation, a lot of stones that we still need to look under, and pieces of evidence we need to acquire but we are confident with how things are progressing."

He could see them taking notes, a couple of people with tape recorders out in front of them getting the sound bites, a couple of others already poised to ask questions.

"I'll be happy to take a few questions now," DI Kidd said. "Not too many, mind, we do have an investigation to conduct, after all."

He looked across the crowd, his eyes passing over Joe Warrington hovering near the back, apparently done with Uni for the day, before catching sight of a middle-aged white man in an ill-fitting grey suit, his tie a little askew, his hair even more so with his hand in the air. Kidd pointed at him.

"Do you think we're looking at a teen runaway or a kidnapping?" he asked.

"We're keeping an open mind at this stage," Kidd said. "As I said, we are tracking her movements leading up to her disappearance." He looked out at the crowd once again, catching sight of an Asian woman in a polka dot blouse. He couldn't really miss her. Maybe that was her tactic.

"Is this being pushed as a high priority because of Laura Harper's online following?" she asked. "If so, what about all the other missing people who haven't been given the same treatment?"

Kidd took a breath, not wanting to lose his rag with the reporter, but it was quite a question. "We treat all of our missing persons cases with the same level of urgency," Kidd said. "In the early part of any investigation, we try to get a jump on things as quickly as possible. However, Sarah is high risk because of her mother's status. That's not something to be ignored. It's all part of the investigation process."

He turned away from the woman and saw another woman wearing a blue blazer, her station printed on the microphone in front of her. She pointed it to herself as she spoke.

"What leads do you have? From what we've seen online not much progress has been made."

"What you've seen online?" Kidd asked.

"Mrs Harper has been posting regular updates and she doesn't seem happy with the way you've been handling the investigation, how do you respond to that?" she asked. It was a totally different question but spoken with the same malice, the same disdain.

"I would say that we are doing all we can," Kidd said, trying not to let the frustration show on his face. When Weaver had told him this investigation would be a doozy, he wasn't joking. If she kept on posting like this, she could end up jeopardising their search. "As I said, we started investigating last night and we are doing our best to keep Mr and Mrs Harper updated as best we can."

There were a few questions thrown out in response to that.

"Do you think you'll find her?"

"Do you have any suspects?"

"Do you think Sarah Harper will ever come home?"

"I think that's enough for now," DI Kidd said, looking out across the reporters and having to shout over their questions. "We will give you more when we have it. Thank you for coming down."

He turned with the intention of walking back into the station, but instead saw a familiar face over by the outside wall of the station. He was smiling, and even from where Kidd was, he could see how bright and white and perfect it was. John McAdams tucked his hands under his armpits as he drew his jacket around himself. He lifted his arm up to wave.

Kidd waved back and mouthed, "Five

minutes."

CHAPTER FIFTEEN

DI Kidd headed back into the station, DCI Weaver waiting for him on the other side of the door.

"Expertly handled," he said.

"Thank you, sir," Kidd replied. "That last question was...interesting."

"She's not wrong though," Weaver replied, taking his phone out of his pocket and showing it to Kidd. "Look at all this?"

Kidd took the phone and scrolled through it as they walked back towards the Incident Room. Laura Harper had posted all about their meeting, pretty much giving everyone on Twitter a blow by blow of everything that they'd talked about. And how it wasn't good enough. #JustKeepBreathing #BringSarahHome Both of them already trending.

"This is a lot," Kidd replied. "Can we stop her?"

Weaver shook his head. "I spoke to PC

McCulloch, she's the Missing Persons Officer, I think you know one another."

Kidd tried to keep his face neutral. "She was at the house today," Kidd said. "And we've worked together before."

"Of course you have, of course you have," Weaver said. "Anyway we asked her to talk to Mrs Harper about not posting all the time but she went off about how it's her career. So what can we do?"

"Can she call off her followers? Whoever's running the Twitter for this place must be losing their minds."

"She won't do that either," Weaver replied. "Believe me when I say we've bloody tried." He sighed and leaned on the wall outside the Incident Room. "I'm not trying to put undue pressure on you here, Kidd, but the quicker we can get this wrapped up the better."

"I agree, sir," Kidd replied. "We're doing our best."

DI Kidd headed back into the Incident Room for the briefest moment to grab his wallet, but stopped as he felt in his jacket for the phone. He rummaged in his desk drawer for a charger and plugged it into the back of Sarah's old phone, hiding it beneath some papers before heading back outside to meet John. When he got back he would look at what was on there, look at the site properly and see what it could tell them, if anything.

John was still waiting by the wall but now there weren't a horde of cockroaches hounding him with questions.

He crossed the car park to John McAdams who immediately wrapped him in a hug, tucking his hands behind Kidd's back and planting a kiss firmly on his lips. Kidd was a little shocked at the contact. He hadn't been expecting it. They hadn't been going out for that long and even though Kidd allowed himself to melt into it and breathe for what had to have been the first time that day, it certainly felt like a weird thing to be doing outside the station.

"What did I do to deserve that?" he asked.

John shrugged. "You met me for lunch," he replied. "I know how busy you are, I hate to disturb you most of the time, but when you mentioned it yesterday..." he trailed off.

"What?" Kidd asked.

"It just seemed like a nice idea, that's all," he replied. "Besides, it breaks up the monotony of working from home. Although," he checked his watch, "they want me in a meeting in an hour and a half, so that's how long we have to wine and dine."

"I'll be heading back to the station afterwards, so no wine for me, unless you mean whining, because I can do plenty of that after the day I've had."

"Maybe just wine for me then," John replied with a waggle of his eyebrows.

"We don't all work in publishing, you know," Kidd replied. "Not everyone can get away with drinking on the job."

"In publishing, believe me when I say, it helps."

Kidd and John crossed the road outside the station and headed down towards the riverside. Kidd could already feel his phone buzzing in his pocket and quickly took it out to switch it to silent. He didn't want to be disturbed when he was supposed to be having a nice lunch. He never took a proper lunch break, never usually had the time, but he was determined to actually spend the next hour with John. He'd promised him after all.

They walked into a pretty nice restaurant overlooking the river, the two of them taking seats by the window. The decor was a little over the top, and way too fancy for somewhere like Kingston, but it was blissfully quiet, the post-lunchtime rush had died down, practically giving them the run of the entire restaurant. There even seemed to be a team of waitstaff over by the bar, waiting for people to arrive.

When they'd walked in the door, a young man quickly approached them. His hair was cropped close to his head and he was wearing a clean, bright white shirt that had creases across the front of it like he'd just taken it out of the packet that morning and neglected to iron it.

"Hello, my name is Alex, I'll be your server

today," he said brightly. "Can I get you started with some drinks?"

"I'll get a lemonade. John?"

John sneaked a quick look at the menu. "A sparkling water?"

Alex wrote them down and swished off towards the bar. Given that there was hardly anybody in here, Kidd didn't anticipate he would be all that long. He looked over at John, who had taken off his jacket to reveal he was wearing a well-fitted checked shirt, tucked into his black jeans. His face cracked into a smile when he caught Kidd looking.

"What are you staring at?"

"Nothing," Kidd replied, flustered, picking up his menu. "You just look nice, that's all."

"Thank you," he said. "Thought I'd make an effort."

"I'm just here in my work stuff," Kidd replied.

"Yes, but Ben, your work stuff is a suit and tie," he replied, still smiling. "If I'd shown up in what I'd been working from home in all day, it would have looked like you were taking a homeless person out to lunch."

"What were you wearing?"

"Day pyjamas."

"What on earth are day pyjamas?"

"Pyjamas...for daytime," he said. Kidd couldn't stifle a laugh. "It's literally a pair of grey sweatpants and a tee, but it's not cute for going out for lunch."

Kidd couldn't really imagine an outfit where he wouldn't think that John was cute, but he decided to keep that to himself. They'd not been seeing each other for all that long and the last thing he wanted to do was scare him off by being too forward.

"Ben?" he said, leaning forward. "I asked what you've been up to."

"Oh," Kidd said, jumping a little. He'd gotten lost in his own head for a moment. "We started working on a new case actually. There's a teenage girl that's gone missing. That's what the press conference thing was about outside the station."

"So I'll turn on the news tonight and you'll be there?"

"Possibly. It might not go national but if it does, I'll be nervously chattering on about Sarah Harper," Kidd said with a sigh. He still wished he'd been able to come up with something a little more concrete rather than vague, politician-style answers that would be torn apart by people online. "It's a pretty big case."

The waiter appeared and placed their drinks on the table, offering a hopeful smile to them both which faded when John politely informed him that neither one of them had yet picked up the menu. He said he would give them a few minutes and scurried off, presumably to stand over to one side and watch them until they picked up the menus and put them back down again.

"The reunion tonight, then," John said, opening his bottle of sparkling water and glugging it into the glass. "What's the dress code? I'm assuming it's also not a day pyjamas kind of place."

DI Kidd winced. He'd forgotten about that.

"What?" John said. "Have I said the wrong thing? I promise I'm not about to wear day pyjamas out, that was a joke."

"I know, I know," Kidd said, taking a quick sip of his drink before turning back to look at him. He was staring across the table at Kidd, his dark brown eyes looking a little sparkly in the light coming in from the window, his hair in that perfect quiff that miraculously seemed to stay there. Kidd had no idea how. His hair always looked scruffy no matter what he tried to do with it. He looked hopeful and Kidd felt like he was about to tell a child that Santa Claus wasn't real. "Something has sort of come up," he said eventually.

"Oh?" It was all John managed. It was clearly still Kidd's turn to speak.

"The reunion is still happening, and I'm still going, but the parents of Sarah Harper, the girl that's gone missing, they are likely going to be there," he said, though he didn't like how readily he was giving out details of what he was working on. He wasn't supposed to be doing that. But this was different, wasn't it? "I thought it would be a good idea to go with DS Sanchez, you know Zoe, so we can scope things out a little. I meant to tell you earlier, but I'd already moved this lunch because of my stupid work schedule and I didn't want to—"

John reached across the table and put a gentle hand on Kidd's forearm. It stopped him from speaking immediately and he looked up to lock eyes with John once again. He was smiling. In spite of the fact that Kidd was blowing him off entirely for tonight, John McAdams was smiling. And it was enough to calm the pounding in Kidd's heart.

"It's alright," he said. "I don't mind not going to the reunion with you. I sort of mind about not getting to spend the evening with you, but we can do that another time. I'm not about to have a breakdown over it."

"You're not?"

John laughed. "Not even close," he said. "You will have to make it up to me some other time though."

"I don't know if I have another reunion around the corner," Kidd said, allowing an easy smile to fall across his face. "So, if you have any other ideas?"

John grinned broadly. "I have plenty." He waggled his eyebrows and Kidd felt his heart skip. He couldn't remember the last time someone had that effect on him. He knew it was probably Craig, but he tried to push those feelings out of his head right now. The last thing he needed was to ruin this.

"We should probably look at this menu," John said. "I can feel the eyes of that waiter burning into the side of my skull. If we don't order soon he's going to have us escorted out for loitering."

"'Escorted out for loitering.' You sure you're not a detective?"

"I've read enough crime novels in my day job to pick up some of the lingo," John replied with a wink. Kidd felt weak. He needed to calm down.

He was about to pick up his menu to see what this place had on offer when a high-pitched laugh from somewhere towards the back of the restaurant caught his attention. It turned out there were other people in here after all.

There was a man and a woman at the far end of the restaurant. They were up on a raised platform, tucked away in a corner, almost in darkness. Even the curtains near them were closed. A man was whispering in the ear of a blonde woman who was giggling, either at what he was saying or at that feeling of someone saying sweet nothings to you.

Kidd was about to turn back to his menu when the man moved away from the woman's ear and came into focus. He locked eyes with

Kidd and his face dropped instantly.

What on earth was Greg Spencer doing here?

CHAPTER SIXTEEN

Kidd's head was spinning, but he couldn't bring himself to turn back to the menu, to break eye contact with Greg. Greg looked ashen, like he was about to throw up right where he was sitting.

The woman hadn't noticed, she was too busy saying something to him and packing her purse away into her bag. She was chattering away to Greg, but even from this distance Kidd could see that he had no idea what she was saying. If there was a pop quiz, he would fail it.

"Are you ready to order?" The waiter had appeared at the table once again, pulling Kidd's attention back to John, who was looking over at him expectantly. "Or do you still need a moment?"

"Ben?" John asked. But his face suddenly dropped when he saw the expression on Kidd's face. Kidd didn't know what it was exactly, something akin to a murderous bear most likely because right now, his sister's husband was out with another woman and his blood was boiling. "Ben, what's going on?"

John turned around and looked at the couple before turning back to Kidd. "You know those people?"

"I know one of them," Kidd said. He looked up at the waiter. "Just a few more minutes, I promise it won't take me much longer than that. Everything looks great." The waiter scurried away and Kidd put his menu down on the table. "I won't be a second. I'm sorry."

He wondered how many more times he would apologise to John for getting distracted when they were supposed to be together, for putting something else first. He hoped it wasn't something that kept happening. He was supposed to be doing better at this, but here he was, leaving a handsome man alone at a table to go and deal with something that was none of his business.

Well. It was sort of his business. He'd always felt a little protective of Liz, but he thought that Greg was a good guy. He was supposed to be anyway. He didn't feel the need to have an, "If you hurt my sister, I will hurt you," chat when they got married because it seemed like a tired old cliché but now he was having second thoughts.

"Greg," Kidd said flatly as he reached their section of the restaurant. "Fancy seeing you here."

"Yes," Greg replied, nervous, sweating profusely. *Good*, Kidd thought. "Small world isn't it?"

"Tiny," Kidd replied. "And you are?"

"Beth," the blonde woman said, her smile never fading for a second. Her lipstick was a little bit smudged around the edges. It was enough for Kidd to put two and two together and come out at the right number. "Nice to meet you."

Kidd smiled and turned his attention back to Greg. "Can I talk to you outside?"

"We're actually just leaving," Greg said, getting to his feet, putting on his jacket.

"Great," Kidd said. "I'll walk with you."

"I don't want to keep you," Greg said, nervously running a hand through his hair. "Aren't you coming over for dinner again next week?"

"It doesn't really feel like the kind of thing to discuss over dinner," Kidd growled. Greg was clearly trying to brush him off, trying to run away from this like he had no say in what was going on right now. Kidd locked eyes with him. "So. Outside?"

Greg sighed and looked over at Beth who, bless her, looked so confused. Either she was none the wiser as to the fact that Greg was a married man, or she was just stupid. Either way, Kidd felt instantly sorry for her being caught in the middle of all this. Whatever this was.

"Sure," Greg said. He turned back to Beth.

"Do you want to come out in five minutes?"

"Sure, I'll go to the bathroom," she said.

"Better make it ten," Kidd replied. "Really wash those hands when you're done."

Kidd walked ahead of Greg towards the doors of the restaurant. He saw John watching them as he walked past, several shades of confused. Kidd mouthed, "I'm sorry," on the way past.

When they were out in the open, Kidd found the chill of the winter sun welcoming. He hadn't realised quite how warm it had been in the restaurant, or maybe that was just his blood boiling at the sight of Greg.

He didn't check to see if Greg was behind him, walking over to a little bridge that passed over an inlet next to the restaurant. When he got to the railing, he turned around to see Greg staring at him, his jacket now on, doing up the buttons on his blue, checked dress shirt. Kidd clocked the fingers. He wasn't wearing his wedding ring.

"Ben, I can explain—"

"Okay," Kidd interrupted. "Try and explain what I saw in there, I dare you."

Greg took a breath. "Beth is—"

"And don't you dare lie to me," Kidd interrupted again, doing his best not to raise his voice, not to cause a scene. "I know what I saw and I won't have you standing here and lying to me about it. Where the fuck is your wedding ring?"

Greg looked down at his fingers like he'd seen a ghost. Maybe he'd hoped Kidd wouldn't notice. Maybe he'd forgotten that it was Kidd's job to notice things.

"She's a colleague from work," Greg said. "I've been working late a lot over the past few months. She's been helping."

"I assume she's been doing more than getting the coffees in," Kidd spat.

"That's not fair."

"No, Greg, what's not fair is the fact that you're off with someone else when you're married to my sister," Kidd growled. "It's not fair that I had to see what I saw in there. It's not fair that I'm having to rip the shit out of you right now and that I can't hit you."

"You want to hit me?"

"I want to beat you to death," Kidd said bluntly. "I want to beat you to a pulp and throw you in that water and never see you again. What the fuck are you thinking?"

"I-I don't know what I'm thinking," Greg said. "It was…it was fun."

"Fun?"

"Yeah," Greg said, joining Kidd at the railing and looking out across the water. "Look, I don't know how much Lizzie tells you about our marriage, about how things are between us, but lately it hasn't been too good. I've been busy at work, she's been busy with the kids, we barely have any time for each other, and then there was Beth..." He trailed off, putting his head in his hands. "It all just went too far."

"How long has it been going on?" Kidd asked, keeping his voice as flat as possible.

"Ben, please don't ask me that."

"How long?" Kidd barked.

"Two months," Greg replied quietly. "They really started riding me hard at work when I came back because I'd been off with Liz and Tim for my paternity leave. So it was a lot of late nights. And late nights with Beth there. One night it went too far and...I never stopped it."

"Did you want to stop it?"

Greg didn't answer right away. "I love Lizzie so much," he said finally, tears choking every word. "Her and the kids mean everything to me. It was a mistake."

"A mistake that you continued with," Kidd said, trying to keep his voice steady. "Keeping it all secret, taking off your wedding ring..." Kidd trailed off. "If you were trying to hide it, might I suggest not taking her to a restaurant in the town where your wife lives, where her brother works."

"I didn't think you'd be out on a lunch date," Greg said. "Who's the guy?"

"That's John," Kidd replied. "He's...new."

"Things going well?"

"Yeah," Kidd said. "I could do without leaving the aforementioned lunch date to come out here and tear you to pieces, but here we are." Kidd sighed and looked at Greg. He was still cradling his head in his hands. "Look at me, Greg. Please."

Greg looked over at Kidd. His eyes looked like they were about to overflow with tears. He'd been caught, and he knew that he'd been caught. He looked terrified.

"Please don't tell her," Greg whispered. "Please."

Kidd took a breath. He knew that the right thing to do would be to go over to their house right now and tell Liz what he'd seen, that her husband had been cheating on her. But then he thought of the kids. When he thought of Tilly and Tim potentially losing their father, all his own doing, of course, Kidd felt his fury fade. He didn't want to be responsible for that. He couldn't bring himself to be.

"I won't," Kidd said quietly. "But you need to end this. Whether you tell Liz or not, that's your prerogative, I'm not getting involved in that part of your relationship, but you finish this today. You put your fucking wedding ring back on and you be the man you're supposed to be for my sister, and your kids."

Greg nodded. He took a few deep breaths, the tears vanishing from his eyes as quickly as they'd appeared. He calmed himself down a little before he spoke.

"Thanks, Ben," he said. "You're a really

good person, you know that?"

Kidd wasn't so sure. He and Liz didn't keep secrets from one another. Whenever things got hard in either one of their lives, their first port of call was to speak with the other sibling about it. But now there was something that Kidd certainly couldn't talk to her about, at least not without causing a heck of a lot of damage. Even so, it didn't feel good.

"Finish it today," Kidd said. "Alright?"

"I will, I promise," he said. "Thanks again, Ben. And I'm sorry."

Kidd shook his head. "You don't need to apologise to me. But you do need to make it up to Liz."

They said their goodbyes and Kidd watched as Greg walked away with Beth. The other woman. He had noticed last night that things between them weren't great, but he hadn't wanted to think that something like this was going on. But here it was, right in front of his face. He couldn't very well ignore it.

He looked back to the restaurant where he saw John looking at him through the window. John waved, none of the wiser, and Kidd offered him a smile. He might not be able to ignore it, but he would have to forget about it. At least for now.

CHAPTER SEVENTEEN

Kidd returned to his lunch with John, trying to explain in as few terms as possible exactly what had just happened. John hadn't even met anyone from Kidd's family, he hardly wanted his first impression of his sister's husband to be that, but he couldn't help it.

John was his trademark kind and understanding self, and no sooner had they spoken about it did the topic get buried under a discussion about what they'd each done that day. With John working in publishing, his morning had mostly consisted of meetings that he was conferenced into so he didn't have to go into the office, and editorial work on the many different authors that he worked with. He loved his work, and it definitely consumed him sometimes, but not quite in the same way that Kidd's did. He wanted to learn from John in that respect, learn how to leave the work stuff at the office and live a somewhat normal life.

John walked him back, the two of them walking hand in hand until they reached the front of the station. Kidd found himself promising that he would make things up to John with the reunion, and John made it his mission to show Kidd that he wasn't altogether bothered about it, that everything was fine and neither one of them needed to panic. It was what Kidd needed to hear.

He turned his attention back to the station, refocussing his mind on the matter at hand. Finding Sarah Harper.

"And who on earth was that handsome man dropping you off?" Diane chirped from behind the desk, her eyes practically on stalks. "You should have invited him in."

"What? So you could interrogate him? I don't think so," Kidd said with a wink.

"He's gorgeous."

"Don't be jealous, Diane," Kidd replied, taking out his key card for the door. "You're my one true love, you know that."

"Oh, stop that, you'll make me blush!"

Kidd pushed through the door and headed back towards the Incident Room. DC Powell and DC Ravel were out, DC Campbell saying through a mouthful of food that they had nipped out to get lunch.

Has he done anything other than eat today? Kidd thought as he passed Campbell's desk and headed to where DS Sanchez was perched, her phone in one hand, a disposable cup of coffee in the other.

"Good lunch?" she said, wiggling her eyebrows at him.

"I've had better."

The playfulness in her face suddenly fell off a cliff and she eyed him carefully. "Why? What happened?"

"Oh, it was nothing with John," Kidd replied, quickly telling her that he'd seen Greg with another woman at the restaurant.

"So you confronted him?"

"Gave him a bit of a bollocking, yeah," Kidd said. "Couldn't help myself. Would have decked him if I didn't have somewhere else to be."

"Ben!"

"What?"

"What did he say?" Zoe asked.

"He's breaking it off with her," he replied. "And we're not telling Liz."

DS Sanchez sighed. "And why are we not telling Liz?"

"Because I'm not about to be responsible for their family breaking up," Kidd said. "If he wants to tell her, that's his choice, but I'm not going to be the one to do it. He said he's going to break it off with Beth."

"And you believe him?"

"I have to believe him, Zoe," Kidd replied flatly. "I don't want to be the one to do it, so Greg

Spencer is going to have to grow a pair and come home to his wife instead of hanging out with some floozy from the office."

DS Sanchez considered this, taking a slow sip of her coffee. She made the tiniest gasp before she looked back up at Kidd. "You don't think that's where he was last night, do you? When he came in late?"

Kidd hadn't even thought about that. If he had, he might have asked. He sighed and looked at Zoe. "I sincerely hope not, but I think you might be right." He headed over to his desk and put his things down, the phone now had enough juice and had switched itself on. He took a seat at his desk and opened it up.

"What the fuck are you doing?" Sanchez groaned. "You can't just—"

"But I am just," he interrupted. "Look, it wasn't the right thing to do but once I saw what I saw I couldn't unsee it." He tapped through the phone again, finding the website and copying down the URL. He typed it into a browser on his computer and opened it up. It looked just as it had done before, the same white background with grey lettering so it was barely legible. "Do you want to look or not?"

DS Sanchez couldn't help herself, grabbing a chair and pulling it round to sit next to Kidd. He scrolled down. There had to be hundreds of posts. Some of them were text, some of them were reposted photographs from elsewhere.

Sanchez looked at him. "This doesn't look good."

"I know," Kidd replied. The photos were definitely concerning. Most of them were pictures of women with text across them about being sad, about being empty.

"You don't think she—?"

"I hope not," Kidd replied. "But we can't rule it out."

He kept scrolling. There had to be hundreds of posts. It would take them days to go through them all. He returned to the top of the page and read the most recent post.

D is on my last nerve. There are too many lies, too many fights and I don't think I can take it anymore. He needs to make a decision but if I force him to, I know that I could lose everything. He probably would too, though I don't care so much about that. D needs to change and he needs to change now.

"Dexter?" Sanchez said.

"Most likely," Kidd replied. He read it over again. *D needs to change.* Everyone at the school had said how strange their relationship was, even Sarah's mum had said he wasn't a good influence. Maybe she was aware of it. Maybe she knew what damage it was doing. Maybe he was who they needed to be focussing on. "Do you want to head out?"

Zoe nodded, downing her coffee and slamming the cup on her desk. "Where we off to?"

Kidd sighed. "We're off to see Dexter Black," he said. "And if that post is anything to go by, I imagine he will have a lot to say."

"You think he'll be at home?" Zoe asked.

Kidd shook his head. "If he's at home, I'll buy you a pint."

❖ ❖ ❖

"So, what time do you think he'll be home?"

Kidd was at the front door of the Black residence. Both Dexter's parents were there, standing in the door frame, neither one of them particularly pleased to have two detectives on their doorstep. It was a fairly common thing. Most people were nice as pie, but you got the occasional family who hated the guts of anyone who worked for The Met on principle alone.

"Not sure," Mrs Black said. She was a slight woman, so thin that the slightest breeze might send her flying off into the sky never to return. But she was well put together, her brunette hair in a severe bob that moved as she spoke like it had a life of its own "He sort of…does his own thing most of the time."

"He's probably just out with his mates," Mr Black said. He was wearing a navy blue dress shirt that was stained with splatters of what DI Kidd hoped was paint. His face was clean-shaven, a couple of spots on his neck where he'd caught himself. Unlike Mrs Black, he didn't look so well put together. But maybe that was just the stained shirt giving that impression.

"Does he do that a lot?" Kidd asked.

"Yes," Mr Black replied. "If he's not off with Sarah, he's out with Jonno, or they're out in a whole group."

"And what about Sarah?" DS Sanchez asked. "How are things between them?"

"Who's asking?"

"The police are asking," DS Sanchez snapped. "We've got a missing teenager on the borough, we're making sure that we're looking at absolutely everything we can."

"And that includes my son?" Mr Black asked, raising his voice a little. His wife put her hand across the door frame, like she was trying to stop him from charging.

"As far as we were aware, everything was fine between them," Mr Black said flatly. "They spent an awful lot of time together, either as a couple or as a group, and we know about the arguments, when he'd come in a strop or something. People fight."

"It's the family you want to watch," Mrs Black barked.

"Philippa," Mr Black snapped.

"What? You say it as much as I do," she snapped back. She turned to the detectives. "They're trouble. Laura with all of her vanity online, immodesty. Him with that crooked company and all those women."

"That's quite enough, Philippa," Mr Black grumbled. "Let he who is without sin—"

"Shut up," she snapped. "They want to know about them so they should know about them." She turned back to the detectives. "Can't keep it in his pants. No respect for the sanctity of marriage."

Kidd looked down at her neck to see she was wearing a cross. So she was religious and the way Mr and Mrs Harper conducted themselves wasn't really in keeping with that. Though, of course, if she didn't like them it could all have been rumours and hearsay. Neither of the parents liking each other, a Romeo and Juliet story played out in Kingston. Kidd had to resist rolling his eyes.

"I'm not here to talk about the Harpers," Kidd said. "I would love to know about your son's relationship with Sarah, if possible."

"I really think you should be talking to our son about this," Mr Black said sharply.

"We would love to," DS Sanchez replied, a sweet smile spreading across her face. "If you tell us where we can find him, I'm sure we can arrange that."

"I told you already, we don't know where he is."

"Do you know where he's been since Friday?" DS Sanchez asked. "Sarah Harper was last seen on Friday, and she was last seen being shouted at by your son at school. Can you vouch for his whereabouts over the weekend?"

"He was here," Mrs Black said quickly. "We were surprised because he's normally out with his friends all weekend, staying up all hours. But he didn't leave the house. That's all we can tell you I'm afraid."

"And what about his lack of attendance at school?" DS Sanchez added. "Did you know he's not been to school this week?"

Mrs Black stared back at them blankly. Mr Black was doing the same. Kidd looked over at DS Sanchez who was waiting on a response that didn't seem to be forthcoming.

"Mr and Mrs Black, when was the last time you saw your son?" Kidd asked.

Mrs Black took a breath. "Sunday morning."

CHAPTER EIGHTEEN

When they'd finally gotten a truthful statement out of Mr and Mrs Black, DI Kidd and DS Sanchez made their way back to Kingston Police Station. Things were getting more and more confusing. Dexter Black was missing, yet hadn't been reported as such. Sarah Harper was missing, and her mother was going spare while the father continued to work all hours of the day, and according to the Blacks at least, was playing away. They needed to get a handle on this and they needed to get a handle on it fast.

DS Sanchez pulled into the police station car park. She shut off the engine and turned to him. "None of this looks good if you ask me."

"I'm worried," he said. "I'm worried that they're both missing, especially since the last time they were seen together he was yelling at her."

"You think he did it?"

"Did what?"

"Kidnapped her."

"I don't know," Kidd said quietly. "You said it yourself, it seems a little too obvious doesn't it?"

"It would explain why he's nowhere to be found." DS Sanchez sat back in her chair and looked over at Kidd. "They could have run away together."

"What, like love's young dream?" Kidd asked.

"It's a possibility, however remote," DS Sanchez replied. "There is always the possibility that no matter how hard we look, maybe Sarah Harper doesn't want to be found."

It wasn't a thought that had occurred to Kidd just yet. Sarah Harper seemed to have a lot more troubles in her life than anyone really knew. From the overbearing parents to the semi-abusive boyfriend, Kidd definitely wouldn't have blamed her if she'd wanted to run away from it all and strike up somewhere new. Who could?

"It's worth considering," DI Kidd said. "I'm wondering if that website of hers can tell us anymore. I may have to look at it a little more closely. Either way, DCI Weaver isn't going to like that idea. He wants this case closed."

"You know more about missing people than most, Ben," DS Sanchez said. "If they don't want to be found, maybe they never will be."

It was a very unsubtle way of talking

about Craig. Two years missing and he hadn't heard a word…apart from what Andrea had sent him last night. With everything that had happened since then, he was surprised to find that it had almost vanished from his mind entirely.

"What?" Zoe said. "You've gone quiet on me. Is this a detective thing or have I made you sad?"

"A little of both," Kidd said, turning to her. "I need to tell you something."

"Oh my god, what's happened?" DS Sanchez said. "Is it about this morning? I knew there was more going on than you said."

She really was good at her job, so it was no wonder DS Sanchez had picked up on that. DI Kidd took a breath and pulled out his phone, bringing up the picture to show her.

"What am I looking at?" she asked, squinting at the picture. "It's a train station, there's a blonde guy on the platform…" She trailed off, her mouth falling open a little. Her eyes widened and she looked up at Kidd. She shook her head slowly. "You don't think—"

"I don't know," Kidd interrupted. "If I'm completely honest, I have no idea, but there it is. There it might be, I don't know."

DS Sanchez pulled the phone closer to her face, looking at the picture. She pinched and zoomed. It wasn't going to help her. It hadn't helped him.

"So this was taken nearly a year ago?" she

asked. Kidd nodded. "Which would mean—"

"Despite everyone's best efforts to convince me to move on and tell me that he's dead, he might actually be alive."

"Wow." DS Sanchez passed the phone back to him. "Didn't the family have a funeral?"

"Yep."

"Do they know?"

Kidd shrugged. "I don't think so. Andrea, his sister, she was the one who sent it to me. So she knows, obviously. She's never given up."

"Just like you."

"Just like me." Kidd sighed. "I don't know what to do with it."

"What can you do?" she asked. "You were looking for him and you couldn't find him. Now a picture has shown up saying that he might be alive, what are you supposed to do?"

"I'm not sure what you're getting at here."

"What I'm getting at," DS Sanchez continued, "is that you do nothing. It's what I've already said, Ben. Maybe he doesn't want to be found."

"You really think that?"

"Whatever it was that made him skip town in the first place has obviously kept him away," she said.

"But if he's in danger shouldn't I try and find him so I can help?"

"Absolutely not," DS Sanchez said. "If he wanted your help, he would come looking for you, don't you think? If he's in trouble with somebody, and he thought you, his former detective boyfriend could help, I think he would have made the effort to track you down at some point over the past two years."

It was a truth that Kidd hadn't really wanted to consider. He had kept looking, of course, he had. He'd sent that message to Andrea, hadn't he? But if Craig had wanted Kidd's help, he would have asked for it. Or at least, Kidd hoped he would have. No one should have to go through bad times alone.

"What are you thinking?" Zoe asked.

"That I don't know what to do with this picture," he said. "It might not even be him."

"I think it is," Zoe said quietly. "And I think you know it is."

"Then what do I do?"

Zoe sighed and looked over at Kidd, her eyes were big and expressive, trying to be there for him even though he could literally feel himself putting a wall up as they spoke.

"You find Sarah Harper," she said. "We have a job to do, so we should do it."

"What about John?"

"What about him?"

Kidd sighed. "Do I tell him?"

Zoe considered it for a moment, looking out of the window and then back at Kidd. "No," she said. "Craig hasn't come to find you. Maybe it's over after all. Maybe this is the closure you need to move on."

Kidd opened his mouth to reply, but any words that he might have had for Zoe died on his tongue. He knew in his heart of hearts that she was right. Craig surely would have come back if he'd needed him, if he'd still loved him. Though he did still wonder what it was that was keeping him away. It had to be pretty bad.

"You gonna be okay?" she asked, reaching across to put a hand on his forearm, giving him a little squeeze.

"I'm going to have to be," he replied. "Like you said, we have a job to do."

They got out of the car and headed into the station, greeting Diane on their way past and heading straight back to the Incident Room. He marched over to his computer and booted it up, returning to Sarah's website.

Kidd moved to the next post down, more things about D. There were phrases that kept coming up, about secrets he held, about the things he had done to her, shouting abuse, sending aggressive messages. She didn't seem to hold a lot of affection for him, which was precisely the opposite of what each set of parents had indicated.

Kidd stared at the screen. He shouted DS Sanchez over.

"Look at this," he said. "Does this sound like the same relationship that their parents were talking about?"

"Christ, '*D has been yelling at me again today. I don't know what he wants but I guess it isn't me. Maybe I should just disappear.*' That's a bit heavy," DS Sanchez said. "You don't think—?"

"We don't have a body, just a missing person," Kidd interrupted. "If a body shows up, maybe we'll consider it."

"But we can't deny the fact that she was vulnerable," she said, grabbing the mouse and scrolling down. "'*Everyone has secrets but D's hurts more than most. Everything about my life is a lie.*' This is all so dark, did none of her friends know about this? Her parents?"

"Every other social media platform is happy-clappy all the time," he said. "It's what you said. It's a highlight reel, all perfectly filtered, perfectly placed, nothing is wrong, but this…this is worrying."

He continued to scroll down to the next post.

Secrets ruin people's lives. I am proof of that today, aren't I? Everything about me and J is out. But what about D? What about all of D's secrets? I know enough secrets to tear D's world apart. He has no idea what's coming for him when I let rip. Or maybe he does? Guess we'll find out.

"Shit," DS Sanchez said. "What do we do?"

"We need to find Dexter Black," Kidd said. "And we need to find him now."

CHAPTER NINETEEN

The world swayed in and out of focus.

How long had she been here? How long had she been out?

It was hard to say.

When she opened her eyes, she could see a small amount of light. Was it coming through a window? The only window she could see was blocked off, boards up against it.

Where was she?

She knew this place. Didn't she?

She'd been here before.

Hadn't she?

She didn't know. She couldn't tell.

"Oh, you're waking up?" The voice was familiar. Deep. Gruff. She shook her head and tried to turn her head to see where the voice was coming from but she couldn't move.

Her wrists were tied, her ankles too. There was something around her neck.

"Can't have you waking up now," the voice

said, getting closer. She recognised it, but she couldn't place it. She was so tired. So, so tired.

They were approaching her, whoever it was.

"I'll be gone for a little while," it said, softer this time, creeping in her ear. "Don't you go doing anything stupid now."

There was a sharp stab in her arm. She winced. She wanted to scream but she couldn't bring herself to. Because here came the dark again, taking her away. She couldn't escape, she was stuck here with the last words of her captor echoing in her mind.

"Goodnight, Sarah," it said. "Sleep tight."

CHAPTER TWENTY

Finding Dexter Black was something that would have to wait until the following morning. DCs Powell, Ravel, and Campbell had already gone home, and without any idea where he could possibly be, going out and looking for a teenager that matched his description was pretty much out of the question.

"I thought you wanted this solved?" DI Kidd barked at DCI Weaver when he told him to go home. "You're saying you've got the Super breathing down your neck, I'm working my arse off trying to get it done, and you won't send people out to look?"

"The Super has calmed down after the press conference this afternoon. Well done again, by the way," Weaver said. "But you are absolutely no use to me whatsoever if you stay up all night looking all over town for a potential suspect. We've put a shout out on social media and the news, so people are looking for him. You don't want to hear this, but Laura has put something out too, so there's a whole community, if you can even call it that, of people trying to find Dexter Black."

He's in so much trouble when they find him, Kidd thought. *If they find him.*

"Tomorrow with fresh eyes, that's when we will get to the bottom of this," Weaver said. "Get out of here."

DI Kidd was about to retort but DCI Weaver had already walked out the door, his jacket on, ready for a night at home with his family. It made him burn. One minute DCI Weaver wanted him on this like never before, the next he wants Kidd to drop it.

Though he was still sort of on duty tonight at the reunion.

He went home, took a quick shower, and pulled on a fresh shirt and a pair of jeans. It was still cold, so he grabbed his denim jacket from his wardrobe and put it on. He couldn't remember the last time he'd gone out. There were dates with John, but going out with work friends was something unheard of. Though, he supposed, this was still work after all.

Even when he'd been off for six months and he took that trip to Europe—mostly to track down Craig—he'd gone out but only to drown his sorrows. That was when he'd gotten in the most trouble. He hoped he'd be able to avoid that tonight.

JOHN: Have fun tonight. Don't forget you owe me. x

Kidd laughed in spite of himself. After their lunch today, he would have much rather have been spending the evening with John. It was no disrespect to Zoe, not at all, but they weren't exactly going out for fun. They were going out to essentially keep working.

                I know I know. Tomorrow? X

JOHN: Until tomorrow then. X

Kidd pocketed his phone and grabbed his keys and wallet before heading outside. He climbed into his car and drove round to Zoe's house to pick her up. He tooted the horn twice and he saw the lights in her hallway click off before she opened the door.

    She was wearing a pair of figure-hugging blue jeans and a white, strappy top, her black leather jacket slung over one shoulder. She'd let her hair down, her curls bouncing free as she walked over to his car.

    "I hate that we're doing this," she said as she climbed into the passenger seat. "And I also hate that you're driving. You're the worst driver."

    "Needs must," Kidd said. "And since I'm

giving you a ride, you can drink tonight."

"We have a pair of missing teenagers to find, I need to be on my game tomorrow," she said with a smirk. "Maybe just one drink."

"Atta girl," Kidd said as he drove them towards the school.

They arrived in pretty good time, struggling to find a space in the almost overflowing car park. People were heading towards the entrance in pairs, in clusters, maybe people that had reconnected over Facebook, maybe people that had never lost touch in the first place like DI Kidd seemed to have done with his school friends.

When they stepped inside, Kidd felt a strange wave of familiarity washing over him. It had been an awfully long time since he'd been in this hall.

The lights were low, the usual rows of chairs cleared to the sides of the room where they surrounded tables that a few people were already occupying, many deep in conversations, and even deeper into their drinks. There was a bar to one side, portable and to be cleared away without a trace before the following morning, and a long buffet table with snacks and nibbles, another place where groups of people were congregating.

No one had dared to step onto the small amount of space cleared for a dance floor near the DJ—Kidd couldn't believe there was a DJ. It was like being at a school disco when you're twelve years old. They got a couple of drinks and stood to one side, their own little cluster. There were a couple of people whose faces Kidd recognised, not that he'd be able to put a name to them. He'd done rather a good job of blocking out most of his school years.

"Do you think they're going to be here?" Zoe asked, leaning in and having to raise her voice to be heard over the music.

"Of course they are," Kidd said.

"What makes you say that?" she asked, raising her eyebrow.

"Keeping up appearances," he said. "They can't miss this event because they've said they're going to be here. Also, and I'm trying not to sound like a miserable old fucker when I say this—"

"Why do I get the feeling you're going to?"

"But she'll want the attention," Kidd said. "Even though it's negative, even though it's not really about her, the amount she's been posting at the moment, she must sort of feed off it."

"Is that not a little bit sick?" Zoe asked.

"I'll say," Kidd replied, but seeing her Tweets about his press conference was enough to confirm that part of this was definitely about getting attention, even though her daughter was missing. He'd never say it to her, he wouldn't mention it to Weaver or put it in the report, but it certainly seemed a little bit weird and a whole lot inappropriate.

The night carried on for a little longer, DI Kidd and DS Sanchez stood to one side nursing their drinks, occasionally wandering as far as the buffet table to pick up a couple of snacks before finding somewhere else to stand or sit and observe. A few people came over and spoke to Kidd and he found himself explaining to most of them that Zoe was his colleague, not his wife. People liked to assume the latter.

"See?" Zoe said. "This isn't so bad."

"It could certainly be worse," he replied.

"I wish we weren't working," she said. "I know we're not officially working, but what I wouldn't give to get you drunk enough that you're the first person to take to that dance floor."

"Not on your life!" Kidd said through a laugh.

The doors to the main hall opened and a few heads turned. There was a whisper that sort of rippled around the whole room and it was enough to draw Kidd's attention away from Zoe. He looked to see Laura Harper walking in wearing all black—of course, why wouldn't she?—with Chris, her husband, at her side. It was the first time that Kidd had seen him in the flesh in twenty years and he looked a lot different than he did in pictures.

In the pictures he had with Laura on her social media, he was every bit the tall, dark, and handsome Prince Charming. But in the flesh, he seemed pale in comparison to her. She was the star in the relationship, that much was clear. All attention was on her, he was part of the supporting cast.

A few people flocked over immediately, women mostly, fawning over Laura, fawning over her outfit, and offering what Kidd assumed would be apologies about what had happened with Sarah. Yes, from the concerned looks painted on each and every one of their faces, he would put money on each of them offering condolences.

"Wow," Zoe said. "She certainly knows how to make an entrance."

"You've got to hand it to her, she knows how to orchestrate a moment."

"How well do you think she could do that?" Zoe asked.

Kidd took a moment. "Not well enough to plan her own daughter's disappearance I would say," he replied. "She played the part of the broken mother far too well. If she could call on that at the drop of a hat, then she should be on stage, not showing people how to clean their bathrooms on Instagram." Though even Kidd wasn't entirely sure he believed it. Should he be thinking of her as a suspect? "Shall we?"

"I think we'd better," Zoe said, noticing a semi-orderly queue forming near where they were standing. "We're going to be here all night just waiting to talk to them."

"Like hell we are," Kidd said, ignoring the queue and walking straight over to Laura's side. He tapped her on her bare shoulder and she about jumped out of her skin. Her face was annoyed until she realised it was him and she softened instantly.

"Of course, DI Kidd, you said you were going to be here," she said, leaving a hand resting on his arm. She turned to Chris and pulled his focus away from a couple of women who definitely seemed to be fawning over him, and pointed out Kidd. "Honey, this is the man who came to visit today, DI Kidd."

Chris' brow knitted together in confusion as he took Kidd in, like he didn't entirely understand what had just been said.

"And this is DS Sanchez," Kidd said, pointing out Zoe who had come around to stand next to him. This seemed to please Chris a little more and smiling, he inclined his head. "We'd love to get a chance to chat to you in private at some point, Mr Harper," Kidd continued. "It's a shame that you weren't in when we came to the house earlier on."

"Well," he said with a shrug. "Houses won't build themselves. There are people counting on me."

"And I'm sure your daughter is too, wherever she is," Kidd said with a smile. "Can I come see you at your office?"

Chris reached into his jacket pocket and pulled out a card, handing it across to Kidd. "I don't really want to get into this right now," he said. "But if you call my office in the morning, they would be more than happy to arrange a meeting. But I warn you, I'm a very busy man."

"Too busy to take the time to help find your daughter?" Zoe said under her breath.

"What was that?" Chris said.

"I hope we manage to find a time that's suitable," Zoe said with a smile. "I'm sure you agree. We just want to find Sarah."

"Of course," he said, his brows knitting together again. "What are you suggesting?"

"They're not suggesting anything at all, honey," Laura said as if she was talking to a small dog rather than her heavyset husband. "However, as Chris already said, now is not the time to discuss this." She turned back to her adoring public. "Alexandra, darling!" Laura exclaimed, throwing her arms wide and wrapping a small, redheaded woman into a tight hug. "It's so lovely to see you tonight, how have you been?"

Alexandra looked a little shaken when she removed herself from the hug. "Oh, you know," she said. "It's been a little bit rough. Caleb has been worried about Sarah, of course. I have been too. It's been such a hard time for him. I can't imagine what you're going through."

Laura straightened up, painting on that warrior's smile she'd had when Kidd had seen her earlier in the day. "It's a rough ride," she said. "But, as they say, these things are sent to try us."

"Well you are a saint for even coming out tonight," Alexandra said. "I nearly didn't want to leave Caleb with his grandparents, given everything that's been going on."

Laura and Alexandra continued to talk, but Kidd found his attention drawn to Chris. He seemed very focussed on their conversation, but at the same time, a little bit shaken by it, like he couldn't take his eyes off of what was going on. His eyes seemed watery, something that Kidd hadn't expected, and without warning he hurried for the double doors leading out of the hall.

CHAPTER TWENTY-ONE

"What on earth was that all about?" Kidd asked.

"Maybe he really didn't want to be here," Zoe said. "If *my* child were missing, the last thing I'd want to do is be out at some party with a bunch of people I've barely spoken to in the last twenty or so years."

But he knew all these people, didn't he? If Laura knew them, Chris must have at least had a passing acquaintance with them since they'd all gone to school together. Though maybe he didn't anymore, if he worked so hard that he was hardly ever in the house. That was how Laura had made it seem anyhow.

"I'm going to go and see where he's gotten to," Kidd said quietly. Zoe nodded and Kidd quickly slipped away and out into the corridor. There was no way of knowing where he'd gone, he'd taken off at quite a speed.

To his left was a door leading to a darkened corridor, so it wasn't likely he'd gone that way. On the way back to the front door, he could see the corridor that led to the offices, to where he'd spoken to Ms Lu and Ms Chowdhury earlier. He slowly shuffled over to it and tried the door, only to find it locked.

Another darkened corridor lay behind him, and then the front door. It was the only one that was open, the only one that seemed like the obvious choice, and if he had been upset like DS Sanchez seemed to think, the first thing you would want to do was go out and get some air, no?

Kidd took a breath and started towards the front doors.

The night air was cold, a few clicks colder than it had been when they'd arrived, though maybe that was the change in going from a room full of people to outside. He pulled his jacket tightly about himself as he looked for Chris. It was quiet out here now, the cars no longer moving around on the gravel and making that dreadful, crunching noise, no footsteps approaching, just the low hum of the lights guiding any latecomers to the front door.

"Mr Harper?" DI Kidd said, perhaps a little too loudly.

"Over here!" A voice came out of the dark, and Kidd could just make him out leaning against the wall a little way away. "Sorry about that."

Kidd approached. "About..." he trailed off when he saw there was another figure with him, mostly cloaked in shadow. But he recognised her all the same. "Ms Chowdhury. Fancy seeing you here."

She straightened up. "It's my school, Mr Kidd—"

"DI Kidd."

"DI Kidd, my apologies. It is my school. I was working late, and given everything that's been going on, I saw Mr Harper heading outside and decided to talk to him about it," she said, her lips curling into a smile. "I hope that's alright."

"It's a free country, Ms Chowdhury," he said. "I was simply doing the same."

"We'll talk later," Ms Chowdhury said, placing a hand on Chris Harper's arm. Kidd watched her closely, she lowered her voice, but not low enough. "I'm working late tonight. You know where to find me."

She locked eyes with Kidd before she walked back into the school. Kidd didn't know where to start with that. He turned to Chris.

"Do I want to ask what that was about?"

"You can ask, it doesn't mean I'll tell," he replied, reaching into his jacket pocket and pulling out a packet of cigarettes. "Do you smoke?"

"No."

"Mind if I do?"

"Free country," Kidd said again. "What did you leave for? Were you coming to meet her?"

"No," he said quickly. "I was struggling with all of the attention in there. That's more Laura's area than it is mine. I just let her get on with it."

"That's how it seemed to me when I came to see her today," Kidd said. "That you were leaving everything to her."

"Did she say that?"

"No."

"Then why are you saying it?"

"I'm doing my job," Kidd replied.

"You're sticking your nose in."

"That's my job," Kidd said bluntly. "I came to check and see if you were alright. You seem fine to me. Not worried about your daughter going missing, but that's your choice."

"I am worried," he said. "I'm terrified. The last things I said to her were so awful. Our relationship wasn't the best but..." he trailed off and took a long drag of his cigarette. "I'm not a bad guy, DI Kidd," he said. "I just...I have needs."

Kidd took a deep breath. He'd had enough of men trying to justify their affairs to him today. That's what this was, an admittance that there was something going on with Ms Chowdhury. And if Sarah happened to know something about that, then maybe they should be looking at her a little more closely. She didn't seem to like Sarah all that much. If Sarah knew that she had been sleeping with her dad, she probably would have been giving her hell.

"I'm not here to judge your life choices, or judge your marriage."

"You must understand," he said. "Are you married?"

"Far from it," Kidd replied.

"Then maybe you don't."

"Don't understand why you're not faithful to your wife?" Kidd asked with a raise of his eyebrow. "I don't think I need to be married to know that it's not the right thing to do. Unless you have some kind of agreement and you're allowed to do that within the bounds of your marriage, but the fact you're sneaking around and justifying it to me suggests that perhaps not." Kidd took a breath. He still wanted to talk to Chris Harper properly, on the record, about what his relationship with Sarah was like. But he'd learned something about the man tonight, and he really didn't like it. "I'll see you back inside."

"You're not going to tell her, are you?"

Kidd sighed. "Of course not," he said. "It's not my place. I'll see you inside, Mr Harper."

Kidd walked back into the school, noticing that Ms Chowdhury was hovering in the corridor as he approached the school hall. She watched him carefully, though when he locked eyes with her she immediately looked away. Was that a guilty conscience? And about what? Her affair with Chris, or something else, something more? It wouldn't be the first time a teacher had abducted a student.

He walked back into the hall and the heat from all the bodies hit him like a tank. Alexandra Kaye was still standing with Laura, an apparent leaning post of solidarity that her husband had failed to provide for this evening.

He walked over to DS Sanchez. She had given up her post next to them and had moved a little closer to the wall, giving them a little bit of breathing room.

"Anything good?" he asked.

"Nothing we can use," she replied. "Most of them are just feeling really sad for her, which I get, and she's playing the role of strong independent woman quite well."

"Not as well as you'd think," Kidd said. "Look at her hands."

She was gripping onto Alexandra's arm so tightly her knuckles were white. If she let go, Kidd wouldn't be surprised if she tumbled to the ground in a heap. She had a lot going on in her life right now, her husband being an adulterous prick was the least of her worries.

"You look furious, Kidd, what's happened?" Zoe asked. "Did you find something?"

He sighed heavily. "You could say that, yeah."

He was about to explain what was going on when the doors to the hall opened once more and Chris appeared. So he hadn't been all that far behind Kidd after all. Maybe one final smooch with Ms Chowdhury before he came back inside, a last little taste. It made him feel a bit sick.

But his appearance sparked a different bit of movement. As Chris made his way across the room and replaced Alexandra Kaye, the two of them exchanging a few pleasantries, a few smiles, someone else had started moving towards them from across the room.

Apart from Kidd, no one seemed to notice a tall man with a buzzcut barrelling across the room at breakneck speed. Without warning, he pushed through the crowd, past the waiting, adoring fans, past Alexandra Kaye, and straight up to Chris Harper, where he threw a punch that landed square on Chris' nose.

CHAPTER TWENTY-TWO

The room erupted with activity. Laura let out a howl and hurried away from where the action was taking place, Alexandra Kaye grabbed hold of the man who had thrown the punch while Chris stumbled back a step holding his face, shock etched into every one of his features.

"What the fuck is happening?" Zoe barked.

"Fucked if I know," Kidd said, immediately heading over to the bloodied Chris and his assailant.

"Stay the fuck away from my wife!" the man bellowed.

"I'm not your wife anymore, Norm. Please, stop this!" Alexandra wailed, but Norm was far too strong for her, yanking his arm away and immediately advancing on Chris again. He threw another punch, one that Chris managed to avoid. It knocked Norm off balance. He stumbled a little to one side, giving Chris a chance to grab hold of him by the shirt.

He yanked the man upright and punched him square on the jaw.

"Fuck's sake!" Kidd growled, barrelling towards the man that Alexandra had called Norm and grabbing him before he could hit Chris again. DS Sanchez did the same, taking hold of Chris by both arms and managing to wrestle him to the ground. She'd twisted his arm around his back, his face twisted in pain. He wasn't going anywhere anytime soon.

"Get off me," Norm grunted, struggling against Kidd's grip. "Get the fuck off me!"

"Calm down," Kidd barked. "Take a breath."

"FUCK! OFF!" Norm tried to break free again, but Kidd grabbed his hand and bent it back, the pain shooting through Norm's arm enough to ground him.

"I'm Detective Inspector Kidd, that over there is Detective Sergeant Sanchez, and unless you want to spend a night in a jail cell or get convicted for assaulting a police officer, I suggest you calm down."

That seemed to stop him. He took a few deep breaths, settling down. When he seemed calm, Kidd released him and Norm took a seat on the floor. The people around them had stopped what they were doing to watch the action, all eyes on Norm.

"Alright," Kidd said, turning to the onlookers. "Show's over folks, please go back to your night."

"What on earth is happening in here?" Ms Chowdhury had appeared nearby, her face flushed, her movements jerky, though Kidd couldn't tell if her being flustered was from the fight that had broken out, or what had happened with Chris a few moments before.

"Could you call the police, Ms Chowdhury?" Kidd asked. "I think we need to take these two in."

"That hardly seems necessary," Laura protested.

"I think it is," Kidd said firmly. "Ms Chowdhury? If you could?"

"I thought you two were the police?" she said, raising an eyebrow before she turned and walked away. Kidd wanted to shout after her that he was off duty and shouldn't be dealing with two grown men who couldn't control themselves, or figure out their issues without the use of their fists.

"I don't think the police need to be involved, Ben," Laura said. "They're already doing so much for me and my family, I wouldn't want to bother them anymore."

"That's precisely the reason we need to take them both in, Mrs Harper," Kidd said, purposely using her surname. "We need to have a talk with them, get to the bottom of what's going on."

"Nothing is going on," Laura said firmly. "Just boys being boys."

Kidd could smell the bullshit a mile off, there wasn't enough expensive perfume in the world to cover it up. He simply offered Laura a smile and escorted Norm outside, DS Sanchez following close behind with Chris.

◆ ◆ ◆

When the uniformed officers arrived and put the two men in the back of separate cars, DI Kidd and DS Sanchez headed out of the building. The second he stepped out of those doors, Kidd felt like he could breathe again. He hadn't wanted the night to go this way, of course, but he had to admit it was nice to have a reason to leave early.

He'd told both Mrs Harper and Ms Kaye that they could follow in their cars if they wanted to, that they would be at Kingston station, but neither one of them seemed all that keen. Perhaps this wasn't the first time their husbands had gone at it like this. Neither one of them seemed particularly shocked by it.

"What was that all about?" DS Sanchez asked as they climbed into the car. Kidd started the engine and quickly pulled out of the car park. It had started raining, just in case the world being like an icicle wasn't enough.

"That's not even the half of it," Kidd replied. "You'll never guess what I saw when I went outside to find Chris."

"You're right," Zoe replied. "I won't guess. Tell me."

"Ms Chowdhury and Mr Harper were a heck of a lot closer than a parent and a headteacher ought to be," he said as he pulled into the Kingston one-way system, driving under the railway bridge and past the Rotunda. "If you know what I mean."

"Really? You caught them?"

"Not exactly," Kidd replied. "I didn't catch them doing anything, but I definitely interrupted them. And then I had him telling me all about how I don't understand and that he has needs."

"Jesus Christ," Zoe groaned, averting her gaze to the window. "He really tried to justify it?"

"He did," Kidd said. "And I'm thinking that maybe this means we need to take a closer look at Ms Chowdhury."

Zoe turned back to him. "You think?"

"It's a little suspicious that she's not exactly Sarah's biggest fan to begin with, and then to have this added on top of it. If Sarah knew about it, then she would be making Chowdhury's life hell, no? Which could explain a lot."

"Or Sarah is just a bit difficult to deal with," Zoe replied. "That's a possibility too."

"There's a lot up in the air right now."

"And our list of suspects keeps getting longer," she added. "What's our next move?"

Kidd pulled into the car park outside the police station and shut off the engine. "First thing we need to do is figure out what's going on between these two," he said. "Then we go from there."

CHAPTER TWENTY-THREE

After Chris and Norman had been booked in, Kidd gave them a little bit of time to get settled, which gave himself and DS Sanchez some time to figure out how they were going to play it. This would be the first time they'd get to properly speak to Chris Harper, at least on the record, so they needed to get it right.

They had him brought to the interview room, a bruise already swelling on his face where Norm had managed to land that first punch. He'd really gotten him good. Chris sat back heavily in his chair, his face drawn, his eyes puffy with exhaustion, and pulled his suit jacket around himself. Though these rooms had a tendency to get too hot in the summer, in the wintertime they were sometimes glacial. Wearing a thin, white shirt and a jacket, Chris Harper was feeling it. It might make him talk faster.

DI Kidd pressed the record button on the in-room tape recorder and saw Chris' eyes widen as he did it. Perhaps, he hadn't been expecting this interview to be recorded. He'd been offered legal representation but had refused. Maybe he had a little more to hide than Kidd first thought.

"I am Detective Inspector Kidd, this is Detective Sergeant Sanchez," Kidd started. "If you could state your name for the tape."

"Uh," Chris said. "My name is Christopher Harper. Does this really need to be recorded?"

"Well, you're not under arrest," DS Sanchez said with a smile as deadly as it was sweet. "We need to record the interview in case you want to press charges against Norman Kaye or if he wants to press charges against you."

"I don't want to press any charges," Chris said quickly, leaning forward in his chair. "If I don't want to press any charges, can I go?"

"He may want to press charges against you," DS Sanchez repeated. "Let's not get ahead of ourselves, you might be here for a while."

"Suppose that means we can get to know one another," Chris said.

"I don't think so," DS Sanchez said. Chris sat back in his chair, looking a little disappointed. Maybe lines like that usually worked, but Zoe was having none of it. Kidd was surprised she didn't leap across the table and lamp him.

DI Kidd cleared his throat. "We have an open case at the moment looking for your daughter and I really think it would be good if we could talk about it."

"I told you, DI Kidd, I'm a very busy man —"

"I know that, Mr Harper, you already told me that this evening," Kidd said. "But right now we have you in custody, so let's kill two birds with one stone, how about that?"

Chris eyed DI Kidd carefully. He didn't like this, he didn't like this one bit. Kidd could see it in the way his eyes narrowed, the way his fists clenched as he tried to hold his suit jacket closed. What was he hiding?

"Do you know why Mr Kaye would have reacted the way he did to you speaking to Alexandra Kaye?" DI Kidd asked.

Chris shrugged.

Kidd sighed. "For the benefit of the tape, Mr Harper just shrugged."

Chris smiled and sat up a little straighter. "I don't know why he would have reacted that way," he said. "Norman is crazy. Always has been."

"Crazy?" DS Sanchez said. "That's a little strong, don't you think?"

"You saw the way he acted, does that look like the behaviour of a rational man to you?"

"It looked like there was more going on than you just being near his wife, at least that's how it looked to me," DI Kidd said. "I imagine it also looked that way to everyone else in that room. Does your wife know why Mr Kaye would have reacted that way?"

"I don't know."

"I'm going to need a little bit more than, I don't knows from you, Mr Harper, it's very late and you're currently costing my boss a lot of money in overtime, and believe me, he doesn't like having to fork out for overtime," Kidd said bluntly. "So either you start talking or I lock you in a cell for the rest of the night and we can discuss this when I'm actually supposed to be on shift. How does that sound?"

Kidd let the words float across the table and reach Chris, who was considering what his next move could be. Kidd could tell he wouldn't want to spend the rest of the night in a cell. Nobody did, given the choice. So he waited patiently until Chris unravelled and started talking.

"We used to be friends," Chris started. "It was a couple of years ago. He used to work for me, but when everything went down with the company, when I had to make lay-offs, he had to go."

So he was one of the people he had upset? A potential enemy.

"Not really the kind of things that friends do, Mr Harper."

"It wasn't about friendship, it was just business at that point, there was nothing else I could do," Chris pleaded. His wife had mentioned people that he made enemies with over the years. Norman Kaye must have been one of them.

"So he attacked you tonight because of that?" DI Kidd asked.

Chris shrugged again.

"Allow me," DS Sanchez said. "For the benefit of the tape, Mr Harper shrugged for a second time."

Chris fixed Zoe with a death stare. She was unmoved. She just smiled at him.

"Why did he tell you to get away from his ex-wife?" DI Kidd asked.

Chris turned his gaze to DI Kidd. "I think you know why," he said quietly. "But it's not what you think."

"Enlighten us," Kidd said.

Chris took a deep breath before he started talking. "It happened a little while back, not too long after I'd had to let Norman go," he said. "Alexandra and I had always been close. She's an old family friend, both her and Norman were really. The business stuff really drove a wedge between us."

"I can't imagine you sleeping with his wife would have exactly helped matters," Kidd said.

"It was a one-time thing," Chris said quickly. "She came over because she was upset about how things were going for her and Norman. She was planning to leave him. I'd been having trouble with Laura, we were on the rocks a little bit. We drank. One thing led to another…" He trailed off. "You don't need the details," he said. "But I thought we were all past that now. Like I said, Alexandra is a family friend."

"And does Laura know?"

"What my wife does and doesn't know isn't any of your business."

"The same way she doesn't know about Ms Chowdhury?" DI Kidd snapped.

"That's my private life, that has nothing to do with what's happening here."

Kidd only wished that were true. When it came to an investigation like this, everything was important. Even the details like that, which seemed like they could be nothing, were something. He didn't want to say it out loud, he didn't want to give anything away, but not only was Ms Chowdhury under suspicion but so was Norman Kaye. How far would one man go to get back at the man who slept with his wife? The man who he believed had caused their divorce?

"I don't think I have anything else to ask," Kidd said. "I'll get an officer to escort you out of the building, if you're definitely sure you don't want to press charges."

"No, I don't," he said. "I just want all of this to go away. Things haven't been the same between me and Norman since everything happened—"

"Sleeping with someone's wife will do that to a relationship," DS Sanchez said.

"But I just want it to go back to normal," he said. "I want my daughter back, I want my friend back, I just want it all to go back to how it was."

DI Kidd stopped the recording and escorted Chris from the room. He wasn't surprised he wanted it all to go away. Like never before, Chris' life was under a microscope. With what was happening tonight with Ms Chowdhury and what happened in the past with Alexandra Kaye, he seemed to be able to get away with absolutely anything he wanted to. Now that he was being watched, he didn't like it so much.

❖ ❖ ❖

Norman Kaye was a little bit more forthcoming once they got him into interview. He seemed rattled when they got him out of the cell, a shadow of the man who had gone at Chris Harper full pelt, who had looked like he wanted to rip the guy's head off. Maybe it was because he'd been taken to the police station, maybe being in a cell had sobered him up, but he'd calmed down considerably.

Kidd once again turned on the tape recorder and sat opposite Mr Kaye. He could really get a good look at him now in the light of the interview room. His buzzed hair was ginger, a light fuzz across all of his head. He was smartly dressed, or at least he had been for the party, they'd taken his tie at the front desk just in case he tried something stupid. His features were harsh, jagged, angular. But his eyes were kind, and looked like they were on the verge of tears the second DI Kidd pressed that record button.

"I'd like to get this done as soon as possible, Mr Kaye," DI Kidd said.

"Of course," he said. "I'm sorry."

Kidd blinked. "What's that?"

"I'm sorry," he said. "I don't know what came over me. Maybe it was the drink. I don't know, but I just saw them together and I saw red." He took a breath. His gaze turning to his feet. "I've got a lot on my plate right now. It's not an excuse, I know, but I just lost it a bit."

"We saw," Zoe said. "Tell us what's going on, Mr Kaye."

"I've been having troubles with my wife, ex-wife," he quickly corrected. "Sorry, I keep doing that. The divorce only finished going through a little before Christmas and I'm just not used to it."

"But you were separated?"

"We were, but I always hoped that she would change her mind," Mr Kaye said, turning his gaze back to his hands on the table. "It's stupid. Because she obviously hasn't and she seemed really happy, didn't she?"

"I can't say I was paying a lot of attention, Mr Kaye," Kidd said. "Carry on."

"Yes, right, sorry," he said. "Well, she keeps talking about Caleb."

DI Kidd had forgotten for a moment about Caleb, the son that she'd mentioned who was particularly distressed about Sarah, at least according to Ms Kaye. He scribbled the name down, something to force him to remember it later. They'd need to talk to him if they could.

"She keeps telling me how awful I am as a father because I work all the time, because I'm still struggling to make ends meet after what happened with Chris' business," he said. "And she's threatening to take Caleb away from me."

"Do you have custody?" DS Sanchez asked.

"No. I see him most weekends, sometimes when Alexandra is working late, but I barely see him as it is," he said. "Since I moved out, we've drifted further and further apart and the last thing that I want to do is lose touch with my son. I don't think I could bear it."

"So you took this out on Mr Harper tonight?"

"In my head, he's the reason my whole life has fallen apart," Mr Kaye said. "It was him firing me for one thing, so now I have no stable income. Then he slept with my wife, which led to our divorce. Now I'm living in a shitty flat I can barely afford the rent for and being threatened with never being able to see my son again." He was only just managing to hold it together. His fists were clenched at his sides and there were tears sparkling in his eyes. He looked at Kidd. "I just lost it tonight. It all became too much."

"It sounds like you're going through a tough time, Mr Kaye," DS Sanchez said. "But violence isn't the answer."

"I know that, I do. I just...I lost it," he said. "I saw them talking to one another and I just saw red. I can't explain it. You must know what that's like? You lose control of your emotions. It's hard to explain."

DI Kidd did know what that was like. It had happened to him in the past. He was never really a fighting man, but when you were in the force sometimes you had to stand up for yourself, throw a punch every now and again. He'd certainly taken more than his fair share over the years. But to lose control? That was maybe a little too far. But Mr Kaye didn't seem like the kind of man who wanted revenge on Mr Harper. At least, it didn't seem that way right now.

"What can you tell us about Sarah Harper?" DI Kidd said.

Mr Kaye sat up straight, his eyes wide. "Their daughter. She's missing, isn't she? Have you found her?"

"No, Mr Kaye, we're just wondering if you can tell us anything about her," Kidd said. "Anything at all."

Mr Kaye took a breath and looked away from them, apparently gathering his thoughts. He turned back. "I knew her quite well," he said.

"Both me and my wife did. We've been friends with the Harpers for years. They're good people. When I saw what happened I... I sent flowers. It seemed like the right thing to do somehow."

DI Kidd remembered the collection of flowers that had been by the Harper's door, how he'd had to shove some of them out of the way just to get inside. Would a kidnapper send flowers to the parents of the person he had kidnapped? Would that be a way of throwing them off the scent? DI Kidd wasn't so sure.

"I didn't take her," he said suddenly. DI Kidd looked up sharply. "I didn't. If that's what you're implying."

"I'm not implying anything at all," Kidd said calmly. "I was just asking a question." He turned to DS Sanchez who was watching Mr Kaye carefully. "Anything to add, DS Sanchez?" he asked.

"Nope," she said.

"Okay," DI Kidd turned back to Mr Kaye. "Then you're free to go, Norman. Mr Harper doesn't want to press charges and we have about everything we need from you here."

Mr Kaye looked shocked. He stared at the two detectives, a little dumbstruck.

"Really?"

Kidd nodded. "Maybe that friendship isn't quite as damaged as you thought," he continued. "We'll get an officer to grab your things and show you out."

They said their goodbyes to Norman Kaye and watched as he left the building, wandering off into the night. Kidd didn't really know what to make of him. All that aggression that had been so fiery just a little while ago had faded and left behind a man who was quite docile, who didn't look like he could fight his way out of a paper bag. It had left Kidd puzzled.

"I can't believe you let him go," Sanchez said as they walked back into the Incident Room. "I would have kept him."

"On what grounds?"

"On the grounds that he has a pretty good reason to have taken Sarah Harper," she snapped. "He could have her locked up in his little flat, everybody around none the wiser, and we've just let him go to do who knows what to her."

"I think you're overthinking it," Kidd said, though the thought had crossed his mind. "I don't see it. We can get a team over there to search his property in the morning. We have his address now, so that part will be easy enough. But I don't think he's got her."

"He's got priors," she said. "It's possible."

"I'll admit that it could be true," Kidd said. "But I don't think it fits. He seems more intent on getting to his son than anything else. If he kidnapped Sarah, if he does anything to her, he's going to get put away for that, it's not going to help his cause."

DS Sanchez grabbed her coat from the

hook by the door. "If you say so," she said. "There's just something about him I don't like."

DI Kidd headed over to his desk, flicking on his computer and sitting down. DS Sanchez hovered by the door.

"What are you doing?" she asked.

"I'm just looking something up. I promise I won't stay for too much longer," he replied, tapping in his login details.

"No, no," she said, crossing the room to his desk and pressing the off button on the computer.

"Zoe!"

"You're not staying here to work, you'll drive yourself crackers, let's go!"

DI Kidd sighed and stood up. "What? Are you dragging me out for a drink? It's late, Zoe, it's been a long day—"

"Don't flatter yourself," she said with a smirk. "You're my ride home. It's freezing outside, there's no fucking way I'm walking. Grab your keys, let's go."

CHAPTER TWENTY-FOUR

After dropping Zoe home, Kidd debated whether or not he should go back to the station to keep working. He had been about to type up his notes and then maybe have a little snoop around to find Caleb online. As far as he was concerned, it didn't count in his work-life balance promise if he was still at the station. When he'd told DS Sanchez his theory, she told him it was bullshit, which made him laugh.

He pulled into a parking space near his house and got out, hurrying to the front door to get out of the rain. The house was quiet when he got inside, just as it always was. He flicked the lights on as he stepped in, locking the door behind him and kicking off his shoes. Thankfully, the heating had clicked on when it realised that it was cold outside and the radiators were pumping out their full complement of heat. Perfect.

Ben made his way up the stairs, quickly

taking a shower before heading into his bedroom to settle down for the night. He just had one more thing he needed to look for before he could rest, one thing that he knew would nag in the back of his mind all night if he didn't just do a quick search.

He grabbed his laptop from its usual resting place on the floor by his bed—a dangerous habit that Liz had told him many times to stop—and pulled it up onto the duvet. Within minutes he'd made his way online, checking through each and every social media site for Caleb Kaye.

There were a couple of accounts there, some that he could quickly dismiss for being in the wrong location, a couple that he had to look through a little before he could establish that the person wasn't in Kingston. But then he found him. The red hair was a giveaway, just like his parents.

He flicked through the photos, through the posts on various pages, trying to find something that would give him a connection to Sarah. But nothing. He checked again, checked the captions under photos, reading comments and hashtags, but there was nothing about Sarah there at all. Some posts were recent, since her disappearance, but there wasn't a single thing about her.

Maybe he's just not the kind of person to do posts like that. But he couldn't help but feel like there was more to it than that. His mother had said he was particularly distressed by the whole situation, that he was worried, and yet he hadn't posted a single thing.

He made his way over to Sarah's account, the one that was monitored—or perhaps controlled, Kidd wasn't all too sure—by her mother. The photos had very much been burned into his memory at this point, pictures of her smiling with her friends, captions that were laden with emojis and inspirational quotes. But Caleb was nowhere to be seen.

He looked at who she was following, searching for Caleb's handle and finding absolutely nothing. Were they even friends? Did he even know her? Was Alexandra just trying to relate to Laura in a bigger way, get closer to her after everything that had happened between them? If Kidd had found one thing tonight it was that they had a deeper history than he ever could have imagined.

He leaned back against his pillows and stared up at the ceiling. Outside, a car drove by at what had to be quite a way over the speed limit, splashing through the newly formed rain puddles, the white headlights flashing through the panes of glass on the window. He took a breath and sat back up, opening his personal email to send the social media handles to his work email. He would have someone look into it tomorrow, he was too tired to deal with it right now.

The message pinged up just as he was about to shut down. It was Andrea replying to his message from last night. There was no attachment so she hadn't found anything more, and there was a part of him, after his conversation with Zoe earlier, that told him to ignore it, to just let it go.

But it was taunting him. That unread message. And he knew that if he didn't at least click on it and see what it said, he wouldn't be able to get to sleep.

He took a breath and opened it.

Dear Ben,

Thank you so much for responding so quickly. It's nice to know that I'm not the only one who hasn't given up hope of finding Craig. I know the picture isn't much, maybe it isn't enough to go on at all, but it is hope, and I think I needed that.

I am going to keep on looking, and I really hope you are too. If you find anything, or you need any more help from me, don't hesitate to get in touch. I've left my phone number below if you want to talk about this in person rather than over email, it can be so impersonal sometimes, don't you think?

Anyway. I'm sending you a lot of love and all the luck in the world.

We will find him, Ben. He is out there, I know he is.

All my best,

Andrea

He read the message a few times, letting the words sink in a little bit. She was still looking. She didn't want to be in this alone and he totally understood why. It was hard when people around him were telling him that Craig was never coming back and he'd never really gotten over it. It must be hard for her, she's holding onto him because he's her last hope of having someone to find him with.

He was about to reply when he remembered what Zoe had said. If he wanted to be found, he would have been found already. If he wanted to see Kidd, he would have come back.

He considered it and he sighed.

He knew she was right. Deep down he knew.

A message pinged up on his phone.

JOHN: Hope you had a good night tonight. See you tomorrow maybe? X

He looked at the message and couldn't stop himself from smiling. Maybe it really was time to let go of all this.

He shut his laptop and set it down on the

floor by his bed. He quickly fired off a response to John on his phone, setting a time for the two of them to meet tomorrow evening before climbing into bed.

It was finally time for him to let Craig Peyton go.

CHAPTER TWENTY-FIVE

Sarah Harper ran down the street at full pelt. She was already out of breath before she'd even started, the wind completely knocked out of her, but she needed to get away, and she needed to get away fast.

The past day had been hell. Drifting in and out of sleep, not knowing where she was, who was talking to her. She could barely remember what she'd seen, it had all happened so quickly.

So she had to keep going. She had to keep running. Her breaths were coming quick.

"Just keep going," she told herself. "Just keep running. Don't stop. Fucking hell, Sarah, do not stop."

The footsteps were coming up behind her at some speed. They were heavy. She knew who it was, she knew that they were coming to get her and they wouldn't stop until they had her. Where could she hide? Where could she go?

She managed to get away from the side streets,

into somewhere that was better lit, where there were roads, where maybe someone would see her running, where someone could help her. But what time was it?

It was dark, the streetlamps were on, bathing everything in a strange orange light that made her feel disorientated. Though maybe that was from her lack of energy. Or the drugs. She felt dizzy.

"KEEP RUNNING!" she told herself again as she made her way towards the centre of town.

The fact that she'd managed to get away felt like a minor miracle. They'd sedated her, she knew that much, left her in a room all by herself, drifting in and out of consciousness. They'd left her for too long. Maybe they'd forgotten she was even there, pushed it to the back of their mind, a desperate attempt to stop themselves from feeling guilty for what they'd done to her.

She almost laughed.

Like they could feel guilt.

They probably enjoyed it.

She'd made it out of the room, she'd surprised them, and it was in that moment that she'd managed to make her escape, out into the night, out onto the streets where maybe she could find someone to help her.

But it was late. There wasn't anyone around. Not a single soul in the whole town.

It was like a nightmare.

She'd had dreams like this before. Where you're running from someone and you just can't get away no matter how hard you try. You can feel them gaining on you, your legs pounding against the pavement. One trip, one slip, and it's over.

Tears broke free from her eyes and started running down her face, mixing with the rain that was drizzling down around her, slicking the pavement, making her escape all the more treacherous.

She turned back.

They were still there.

Of course, they were.

They would never stop.

Without thinking of where she was going, Sarah Harper started through the middle of town. She barrelled past the darkened shop fronts, past the M&S with its shutters down, past the Bentall Centre that still seemed to be lit up like a beacon, even in the middle of the night.

When she carried on out of town and started over Kingston Bridge, she didn't realise the mistake she'd made. She was running out of steam, running out of places to go, running out of ideas, if she had any ideas at all in the first place.

Then she made her final mistake.

She took a left towards the riverside, heading out of the light and into the dark. She ran down the paved road and towards the river, heading past the houseboats with their twinkly lights still on even though it was the middle of the night, even though Christmas had long since passed, and she kept going.

She kept going until the ground seemed to give way under her feet, or maybe it was her legs giving way, finally giving up.

Sarah Harper fell near the water, her head smashing onto the concrete and as the blackness enveloped her and took her away, her assailant stopped and watched her. They watched her lying there, the blood pouring from a wound on her head, her jacket covered in mud, her legs scraped and bleeding too.

They walked over, shoes squelching in the mud along the riverbank. They watched her move, slowly coming to. She locked eyes with them and moved her mouth, trying to say something, maybe even trying to scream.

It was a risk they couldn't take.

CHAPTER TWENTY-SIX

DI Kidd wasn't prepared for what greeted him when he made it into the station the following morning. He'd woken up determined to get to the bottom of what was going on. They had more suspects than they could count, everyone from Norman Kaye to Dexter Black, with the headteacher and Caleb Kaye in-between. They needed to narrow it down and every second that passed was putting Sarah in more and more danger.

He'd walked into the Incident Room with that renewed vigour, a spring in his step almost as he approached DS Sanchez and told her what he had found out about Caleb. She was interested, more than interested. They broached it with DC Ravel, who dug a little bit deeper and found that he had no online connection to the family at all, his social media presence was almost nil. If he had a relationship with Sarah it was either analogue or non-existent. Which put many questions in Kidd's head about Alexandra Kaye.

They were about to get to work on trying to narrow this down, wanting to bring people in, when DCI Weaver walked into the room.

And that was when DI Benjamin Kidd knew something was wrong.

He'd worked with DCI Weaver long enough to know that he barrelled into rooms like a bull in a china shop, knocking anyone and anything out of the way to make sure everybody knew that he was there. But this morning was different.

Kidd turned to the door, the smile quickly slipping from his face when he locked eyes with DCI Weaver.

"Boss?" Kidd said. "Everything alright?"

"We've got a body," he said. "Sarah Harper's body."

He wandered over to the evidence board where the pictures of their suspects were, every single one of them, Norman's mugshot from last night, Ms Chowdhury's school photo, a family photo of the Harpers, all of them surrounding a picture of Sarah Harper. He wandered over to the picture of Dexter Black, tapping it.

"I think we've got your man too."

DI Kidd was confused, he needed Weaver to go back a few steps. He must have noticed because he shook his head.

"We've found Sarah Harper's body at

Kingston riverside," he said. "Her head had been caved in, blood everywhere, all over her, there are marks around her wrist, marks around her neck too, strangled we think and covered in mud, looks like she was running from someone. Though that remains to be seen, we've got some detective work to do on that."

"What about Dexter Black?" Kidd asked.

DCI Weaver took a breath before he spoke. "Response team found him with the body. Turns out he was the one who called it in."

CHAPTER TWENTY-SEVEN

There was already a Family Liaison Officer on their way to see Mr and Mrs Harper to break the news. DC Powell was sent to meet them at their house. They would need to identify the body, even though Dexter Black had already done that for them over the phone.

The team wasted no time gathering their coats and heading to the riverside to see what was going on. Every single one of them went along, like it was some kind of strange family outing, not a group of detectives going to see a dead body.

DI Kidd cursed himself on the way there. Had they not worked fast enough? Had they not been working flat out since they found out...? He traced it back in his head. Yesterday morning. They'd found out about it yesterday morning, they'd conducted interviews, they'd even gone to that bloody school reunion to see if they could figure out who it was that was doing this and all they'd ended up with was a body.

The last thing Kidd had wanted was for it to turn into a murder investigation. He'd wanted to bring her back alive. There had been too many young girls that he had seen suffer in this borough and now Sarah Harper was another one to add to the list.

The fact that DCI Weaver looked rattled by it also wasn't a particularly good sign. He knew that the Superintendent had been on his case about it since the beginning, the rushed press conference, the determination to get someone arrested, but now it was only going to get worse. DCI Weaver was going to get the blame for this, which meant it was DI Kidd's head in the smasher too.

The riverside was crowded. There were marked police cars, sparkling white in the morning sunshine, a couple of uniformed officers stood at the cordon, stoically watching people pass by and rubberneck. The traffic on the bridge was obscene, everyone and their mother trying to see what was happening down there.

A couple of cyclists had stopped at the tape, talking to one of the officers, wondering why they couldn't cycle down there. Some people needed their bloody heads examined.

"'Scuse me," Kidd growled at one of them as he made his way past.

"Why can he go down there?" A middle-aged man whined.

Kidd turned back to him, his eyes ablaze. He didn't know whether to rip the man to shreds for wearing that much Lycra at his age or just bite his head off for the question.

"I'm the investigating officer," he barked. "You got a problem with that?"

The man winced, stepping back from the cordon and starting away on his bike.

The press had arrived too, cameras being set up around the cordon. Kidd half expected to see Joe Warrington there somewhere, but maybe this was a little bit too early for him. Or he had a class. This was going to make national news because of Laura's profile. The shitstorm was just beginning. And it was his fault.

"You alright?" Zoe asked falling into step with him.

"No, Zoe, I'm not alright," Kidd growled. "We lost her. We bloody lost her. Fuck."

"Okay, look, I know you're hurting right now, but this isn't the place for it," she said. "We'll get a drink later and you can rage about it to your heart's content. Or save it for Weaver, I imagine he'll give you a run for your money," she added.

He smirked. "He really looks like he's going to explode at some point, doesn't he?"

"Wait until he's had the call from the Super, you'll be in that office so fast."

Kidd and the team pulled on coveralls, white puffy suits so they didn't contaminate anything, and headed down towards the riverside, joining the forensic team who'd beaten them there. They'd already set up a small tent where Sarah's body was so it was hidden away from prying eyes and to protect the crime scene. They were collecting everything they could, anything that could possibly help. Kidd could feel himself sweating beneath the suit.

The team walked down to take a look at her. Kidd found himself holding his breath.

How many bodies had he seen over his years? Too many to count, that much was for sure, definitely too many for him to name, but there were a few that seemed to stand out in his head. He'd never forget the names of the women who'd been killed in the first Grinning Murders case fifteen years ago. And he didn't think he would forget Sarah Harper in a hurry either.

She was lying on her back. He wondered if she had fallen that way, the last thing she would have seen being the sky. She was pale, the tanned complexion that they'd seen in all of her photos not there. Kitt wondered whether it was because she was without a filter or because the life had drained from her. Kidd couldn't tell.

Her eyes stared upwards, glassy, unseeing, and it was enough to chill him. The rest of the team was by his side, looking down at her body as the forensics team swept around her, digging beneath her fingernails, taking photographs.

She was wearing a jacket, though now it

was covered in mud. Most of her body was from where she had fallen. You could see it on the ground, where she had slipped, tripping over the dirt, over her own feet and…Kidd looked at where she was now. There was a rock jutting out of the shore. That must have been where she hit her head.

So an accident. But why was she running?

He looked at the markings around her neck, just as DCI Weaver had pointed out. A combination of the two? Did she slip and fall? Did someone come along to finish the job?

"Thoughts, DI Kidd?" DCI Weaver asked.

"We need to look for any footprints that don't belong to us," he said. "The scene is likely already contaminated with our footprints, other officers, Dexter's, but we need to find the prints of whoever it is that was chasing her."

"A good start," Weaver said. "The houseboats?"

"Owen, Janya, can you do some door knocking on the houseboats both on this side of the bridge and on the other, see if they heard anything, saw anything," he said. "I feel like we'd be pushing our luck to think that one of them might have CCTV."

"They don't have proper plumbing, Kidd, I think asking for CCTV would be a lot," Weaver replied.

"Fair point," Kidd said. He looked over at DCs Campbell and Ravel, both of whom were watching him with careful eyes. "No time to stand around," he barked. "Knock on those doors, see if we can track down the bastard who did this."

"Ben," Weaver said. "We have Dexter Black in custody. He was found with the body. We have evidence...I think—"

"With all due respect, sir," DI Kidd said, without a hint of respect whatsoever. "You handed the case over to me. And we didn't move quick enough and now a girl is dead, I want to do this properly."

"I just think that Dexter—"

"He needs to be interviewed, sir, I know that," Kidd said. "And I will get to it. But I want to knock on these houseboats, I want to see if they heard anything or saw anything. We need a timeline on this. She was last seen on Friday, we need to know what happened between then and now."

He kept his gaze on DCI Weaver, unable to stop the fire that was running through his veins. He didn't want Weaver muscling in on this, he didn't want Weaver making the wrong call and letting someone else get away with murder. He was determined to make an arrest, to charge somebody, DI Kidd was concerned with getting this right. He'd already gotten too much wrong.

"He's at the station, in a cell," Weaver said. "We've arrested him on suspicion."

Kidd opened his mouth to speak but Weaver stopped him.

"The interview is yours, the case is yours, but I want someone charged with this," he said his voice firm. "I've got the Super and I've got the media breathing down my neck, they are all over my arse, I want this closed."

"So do I, sir," Kidd said. He hated the implication that he didn't. It made him want to tell Weaver to stuff it and figure it out himself, but he knew he couldn't do that.

That was the problem with working on cases like this. There was a strange sort of addiction attached to it. It became a game, a puzzle that you needed to work out. The only problem was, it was a game that had people's lives at stake, not just bravado or the thrill of figuring it out. Weaver knew that. But Weaver also had higher-ups to impress and the fact that Sarah Harper was a pretty high-profile case and she'd wound up dead wouldn't look good on his record.

"We'll come back to the station when we're done here," Kidd said, turning away from Weaver once again to look down at Sarah's body. The camera flashes kept going off, close-up shots of the wound on her head, of her eyes staring into nothing, of the cuts and bruises on her wrists, on her legs, the strangulation marks around her neck.

To Kidd, she looked like she'd been held captive somewhere, that she'd possibly been restrained while she'd been there. It was enough to make his blood run cold. The fact that she'd ended up here, on the riverside, meant that it was somewhere in this town, right under their noses. And whoever it was, they were still out there, thinking they'd gotten away with it.

Not on Kidd's watch.

CHAPTER TWENTY-EIGHT

While DCs Campbell and Ravel collected statements from the nearby houseboat residents, and from the people who had seen Dexter with the body that morning, Kidd and Sanchez made their way back to the station.

He stayed quiet on the short car journey, watching life carry on outside the glass, people who were none the wiser to the dangers that existed in the world around them. He thought about what they had so far. Dexter was seen yelling at Sarah, very publicly. A lot of people witnessed that at the school. He was nowhere to be seen for the days after that, which lined up with her disappearance and he reappeared in time to find the body.

It all seemed to work. And maybe finding the body and calling it in meant that he looked less guilty. Could a boy so young really be that conniving? Could he really plan that?

Kidd didn't know, but he was determined

to find out.

◆ ◆ ◆

"Good morning, Mr Black," Kidd said when he walked into the interview room, DS Sanchez at his side.

Dexter Black looked up at them, his dark, floppy hair falling into his face. He flicked it out of the way with a movement of his head, a move that Kidd associated so strongly with Craig that it took him by surprise. When they could see his face, Kidd could see the terror in his light brown eyes. He was ghostly pale, with a strong jawline and a slightly crooked nose, which told Kidd that maybe he'd been in one or two fights at school. Given the reports of his anger issues, that wasn't exactly surprising.

Dexter had needed an appropriate adult, given that he was underage. His parents had sent a legal representative—a short, squat man with a bald head that looked like it had been freshly shined. The solicitor's grey suit was about three sizes too big for him, his shirt, on the other hand, looked three sizes too small, the buttons screaming where they sat across his chest. Kidd vaguely recognised him.

"Andrew Grace," the man said, reaching out a hand for Kidd to shake, dark hair snaking out from beneath his shirt cuff. "I think we met a few years ago. The Peter Walters case?"

There it is, Kidd thought to himself. Andrew Grace had represented Peter Walters, a notoriously vicious killer who had dismembered several men and women across London before Kidd had managed to catch him. Andrew Grace had been assigned to defend Peter. Kidd got the impression that he hadn't really wanted to get Peter off, though he did try.

"Yes, of course," Kidd replied, shaking his hand. "Nice to see you again."

"Is it?" Andrew replied. "Would be nicer under less saddening circumstances."

"Yes," Kidd said. He turned his attention back to Dexter. Dexter's gaze was focused on the table. He was picking at his fingers, pulling at the skin on the sides of his nails. He could see they were already red raw. A nervous habit. "Mr Black." He looked up sharply, eyes wide, attentive. His lips quivered a little. "Shall we get started?"

Dexter nodded. He was wearing a pair of jogging bottoms and jumper that were provided by the front desk, the greyness of it matching his skin.

DI Kidd pressed record, announced the date, who was present, and sat back in his chair.

"Would you mind telling us in your own words what happened today?" DI Kidd said.

Dexter took a deep breath before he started. "I didn't kill her."

"Deep breaths," Mr Grace said beside him. "Just tell them what you told me. You don't have to answer any questions if you don't want to."

Kidd sighed. "I never said you did," he replied firmly. "I just want to get to the bottom of this, so I need you to start talking."

"But I've seen it on TV," he said. "I've seen what you do. You find someone who looks like they've done it and you make it all fit so you can put them away. But I didn't kill her. I didn't. I found the body, but I didn't…" He trailed off, the tears rolling down his face as he sat there, trying to get control of himself.

DS Sanchez leaned forward in her chair and lowered her voice. "No one is accusing you of that right now."

"They arrested me on suspicion of the murder of Sarah Harper," Dexter snapped. "They think I— You think I did it. I know you do."

"Suspicion," DS Sanchez said firmly. "It's suspicion because you found a dead body and we were looking for you to ask you questions about it."

"It seems a little bit suspicious, don't you think?" DI Kidd chimed in. DS Sanchez looked at him sharply. "You disappear, no one has seen you since shortly after you were shouting the odds at Sarah in front of your school. Suddenly you show up, and so does her dead body."

"I didn't kill her!"

Kidd banged his fist on the table, making Dexter—and his legal representation—jump. "Then you'd best start talking so we can figure out who did," Kidd barked. "I want to get to the bottom of this. I want to know who kidnapped her, I want to know who killed her, and I need you to talk to me so I can figure that out. I'm not accusing you right now, but there is a lot of damning evidence that I think could put you away for a long time. So, Dexter Black, I am asking you once again, would you mind telling us, in your own words, what happened today?"

Dexter was rattled. His hands were shaking, the tears were still rolling down his face despite wanting to stop them. He steadied himself, Mr Grace telling him to take his time, and he looked back at Kidd, apparently ready to speak.

"I was out for a run," Dexter said quietly. "I...I'd not been out of the house for a few days, and my parents were out."

"They were out?" Kidd interrupted.

"We went around to your house to talk to you and—"

"I know," he said. "They...they didn't want me to talk to you."

Kidd could feel his blood starting to simmer in his veins once again. He added it up in his head. They'd kept Dexter from them and possibly cost Sarah Harper her life. He clenched his fists under the table, not wanting to scare Dexter now that he'd started talking.

"Go on," he said through gritted teeth.

"They went out, shopping or work or something, they'd not been out together for days, that's why I couldn't leave. Even when I tried to go to school they..." He trailed off. "Anyway, I thought I would take a run," he said. "It was early and I went down by the river, like I always do, I have a route you see, like, a regular running route. And I went down by the water and...there she was."

He got this far-off look in his eyes, one that Kidd had seen far too many times in people who had found bodies in the past. He was going through it all in his head again, reliving every one of those feelings he had when he first saw the body, when he walked up to it and realised it was somebody that he knew. Kidd felt sorry for him.

"There was a body, someone, just lying there and I figured she was in trouble, so I went over there," Dexter's voice had gotten very quiet all of a sudden. "And that's when I realised it was Sarah and...I didn't know what to do. I froze. There were a couple of people who came down when they saw me standing next to the body. I don't know how many people must have gone past her this morning and not even noticed, but I did. And she was just...lying there. So still. So pale."

He pulled his sleeve over his hand and rubbed at his eyes, dabbing up the tears. He wiped his nose and then looked across at Kidd and Sanchez, panicked.

"I'm sorry, this isn't even mine and I'm—"

"It's okay," DS Sanchez said, offering him a smile. It seemed to calm him a little bit. "What else?"

"Well," he said. "I took out my phone. I didn't know who to call at first, I thought about calling my friends, I don't know why, but then figured that this was bigger than that and called the police. They arrived pretty quickly. But then they put me in cuffs and arrested me on suspicion of murdering Sarah and I got real scared. I panicked and I tried to pull away and I told them that I didn't do it but they weren't listening."

The response team would have known they were looking for Dexter Black after they couldn't find him so they would have gone in all guns blazing when they realised who he was. Kidd, once again, found himself pitying Dexter Black.

"They wanted to call my parents but I have Andrew's number because, like, he's friends with my dad and I thought he could help." The tears were coming fast now, flowing down his cheeks, cascading off his jawline, and onto the collar of the jumper.

"She was wearing my jacket," he sniffed. "I gave her that. She got cold one night when we were all out as a group and I gave her the jacket and she just kept on wearing it. I didn't want it back. I never wanted it back. It was hers as far as I was concerned but…" He trailed off, crying again.

Kidd needed him to keep talking. "I know this is very distressing, Dexter, but I need you to take us back to Friday. I need you to tell us everything that happened to you from Friday when you shouted at Sarah in front of everyone. We spoke to people at the school, they were really worried you were going to hurt her. Was your relationship with Sarah like that? Did the two of you get into fights often?"

Dexter scoffed and looked away. "It wasn't even a fight."

Kidd straightened up. This lad was really taking him on a ride here. One minute he felt sorry for him, the next he wanted to reach across the table and smack him in the face.

"What was it then?" Kidd asked, firmly. "Because everything that we've heard is that it was a fight. And from what we were told you fought a lot, and your relationship was strange. A lot of people were confused."

"We were putting it on."

"Putting it on?" Kidd repeated. "The people watching seemed to think it was pretty real. I've been told you were screaming in her face, threatening her. Is that what people do in relationships, Dexter?"

"We weren't in a relationship!"

"What?"

"I'm gay."

Kidd sat back in his chair and blinked. He

hadn't been expecting that at all.

CHAPTER TWENTY-NINE

Going off of Kidd's silence, DS Sanchez chimed in. "So you were in a fake relationship?"

Dexter sank a little further down in his chair and Kidd suddenly felt a strange affinity with the lad. He remembered what it was like being young and gay, not being able to say it out loud for fear of getting in the shit for it. Maybe that was the first time Dexter Black had ever said it out loud.

"I...I'm gay," he said again. "And Sarah knew about it. We've been friends for years, since we were babies, and she knows my parents, knows they're super religious and the biggest pair of arseholes you could possibly meet." He stopped and looked up. "I mean, I know they're my parents but...they're not, like, accepting. They're pretty far from it actually. That's why I wasn't allowed out all weekend."

Kidd was lost. "Circle back," Kidd said.

"My dad found...he found that I'd been looking at...*websites*..." Dexter trailed off. Kidd didn't need to know what kind of websites. He could imagine what kind of websites a curious sixteen-year-old would be looking at. "We got into a big fight and they...they said some things to me and they...they locked me up in my room for the weekend, longer actually, they wouldn't let me go to school."

Kidd nearly said that's the last thing they should be doing to a horny teenager with access to the internet but he held his tongue. "Go on."

"So when I had a chance to go out for a run, I took it. They'd left me breakfast outside the door and left the door unlocked so I could get it and when I realised they weren't home, I went running," he said. "But Sarah was trying to protect us from all that, from my parents finding out, but then I got stupid and they found out anyway."

"You said us," Kidd said. "Who is us?"

"Me and Nick," he replied, looking down at his hands again, furiously picking at the skin until he started bleeding. Kidd winced. "She was...she was trying to protect us. We've been seeing each other for about a year, getting to know one another, both of us doing it in secret, really. He's not out to his parents either. His parents would probably be fine with it, but if he came out to his parents and I met them, then maybe my parents would have found out too and I didn't want that." He lowered his voice. "But they found out anyway."

"So since Friday, you've been locked up in your house?" DS Sanchez asked. "Your parents could confirm that?"

Dexter nodded. "They wouldn't want to, but they could, yes."

"Alright," Zoe said, turning to DI Kidd. "Any further questions?"

"Yes, just one," he said. "Who is Nick? We may need to speak with him, just to corroborate your story, you understand?"

Dexter nodded. "He goes to my school. I can give you his phone number if you like?" Dexter said. "His name is Nicholas Ayre."

Kidd sat up a little straighter. The name triggered something in the back of his brain, it was a name he had heard before. He closed his eyes and thought back before he turned to DS Sanchez whose eyes were wide, staring over at Kidd.

"He's been a little bit off-grid for the past couple of days, but he's still been going to school like normal. He said he was going in today, and I said I'd see him there because I thought maybe my parents were going to let me go. I mean, I was going to go anyway, when I got back from my run but… " He trailed off. He didn't need to finish that thought. "I thought he might have been mad or something, or worried because of what happened to me with my parents, but if I told him it was urgent I'm sure he would reply. I'm sure he'd come and meet me," Dexter said. "They've got my phone so I can't do it right now."

Kidd sighed and looked back at Dexter. "We've heard of Nicholas Ayre," Kidd said. "Was he aware of your arrangement with Sarah?"

"Of course he was," Dexter said, confusion flickering across his face. "He didn't like the arrangement, I don't think he did anyway, but he went along with it. He thought Sarah was taking advantage of me."

"Did you think that?"

"No," Dexter replied quickly. "She was trying to help me. She's known my parents long enough to know that they take their religion very very seriously and they didn't agree with…" He trailed off, silencing himself, something Kidd imagined he had to do on a daily basis. Again, there he was, feeling sorry for the lad. "Why?"

"Nicholas Ayre is someone who has come up in our investigation, someone we've not actually had a chance to speak to yet," DS Sanchez said. "We understand the website that posted the pictures of Sarah and Jonno was set up and run by him."

Dexter stared at the two of them, his face blank. He looked down to his hands, back up to them, his eyes getting that faraway look in them again as he tried to figure out just what the heck was going on.

"That can't be right," Dexter said. "He didn't do anything to Sarah either, I know he didn't."

"We can't be sure of that."

"He was with me," Dexter said quickly. "On Friday night, Nicholas was with me. After school, after everything that went down outside the school with Sarah, we spent the rest of that afternoon together at his house. It was when I got home late from his that my parents confronted me about the...about...the websites."

"Okay," DS Sanchez said. "Nicholas can confirm that?"

"Yes."

"Well, we need to speak with him then," DI Kidd cut in. "You said he's been off-grid for the past couple of days?"

"Yeah," Dexter said quietly. "I guess I know why now. He was laying low."

"I imagine he was," Kidd replied. "You said he's at school today? You're sure about that?"

"He messaged me this morning," Dexter said.

"Okay," Kidd said. "We may need to ask you some more questions later, is that okay?"

Dexter nodded. "I'll do whatever I can to help her," he said. "She's...she was my best friend." And the tears started rolling again. Kidd took the opportunity to finish the interview, a high-pitched beep ringing through the room from the recorder as silence fell upon them all.

DCI Weaver wouldn't be happy about this, not one bit.

CHAPTER THIRTY

DI Kidd had figured out his next move by the time they were finished with Dexter Black. They'd given the lad some time to calm down before taking him back to his cell. He hadn't wanted to go and Kidd could hardly blame him, but they needed to keep him there until they could be one hundred percent sure. He understood that.

"I want to talk to Caleb," Kidd said as they walked into the Incident Room. The other members of the team had returned from their door-knocking. DC Powell was just taking his coat off from being out with the FLO and the Harpers. Everyone seemed eager to hurry over to Kidd and report back. He kept talking regardless. "And we definitely need to talk to Nicholas Ayre. If he's not at school, Dexter can help us track him down."

"You think he's innocent then?" DS Sanchez asked.

"Absolutely."

"DCI Weaver is going to be pressing you to get that arrest," Zoe said. "You heard him down by the river. He thinks it's him."

"Yeah, but I'm not about to convict Dexter for the sake of it. We know different."

"The evidence is there," Zoe said. "For the record, I think he's innocent too, but there are a lot of things that point to it being him."

"The thing pointing me away from it being him is that he wasn't even with Sarah in the first place," Kidd said. This case kept twisting around in all different directions, it was hard to get a handle on it. Or to have any idea where it was going to take them next. "There's no way to prove it, of course, but who the hell is Sarah talking about on her website?"

DI Kidd was about to move over to the computer to check the entries again when the door burst open, DCI Weaver barrelling in with such force that DC Powell practically fell out of his chair.

"Why the bloody hell is Dexter Black back in his cell and CPS hasn't been called to charge him?" he barked.

DC Campbell looked up from behind his computer screen, a gleeful smile spreading across his face. Kidd wanted to throw something at him. He made a mental note to do it later.

"He's not our prime suspect, sir," Kidd said.

"This is a murder investigation, he was found with the body!"

"And she was wearing his jacket," DI Kidd said. DCI Weaver's eyes widened at this new information and opened his mouth to speak. DI Kidd started before he had the chance. "I know, sir, it's damning, but after interview he's not our guy. He's going to help us get to the bottom of this though."

"I don't think you understand what I'm saying here, Kidd—"

"I think I do, boss," Kidd interrupted. "You want me to charge this lad, even though we're fairly certain he didn't commit the crime, right, DS Sanchez?"

"Right."

"We have his statement recorded from the interview," Kidd continued. "We're working with him to track down his alibi who will be able to corroborate that statement, and DS Sanchez here is going to go and carry on with the other enquiries that we have. Right, DS Sanchez?"

"Absolutely, sir. I'm just about to grab my coat," she said with a smirk. "DC Ravel, can you give the school a call and see if Caleb Kaye is in today?"

"Sure thing," she said, immediately picking up the phone and dialling.

"Caleb Kaye?" DCI Weaver repeated.

"This lot," he said, pointing over Weaver's

shoulder, "were getting ready to tell me all about what they found out down by the riverside, and DC Ravel is already in contact with the pathologist so we can find out exactly what happened to Sarah Harper," DI Kidd said, leaning around DCI Weaver to take in the rest of his team.

DC Powell was watching him with his mouth hanging open, probably scared that he'd be next in the firing line if Weaver couldn't take his frustrations out on DI Kidd. DC Campbell couldn't stop grinning. DC Ravel looked like she was about to burst out laughing as she dialled.

"Isn't that right?" DI Kidd prompted.

DC Campbell sprung into action, grabbing his notebook from his desk and walking a little closer. "We spoke to the people who are staying in the houseboats by the riverside and they didn't see anything that night. Apparently, there are Uni students down there all the time so they've sort of learned to tune it out."

"However," DC Powell piped up. "One of them does remember being woken up by a scream. They thought maybe it was a fox because, you know, wildlife out there. That might have been when Sarah fell, right before she hit her head." DCI Weaver rounded on Powell, and while Kidd couldn't see his face he could imagine it was screwed up like a raging bull ready to charge. "Just a theory, sir."

"Caleb Kaye is off school today," DC Ravel

called across the room. "Mother called in this morning."

"Perfect, thanks, Janya," Zoe said.

"What happened with the FLO at the Harpers?" DCI Weaver asked, his rage appearing to subside.

"They were distraught, sir," Powell said quietly. "Caitlyn is there doing all she can. They didn't want to come and identify the body. They know they're going to have to, but neither one of them want to. It's…it's shit, sir."

"One, or a couple of you, need to go and make sure they're doing alright. Things have obviously changed quite drastically now and I want this sorted."

"We know, sir," Kidd said. "We'll follow up later on today if we can."

"Fine, fine, fine, good work." Weaver grunted, turning his attention back to Kidd. "I want this wrapped up as soon as possible, DI Kidd. Otherwise, I'll take it out of your hands. You've got until the end of the day or I'm calling CPS, is that clear?"

DI Kidd resisted the urge to say that he would like to see him try, but instead, he nodded and said, "Of course, sir," and let DCI Weaver storm out, slamming the door behind him. The air in the room was thick with the tension DCI Weaver had brought in. It was Owen who broke it.

"I thought he was going to rip your head

off, sir," he said. "Honestly, he looked like he was about to properly erupt."

"Bold move," DS Sanchez said.

"I told you I was going to give him hell," he said. "Are you alright to go and see Caleb at his house? Might give you a chance to talk to the mother as well. I know I sprung that on you a little bit there."

"Of course," she said. "Powell, grab your coat, we've got work to do." She started towards the door, DC Powell quickly collecting his things and heading out of the room behind her.

"I'm going to talk to Dexter Black," he said. "Apparently, he knows Nicholas Ayre quite intimately, that's what I have as proof that he didn't hurt Sarah."

"But Nicholas posted the article?" DC Ravel said. "Doesn't look good, sir."

"It doesn't look good for Nicholas, no, but if Dexter can get him here then at least we can question him about what's going on," DI Kidd said heading back towards the door.

"Hold up, sir," DC Ravel said quickly, getting to her feet to grab his attention. "We've got a problem."

"What's that?"

"Joe Warrington."

DI Kidd's face screwed up in confusion. What on earth did Joe Warrington have to do with this?

"What about him?"

"He's just updated his news page, sir," she said. "He's outed Nicholas Ayre as the guy who made the post about Sarah."

"Shit," DI Kidd grunted. Nicholas Ayre was in big trouble.

CHAPTER THIRTY-ONE

DS Sanchez headed out to the car park with DC Simon Powell hurrying along behind her, having to take two steps for every one of hers. By the time they made it to the car, he was a little out of breath, his face sort of red, and he seemed nervous.

"You okay?" Sanchez asked as she pulled on her seatbelt. He really didn't look well. "You look like you're about to vomit."

"DCI Weaver just makes me nervous, that's all," he said. "I had a Sarge like him once and honestly, every time she came into the room I thought I was going to shit my pants." He looked up at her, like he'd suddenly heard the words that had come out of his mouth. "Oh my God, I'm so sorry. I didn't mean to say that out loud."

"It's alright," she said, putting the car into drive and pulling out of the car park. "DCI Weaver is all bluster," she continued. "He'll absolutely give you the hairdryer treatment if you put a foot wrong, but mostly he just wants to get the job done." She thought about it a little. "Not that I'm excusing his methods, it's not how I would do things if I were a DCI."

There was a lot of masculine bullshit in the job. She'd had to deal with it daily since she'd started. She didn't want anybody, especially not somebody new, thinking it was okay to manage people through fear.

"You'd make a good DCI," Simon said. "A good DI, too."

"You think?"

"You're a lot like DI Kidd," he said. "But without the short fuse. You're calm under pressure, but you have an edge."

"You think I have an edge?" Zoe asked with a smirk, looking at Simon out of the corner of her eye. He stiffened, his gaze fixed on the road.

"Um...I don't know what the right answer is to that question."

Zoe laughed as she continued to drive, DC Powell directing her as she went. It seemed to ease the tension. They'd not worked together an awful lot, Sanchez usually paired with Kidd because that was the way he liked to do things, or she would pair herself with DC Ravel if possible because, as far as she was concerned, women in this job needed to stick together.

But she liked him. He was a little clumsy at times, and his nervousness needed to fade away pretty sharpish if he was going to survive as a detective, but he was nice. And when you sat him next to someone like DC Campbell, she would choose Simon Powell eight times out of ten. The two times she wouldn't were maybe when they were going into something dangerous. At times like that, she was more than happy to use DC Campbell as a sacrificial lamb.

They drove right past Sarah Harper's family home. Zoe Sanchez shook her head, her heart going out to them. They would be in that house right now probably going through Sarah's last movements in their head, trying to figure out who on earth would do something like this.

"How were they?" DS Sanchez asked. "I mean, I know they wouldn't have been good but how did they take it?"

DC Powell shook his head. "A left here," he said. "Neither one of them took it well. Surprisingly enough, it was Mr Harper who broke down. Mrs Harper was fairly solid. I think she'd come to terms with it in her head." He swallowed. "Caitlyn did a good job at calming him down."

"She's a good egg, Caitlyn," Sanchez said, following Powell's instructions and turning left. "We'll check in later, see how they're getting on."

"Sounds like a plan," he said. "It's just here," he added quickly, pointing to the house.

The Kaye residence wasn't too far from the Harpers' house, just a couple of minutes around the corner. Mr Harper had said that they were family friends, so that was clearly facilitated by them living so close to one another. There was probably a whole street of people who knew each other and were in and out of each other's business. Maybe some door knocking here wouldn't go amiss.

The Kaye residence was definitely different from the Harpers' house. It wasn't quite as large, the house seemingly squeezed in between one that seemed to match the rest of the street and a one that only looked about half-finished. There was a skip out the front of the half-built house, mud covering a half-paved driveway, bits of plastic hanging off the double glazing that flapped about in the wind like a half-arsed flag parade. It made everything around it look a little more untidy.

But the Kaye Residence itself was meticulous. It looked clean, the yellow bricks on the outside looking like they'd been freshly jet washed. They had to be paying a window cleaner because there wasn't a spot on any of the windows and the bright white door seemed to have a strange glow to it in the late winter sun.

DS Sanchez got out of the car, Powell following suit, and headed towards the front door. The gate didn't even squeak when they opened it. Everything about the house was a well-oiled machine—in the case of the gate, that was literal.

Zoe knocked firmly on the door, the gold

knocker jumping each time her fist landed on the plastic. She heard the shuffling about inside, the sound of a lock being pushed to one side, before the door opened.

Alexandra Kaye opened the door just a crack, poking her head into the gap and looking out at DS Sanchez and DC Powell. Her eyes widened as she saw them. She looked, for want of a better word, exhausted, as far as DS Sanchez could see. The rings beneath her eyes were heavy and dark, her hair didn't look like it had even been touched with a brush that morning.

"Hello again," she said. "Is this about Norman?" she asked. And it was so sudden that it threw Zoe a little bit off balance. She righted herself and smiled at Ms Kaye.

"No, we released Norman last night," Zoe said. "We're actually here hoping we can have a chat with Caleb. We called the school but they told us that he was off. Could we have a word?"

"He's sick," she said. "He won't come out of his room, the poor lamb. But I don't feel all that well myself so I'm wondering if whatever he's got I've managed to pick up."

She backed away from the door a little, allowing it to open further. Zoe would have taken that as an invitation to step inside, but Alexandra Kaye seemed to be blocking the whole of the hallway. She didn't want them to come in, that much was for certain.

"It would be really useful if we could talk

to him," Zoe said. "It shouldn't take too long, just wanted to have a word about Sarah."

"He's been so upset since she went missing," she said, just like she had done last night. Her eyes looked red upon closer inspection, her face a little bit puffy. She had obviously heard the news. "Honestly, he hasn't known what to do with himself. With news of the body I..." she trailed off. "I can't imagine what he's feeling."

"We'd love to hear that from him if possible," DS Sanchez said, a little more firmly now.

"I really don't think he should be seeing anyone right now," Ms Kaye said. "He's very sick. I would be more than happy to have him call you?"

DS Sanchez watched Ms Kaye carefully. It was hard for Zoe to put her finger on it, but there was something about her that unsettled her. Like she wasn't just trying to stop them from talking to him, like she was hiding something else.

"Can I talk to you a little bit about Mr Harper while I have you?" DS Sanchez said carefully. It felt as good a time as any. "We spoke to him last night after the altercation with your ex-husband, and we'd love to know about your relationship with him."

"Well, we don't really have a relationship," she said with a slight laugh that was more like an expelling of breath. It told Zoe more than she probably intended. There was a lot of history there, it was obvious. "We're old friends, of course. I've been friends with Laura and Chris for a number of years. I think my husband just gets jealous sometimes."

"Because you slept with Chris?" DS Sanchez said quickly.

Alexandra Kaye's face slipped, but only for a moment. She obviously hadn't expected Chris to gift them with that sort of information. Maybe they'd agreed never to discuss it again, but the fact she was so willing to keep it from Zoe made her wonder what else she might be hiding.

"Well," Ms Kaye said, brushing her hair behind her ears, a nervous habit maybe. "It was a one-time thing. I was having problems with Norman and..." She looked up the stairs and lowered her voice. "I don't know how I feel about discussing this with my son just upstairs. I don't like to speak badly about his father if I can help it. He doesn't make it easy, of course, but I still want him and Caleb to have a relationship."

"Well, I'd be more than happy to chat to you about this down at the station, Ms Kaye," Zoe said. "We can take you there, we have a car outside."

"I shouldn't leave Caleb, really."

"Then please, tell us more about Mr Kaye," DS Sanchez said. She lowered her voice, conspiratorial, vaguely threatening. She wanted Alexandra to know she wasn't to be messed with. "You can speak softly if you want to."

Ms Kaye locked eyes with DS Sanchez before her gaze drifted to DC Powell and back again. She plastered that smile back onto her face and took a breath before speaking.

"The way he acted last night wasn't exactly out of character," she said quietly, her voice trembling. "Even when we were together he had a tendency to fly off the handle at the slightest thing. Caleb has a very close relationship with my mother, his grandmother, because I would often send him off there when it felt like things were getting a little too much here."

"Too much, how?" DS Sanchez asked.

"He would yell, as you saw last night," she said. "And would often get physical."

"Did he ever hit you, Ms Kaye?"

"No, no, nothing like that," she said quickly. "But the threat of it always felt like it was there. And it was enough to keep me scared and keep me in the relationship perhaps longer than I should have."

Zoe considered this. She hadn't wanted to speak about it, but once she'd unlocked the flood gates it had all come out. And everything that she had said matched with the way that Mr Kaye had behaved the previous night. She took down a few notes.

"And what about you taking Caleb away from him?"

"Is that what he told you?" she scoffed,

shaking her head, pulling her gaze away from the DS. "He has quite an imagination, that man."

"What makes you say that, Ms Kaye?"

"Well, I've never threatened to keep him and Caleb apart," she said. "Like I said, I want them to have a relationship. I don't want to keep them apart. Caleb's decisions are his own to make, he's a big boy, he can do what he wants. The fact that he has seen his father for who he is, or maybe doesn't want to go and spend time in his sad little flat is his own decision. Norm can't accept that."

"Why can't he accept that?"

"Because he is so sure that the world, or me, are entirely against him," Ms Kaye snapped. She stopped and steadied herself. "Ever since what happened with Chris, the job loss, the..." She lowered her voice again. "The affair." She shook her head. Was that shame? "It's the way he is. It's frightening and it's sad, but it's true."

"Do you want us to raise anything against him?" DS Sanchez asked. "If you're feeling frightened I wouldn't want—"

"No, please don't," she said suddenly, quickly. "He can be dangerous, I know, but I don't think...I don't think he would do anything to hurt me."

And Zoe saw an opportunity in front of her, one that only someone who had known Norman for many years would be able to answer.

"Do you think he's capable of hurting

other people?" Zoe asked.

Ms Kaye took a breath and locked eyes with DS Sanchez, she looked almost too nervous to speak. What was that? Was she afraid to speak against him, or was it something more? "I think he is capable of absolutely anything once he sets his mind to it," she whispered. "Absolutely anything."

CHAPTER THIRTY-TWO

DI Kidd headed out to the car at a run, taking Owen along with him for support. Owen seemed beyond thrilled to have been chosen, practically bouncing into the passenger seat. Kidd barely waited long enough for Owen to shut his door before he floored it and took off around the Kingston one-way system to make it to the school.

Bloody Joe Warrington, he thought. *I thought I was going to have more time to track him down.*

"This is brilliant," DC Campbell said, absolutely buzzing. He was like a kid in a sweetshop. "We never work together, boss."

"And there's a bloody good reason for it," Kidd grumbled. "But, you never know, I might need your help on this."

"How's that?"

"Well, if I'm right, and I really hope I'm not right this time around," Kidd said, whizzing through an amber light at the crossing and swinging the car into the car park. "Nicholas Ayre is going to be in a heap of trouble when people see the news on Joe's socials, assuming they're looking at them of course."

"Because Sarah's dead?"

"Because she's dead, because there were a bunch of his classmates already out for blood when she was only missing," he said. "With Sarah being dead, Nicholls Ayre could end up being in deep shit when people find out."

"And why is it our responsibility to stop that?" Owen asked. "Isn't this just school drama?"

Kidd had the sudden urge to hit Owen, though he wasn't wrong. The website stuff was definitely petty school drama, but a dead body and a pissed off and grieving student body with a large vendetta against whoever posted it, felt like something he needed to get involved in. Especially as he wanted to talk to the lad, and he needed to be conscious for that to happen.

"Just follow me, yeah?" Kidd said, turning off the car and undoing his seatbelt. He got out of the car and started towards the front doors as he had done the day before, purpose in every step. He needed to get to Nicholas before the rest of the student body did.

Ms Lu was behind the front desk once again, her face lighting up when DI Kidd walked in. "Good afternoon," she said brightly. "We can't seem to keep you away, can we?"

"Hello," he said. "We're actually looking for another one of your students."

"Caleb Kaye?" she said, looking a little surprised. "I got your phone call earlier on, were you not told he's not in?"

"Nope, not Caleb," Kidd said. "We're looking for Nicholas Ayre. I don't suppose you know which class he would be in?"

"He's not in classes right now," Ms Lu said. "The students are on their lunch break, will be for the next," she checked her watch, a sparkly little thing that dangled from her wrist. "Oh, thirty minutes or so."

Kidd was too late. He knew he was too late. He'd been beaten up enough times on that playground to know that once the lunch bell rang, teachers weren't likely to give a toss what you were doing or who was kicking the shit out of who.

"Fuck."

"Language, Mr Kidd, we are in a school," Ms Lu scolded, though it wasn't really much of a scold as it was all done with a smile on her face.

"What do we do now?" Owen asked. "Wait?"

"We can't wait," Kidd said, agitated. If he didn't get a confirmation of that alibi from Nicholas, DCI Weaver was going to call CPS and chances were Dexter was going to get charged for this and he didn't want that to happen.

There was a crackling of static from somewhere in the office. A burly mixed-race man in a high-vis jacket with a bald head grabbed hold of it and grunted something indistinguishable into it. Kidd listened in, trying to pick up whatever was being said.

"Where?" the man grunted.

The crackle came through again. Kidd just managed to make out the words "fight" and "playing field."

Jesus Christ, he thought, cursing his rotten luck that they hadn't gotten here sooner, that Joe Warrington hadn't held off for a little bit longer. Nicholas probably didn't even know what was coming for him.

"Which playing field, Ms Lu?" There were the athletics track and the cricket field and he didn't have time to look at both. Nicholas didn't have time.

"DI Kidd, I can't—"

"Ms Lu, I'd like to talk to Nicholas Ayre before he ends up eating through a straw. Which playing field?" Kidd watched as the man in the high vis jacket ran from the office and out into the corridor. He barrelled past the reception desk and out the front door. "Never mind. Owen, shift it!" Kidd barked, running out of the door and after the man in the high-vis jacket.

The man didn't realise he was being followed until Kidd ended up jogging alongside him. He looked confused, possibly wondering if he had ended up in some kind of footrace.

"Detective Inspector Benjamin Kidd," Kidd panted. "This is DC Owen Campbell. Don't mind if we tag along, do you?"

The man shrugged as he ran, still looking confused. They rounded the corner and headed down towards the playing fields where the athletics track was, a great expanse of green where a cluster of students had gathered somewhere near the middle, white paint barely visible on the grass around them. That had to be what he was looking for.

The closer they got, the louder the chants of "Fight! Fight! Fight!" became. Kidd put on a turn of speed, bolting past the security guard and towards the crowd of students. He could see Jonno Edwards in the thick of it, his blazer off, his white shirt like a beacon in the grey. Across from him was another boy, soft-looking, a little bit chubbier than Jonno. He was backing away, but there were people on the edge of the circle not letting him get free, the people chanting "Fight!" pushing him back into the circle.

Kidd kept up his pace despite the slipperiness of the grass. The rain from the night before had made the whole thing a squelchy death trap, but he needed to get there and he needed to get there now.

He heard someone take a tumble behind him, a small part of him hoping that it was Owen, just because the thought of it made him laugh.

He reached the circle of students and broke through them, the security guard not too far behind. In shock, some of the students immediately starburst off in various directions, screaming, adding to the cacophony of noise that was already assaulting his ears. But some stayed, some stayed because they wanted to see Nicholas get punished for this.

"Knock him out, Jonno!" a voice that Kidd recognised shouted. He turned to see that Taylor was stood there, egging Jonno on, not running away like the rest of them. She was as committed to this as Jonno was. She watched on as Jonno pulled his fist back and threw a punch that connected with Nicholas's face.

He fell into the mud, the dirt splattering all over his uniform.

"Get up and fight me, you coward!" Jonno shouted, spitting at Nicholas. "Just a pathetic little keyboard warrior, aren't you? You're disgusting." He went in to kick Nicholas in the stomach, but DI Kidd got there first, pulling Jonno out of the way.

It surprised him, Kidd could see that in the way he stumbled, nearly losing his footing on the mud. Jonno glared at DI Kidd for a moment, only straightening up when he realised who he was staring at.

"What the fuck are you doing here?"

Kidd was out of breath, panting, his shirt

stuck to his back, splatters of mud all up his front. "I...phew...I wanted to talk to Nicholas," Kidd said. "You know, before you hospitalised him."

"You know what he did!" Jonno barked, his voice cracking as he shouted. "He posted all that shit, he might as well have killed her, he's the one who caused all this. Oi, prick, Dexter's gonna fucking murder you when he finds out you did it."

"I highly doubt that!" Nicholas parried, smug despite the fact he was covered in mud and would probably be unconscious had Kidd not shown up.

Jonno looked like he was going to go for him again but Kidd put his hand up to stop him. He turned to Nicholas.

"You want to shut your fucking mouth for a second before he breaks it?" Kidd snapped. He turned back to Jonno. "We'll take it from here," he said. "You guys go back to your break."

"He might as well have been the one that killed her," Taylor said. Her rage had subsided and she was looking past Kidd, right at Nicholas, her face scrunched up in disgust. "If it hadn't been for him, she'd still be alive. I hope you can fucking live with yourself."

Kidd didn't argue with them. They were hurting, and it was possible that what they were saying wasn't entirely untrue. He didn't know the root cause of Sarah's disappearance yet. It could have been anything. He still needed to find that out, which meant he needed to talk to Nicholas Ayre.

The security guard appeared, out of breath, his high-vis jacket undone. He bent over and put his hands on his knees, willing the air to get back into his lungs.

"You want me…you want…me to take 'em in?" he asked Kidd, gesturing towards Jonno and Taylor. Jonno had his arm around her now and she was crying. He didn't want to cause them any more pain.

"Leave them," he said. "I've sorted it."

"Sorted it? The second you leave they're going to attack me again—"

"I'd stop talking if I were you," Kidd interrupted. "I've got some questions for you, alright? And I'm going to need you to answer them pretty quickly."

"What's happening, boss?" Owen's voice pulled Kidd's attention away from Nicholas. "Did we save him?"

Owen was covered head to toe in mud all across one side. Somehow, he'd even managed to get it in his hair. Kidd couldn't keep the grin off his face. He looked utterly ridiculous, and even if it was just for a moment, it did feel good to laugh.

CHAPTER THIRTY-THREE

They all headed back into the school, Ms Lu getting one of the PE Teachers to open the changing rooms so Nicholas could clean himself up. DC Campbell didn't get such a luxury, though he did spend a solid forty minutes in the toilets trying to scrape the mud off of his face and out of his hair. Kidd found himself wishing that he'd taken a picture to send over to Zoe, she would have lost her mind.

They waited for Nicholas to get changed into his PE Kit—a pair of black jogging bottoms and a light blue polo shirt—and be escorted to see them in the same office that Kidd had conducted interviews with Sarah's friends in the previous day. It seemed smaller in there somehow, like the walls were pressing in a little bit closer. Though maybe that was just Owen talking at a million miles a minute the whole time they were in there.

"I just can't imagine you being here, sir.

Can't really imagine you as a student, to be honest," he said. "In my head you're like Mrs Trunchbull."

"Who?"

"From Matilda, sir," he said. "There's a line where she says she hates children, glad she never was one."

"You don't think I was ever a child, Owen?"

"Erm, I don't know, sir. I've never really thought about it."

Kidd sighed. "Have you thought about not voicing every thought you have?"

When Nicholas arrived, Owen seemed to put his more professional hat on, which meant he was going to let Kidd do the talking, which certainly appealed to him. It was getting on for two o'clock, lunch was long since over and Nicholas would likely be hoping he could get out of school and away before the rest of his classmates finished. At least this way, he might not get into more trouble.

"I heard about Sarah this morning," he said quietly before Kidd could even get a word in. "I...I felt terrible. The news said you'd arrested someone but wouldn't say who. But I just felt awful for what I posted. I didn't...this isn't my fault, is it?"

Kidd hesitated. He didn't know whose fault it was at this stage, that's what he was trying to figure out. All he knew was that it was possible this had sparked off the chain of events that had caused her death. But he didn't want to lay that on someone who was barely sixteen years old.

"We're trying to figure that out," Kidd said. "I just had a few questions to ask you. I need to know what your movements were from Friday to today, if possible."

"What? You don't think I killed her, do you?"

"We need you to answer the questions so we can figure that out," Kidd said firmly. "It's not about tricking you into a confession or anything CSI: Stupid like that, it's about getting to the truth." Kidd didn't want to bring the next part up, but maybe tugging on his heartstrings would be the right way around this. "We've arrested Dexter on suspicion," Kidd continued. "And I have enough evidence to charge him with it, so I'm looking to find out what really went on."

"So you're trying to prove him guilty?"

"I'm trying to get the bloody truth," Kidd said, raising his voice a little. "So, Mr Ayre, tell me what the bloody truth is, alright?"

Nicholas sighed and sat back in his chair. Kidd could see the goose pimples on his arms. Either he was cold, or he was nervous. Kidd would put money on both.

"We were together on Friday night," Nicholas said quietly. "My parents were out, and they're *never* out, and we never get any alone time so...he came over to mine, it got really late, and then he went home. There's no way he could have done anything to Sarah."

"And did you see him over the weekend?"

Nicholas shook his head.

"Or this week?"

"He wasn't coming into school," Nicholas said. "Something happened with his parents when he got back on Friday, they took his phone away but he managed to message me on an old computer. I...I didn't really know what to say to him."

"Why's that?" Kidd asked.

"He and Sarah were really close and the fact that she had gone missing right after I'd posted that thing...it felt like it was my fault," he said. "So I didn't know how to be with him. He probably thought it was because I was trying not to get him in trouble. He's sweet like that, always thinking the best of me, but actually, it was because I was just being an asshole and distancing myself because I felt bad."

And now came the million-dollar question.

"So why did you do it?" Kidd asked. "You say that you regret it and that you feel terrible about what you've done, about what you posted. But why did you do it in the first place?"

Nicholas shrugged. "I'd heard what was going on and investigated it. I took the pictures and...I don't know. I didn't like the way she was treating him. Sure, they were best friends and she was keeping his secret for him, but he had to be available to her whenever she wanted him and it…it just…"

"It pissed you off?"

"Yeah," he said.

"Were you maybe a little jealous?" Owen chimed in. Kidd didn't shoot him a death stare because he actually had a good point for once.

Nicholas shrugged again. "Maybe a little," he said. "We couldn't hang out because she wanted to hang out with him, or they were doing something as a group and he had to be there to play the perfect boyfriend."

"And he played it a little too well for your liking," DC Campbell said. "I take it you also had to see them in school as well, canoodling on the playground and such."

"Yeah," Nicholas replied, his cheeks going a little pink, his eyes seeming to fill with tears. "And it didn't seem fair. It was like our relationship was part-time, a second thought."

"It wasn't a second thought to Dexter, I don't think," Kidd said. "I think we'll need to take you down to the station, get you to write a proper statement for us, and then we can wrap this up. Is that okay?"

He nodded and started to gather his things. DC Campbell went and told Ms Lu that they were taking Nicholas with them to the station and that they would make sure he got home safely, something DI Kidd wanted to make sure happened to Dexter too. He felt a weight lift from his chest knowing that he had likely just saved Dexter from being charged, and managed to cross two names off of his suspect list. But he knew that this was far from over. If it wasn't Dexter or Nicholas, who did that leave?

◆ ◆ ◆

It took a good few hours to get Nicholas' statement down and to convince DCI Weaver to let Dexter go once he'd seen it all. CPS wouldn't be able to charge him with Nicholas' statement on file, and if his parents confirmed that he was in the house with them all weekend, they would be more than fine to let him go.

He took it upon himself to drive Dexter and Nicholas home, dropping Nicholas off first so he could accompany Dexter to his front door and have a word with his parents. When they pulled up outside Dexter's house, he seemed nervous. Incredibly so. He was practically shaking the screws of the passenger seat loose.

"They'll be happy you're okay," Kidd said. "They'll have been worried sick about you all day."

"They won't," he mumbled. "They'll yell at me."

"No reason to yell at you, lad, you didn't

do it," he said. "And you did a good thing by reporting it."

"But I broke out of the house—"

"That they shouldn't have been keeping you locked up in, in the first place," he interrupted.

Dexter opened his mouth to speak but thought better of it. He reached for the door handle but DI Kidd stopped him.

"Hang on, lad," he said, taking a card out of his jacket pocket. "I know it's not much, and maybe keep it from your parents, I have a feeling that they're not going to like me much after tonight, but if you need anything from me, at any point. Just give me a text."

Dexter took the card and looked at it carefully before putting it in his pocket. "Thanks." And without another word, he got out of the car and started towards the house. Kidd followed suit.

Right, he thought. *Time to piss off some parents.*

CHAPTER THIRTY-FOUR

Kidd hated that he'd had to leave Dexter in that house with those people. They hadn't been too impressed with him coming home so late, nor about the fact that he'd been arrested in the first place. Paying out for Andrew Grace's time was a huge inconvenience to them apparently, which was enough to make Kidd hate them even more than he already did.

He told them how helpful he'd been, and also got statements off them regarding Dexter's whereabouts over the weekend. He wanted to let them know that their darling son wouldn't be able to pray the gay away no matter how hard he tried, but he imagined that it would fall on deaf ears and would only get Dexter in more trouble. The lad had it hard enough without Kidd adding to it.

He made sure to let them know that he wasn't charging them with perverting the course of justice, tempting as it may have been, and made sure to get statements as to their whereabouts for the whole weekend. He didn't believe they had anything to do with it, but he wanted to scare the shit out of them if he could.

The station had quietened down as the afternoon had turned into evening. Owen had been sent home to clean himself up, though his appearance had caused Zoe to laugh so much that she had fallen out of her chair. DC Ravel had to hide behind her computer screen because the tears were streaming down her face when she saw him.

That had made it worth taking Campbell with him. And the fact he had actually asked a few good questions. He might have been a little unbearable some of the time, but Campbell was a pretty decent DC. Not that Kidd would ever tell him that.

DCI Weaver joined them in the Incident Room as Kidd updated them on everything that had happened and then he sat back while Zoe did the same.

"He was in the house, but he wasn't coming down," she said. "Well, there was no way that Alexandra Kaye was going to let him come down, she told us how sick he was, so I don't really know what to do with that."

"Did she seem upset at all?" DCI Weaver growled.

"Yes," Zoe replied. "She looked like she'd been crying. She commented on it regarding

Caleb too. I think she's worried about him."

"We need to talk to him," Weaver said.

"I know," Zoe said. "We'll get there. She seemed concerned about his health, and her own safety too."

DCI Weaver didn't seem convinced. DI Kidd wasn't feeling it either. There was something about Ms Kaye that he couldn't quite put his finger on, something that told him they should be watching her a little closer than they were. But she'd given them no reason to doubt her yet, had she?

"Is she not close with the Harpers?" DCI Weaver said. "I'm sure I read in someone's notes that they were close friends."

"Given everything they've been through, I do wonder if it's a little bit for show," DI Kidd said. "They were friendly with one another at the school reunion, but looking back, I wonder if it wasn't more like keeping up appearances."

"She was a little secretive when it came to the affair with Mr Harper," Zoe said. "Didn't bring it up until I mentioned it."

"So she was trying to hide it then?" DC Ravel chimed in. "She definitely wouldn't have brought it up if you hadn't said it?"

"I'd say not."

"Definitely not," DC Powell added. "She seemed flustered when you brought it up."

"So it's a touchy subject," DCI Weaver said. "Hardly surprising. I don't think anyone is about to go around flaunting their infidelity."

DI Kidd kept his mouth shut. Given what he'd seen with Greg the previous day, it wouldn't be surprising if *he* was.

"One last thing," DS Sanchez said, heading to the opposite side of the Evidence Board and tapping on the picture of Norman Kaye. "Norman came up a little in conversation."

"Norman Kaye?" DCI Weaver asked. "Guy you brought in last night."

"Yeah, he got into a fight with Chris Harper at the reunion," Kidd said. "It's all in the paperwork."

"Well, she brought him up because she's apparently frightened of him," Zoe said. "Given what we saw, I'd be frightened of him too, but it makes me wonder if he might have more to do with this than we thought."

DCI Weaver stood up, clapping his hands together. "Then it looks like we have a new prime suspect on our hands," he said, turning to DI Kidd. "Good work on getting the Dexter lad cleared. Now work on getting me the real bastard who killed that poor girl. Is that everything?"

"Just about," DS Sanchez said, offering him a smile as he walked towards the door.

"Back at it again tomorrow then," Weaver said, looking at his watch. "Onwards!"

He left the room and everyone seemed to take it as their cue to let out a breath. Given how he'd been earlier that day, it was a wonder that he'd taken the news that they'd let Dexter go so well. It was a minor miracle.

"You heard the man," Kidd said. "That's us done for the day. Tomorrow we need an interview with Ms Chowdhury if we can, I'll go and see the Harpers on the way home, and we'll bring in Norman for more questioning." He turned to DS Sanchez. "You might have been right about that one, maybe we shouldn't have let him go so soon."

"If it's him, you owe me a pint."

"If it's him, you're getting all the credit for it," he said. "I'll see you all in the morning, bright and early."

They started to gather their things to leave, DC Ravel still clicking away on her keyboard while she put her things back in her handbag. DS Sanchez stopped by her desk.

"Janya, you'll work yourself into the ground," she said. "Clock off, the emails will still be here tomorrow."

"Not emails," she said, her face looking panicked as she clicked through screens faster and faster, a sheen of sweat across her brow. "Shit, shit, shit."

DI Kidd's ears pricked up. "What's happening?"

"It's Sarah's phone," she said. "I've been tracking it since this all started, it's been off this whole time."

"Yes, and?" Kidd breathed, his heart pounding hard in his chest.

Janya Ravel looked over her computer monitor like she'd seen a ghost. "It's just been switched on."

CHAPTER THIRTY-FIVE

After much "what the fuck-ing" and trying to make sure the signal was real, DI Kidd was back out once again, DS Sanchez driving him to the last place they thought they would be going to track down Sarah's phone.

"Didn't think I'd be back here so soon," DS Sanchez said as she parked the car. "So...you think it's her?"

"Sarah?! Zoe, we're not ghost hunters."

"I mean—"

"I know who you mean," DI Kidd said, taking off his seatbelt. "Best find out, eh?"

They got out of the car and marched towards the house. It was dark, all the windows facing the road had their lights switched off, even from the hallway there wasn't any light pouring out onto the street through the glass.

"You sure it was here?" DI Kidd asked.

"Positive," she said. "I was here earlier on, the address is Alexandra Kaye's house."

DI Kidd nodded. "Alright then."

He marched up to the front door and rapped his knuckles three times. The gold knocker jumped and immediately there was movement behind the door. Kidd braced himself for some kind of fight, for Alexandra Kaye to try and do a runner.

"Keep an eye on the side gate, Zoe," he said. "If she's—"

The door opened and Kidd was ready to read Alexandra Kaye her rights but it wasn't her that greeted him. In her place stood a boy that he'd only seen in pictures. His eyes puffy and red from crying, his nose streaming.

Caleb Kaye.

And Kidd was just about to ask him where his mum was when he saw the phone in his hand, lighting up his face.

They'd got him.

CHAPTER THIRTY-SIX

"Where did you get that phone?"

"None of your bloody business, who the hell are you?" Caleb snapped, backing away.

"I'm Detective Inspector Benjamin Kidd, this is DS Zoe Sanchez, we're investigating the disappearance and death of Sarah Harper," he said, advancing on the boy. "Your turn. Where the bloody hell did you get that phone?"

"This phone is mine."

"Strike two, that phone is Sarah's," Kidd said. He'd seen it in pictures enough, the sparkly case, the pop socket on the back, her and Dexter as her wallpaper. "You've got one last chance to tell us the truth or we're taking you down to the station."

"I—it's—I—" he stammered and started walking backwards down the hallway. Kidd could practically hear the cogs turning in his head as he tried to figure out just how he was going to get out of this one. They had him backed into a corner and Kidd had that feeling that he was getting closer to solving this particular puzzle, at least. "She was here."

Kidd eyed him carefully. The lad looked terrified, and Kidd honestly couldn't blame him. He was about to be arrested.

"Explain yourself," Kidd barked.

"She was here when she first went missing," Caleb said. "When everything went down at school, I saw her in town just…just wandering around looking sad and I asked if she wanted to come back to mine and talk. We were…we were sort of friends I guess. And then she just…she stayed."

"Why the bloody hell didn't you tell anyone?" Kidd barked.

"Because she asked me not to," Caleb replied. He was terrified, literally shaking, the phone about to fall out of his hand. "When the police got involved, I told her. Then when I was at my grandma's, I came back and she'd gone. I assumed she'd gone home. Then…then I saw the stuff on the news."

"Why did you switch on her phone?"

"I was looking for a clue, a note or something, and I found the phone," he said. "When I saw on the news that she'd…that she'd…" He couldn't bring himself to say it. He was stood in front of Kidd and Zoe looking like he was about to burst into tears, and Kidd couldn't blame him. It was definitely a lot to deal with. "I turned it on. Because it didn't seem right. I thought she might have been messaged by someone."

"And has she?"

Caleb shrugged. "The phone is locked," he said. "I was going to try and unlock it but I got scared and didn't, and then you arrived."

DI Benjamin Kidd looked over at DS Sanchez, giving her a tight-lipped, half-smile. She shrugged at him, a silent conversation passing between them. Neither one was sure what to make of this news, of his story. He could, of course, be telling the truth, but there was so much room for error, so much of Sarah's final days that had gone unaccounted for. Maybe he would be able to help fill them in.

DI Kidd turned back to Caleb.

"Is your mum home?" he asked.

Caleb shook his head.

"Right," he said. "Then you're coming with us."

◆ ◆ ◆

When they made it back to the station, the rest of the team had gone home. DI Kidd had told them to. DS Sanchez had volunteered to stay on with him to help deal with Caleb. She wanted this finished with as much as he did, and maybe the anticipation of waiting until tomorrow was too much for her. Keeping the rest of the team around for the night wasn't necessary.

Before they went into the interview room, Kidd slipped into the Incident Room and quickly dialled John's number. He picked up on the second ring.

"Hey," John said down the phone, a little out of breath. He was moving around as he spoke. "I'm not late, am I? I was just getting my things together to come and meet you."

"You're not late," Kidd said. "I'm glad I caught you. Look, something's come up." They were words that he'd said to Craig a thousand times before, words that he didn't want to be saying to someone as kind and sweet as John, at least not at such an early stage of their relationship, if he could even call it that. "I wouldn't do this unless I had to, I promise."

John let out a breath that distorted into Kidd's ear.

"Ben," he said. "It's fine."

"It is?"

John sighed. Kidd could hear him sitting down. "Sure," he replied. "You've got a whole investigation thing going on. It was only a drink, right?"

He sounded disappointed. Ben could hear it in his voice, and he hated that. He hated so much that he was making someone else feel that way.

"No, no, it wasn't just a drink," he said, perching on the edge of DC Campbell's desk.

"This was supposed to be me making it up to you that we didn't get to see one another last night. And then..." he trailed off. He didn't want to get John too involved in it. The world was hard enough without knowing about all the darker things that happened in it. "Like I said, something came up in the investigation. We're about to interview someone, it shouldn't take long."

"Ben, honestly, we can reschedule for tomorrow if—"

"No," Kidd interrupted. "Give me an hour, an hour and a half and I'll call you. I want to see you."

Kidd could hear John smiling down the phone. "I want to see you too."

"Good."

"Okay," John said. "I await your call."

"I'll be as quick as I can."

"Be quicker," John replied.

They hung up the phone and Kidd found himself staring at it, the backlight illuminating his face in the darkened Incident Room.

"Everything okay?"

Kidd practically jumped out of his skin, nearly dropping his phone in the process. "Christ, Sanchez, you nearly gave me a heart attack."

"Alright, skittish," she said. "Caleb is ready, if you are."

Kidd nodded. He needed to get his head back on the case.

He followed DS Sanchez out of the Incident Room and down the corridor to one of the interview rooms. Caleb was sat at the table, a disposable cup steaming in his hands, the phone face-up on the table. There were notifications popping through on the screen, hundreds of them at a time.

"How long has that been happening?" Kidd asked.

"Pretty much since I turned it on," Caleb said. "People were worried about her, I'm not surprised she switched it off."

"If it had been switched on, we would have found her," DS Sanchez said as she took a seat across from Caleb.

"She didn't want to be found," Caleb said.

"What makes you say that?" Kidd asked.

"She told me," he said. "At first, I think she was just out to punish her parents a little bit. After that, I think she just didn't want to deal with everything anymore, all the pressures of her life."

"The popularity?" Zoe asked.

Caleb nodded. "She didn't really want it, I don't think. It happened because she is... was pretty sociable, fell in with the right crowd. Or the wrong crowd, depending on how you looked at it. But it meant that, with everything happening for her mum too, everybody was always looking at her. She had nowhere to escape to."

"Which is why you think she escaped to

you?" Kidd asked.

Caleb shrugged. "Maybe. We were friends, like I told you, but I wasn't part of her group."

"There were no pictures anywhere of the two of you together," Kidd said. "Doesn't that seem odd?"

"No," Caleb said bluntly. "Just because it's not been obsessively documented online doesn't make it any less real. She was my friend. We'd hang out in the library sometimes when we both had work to do. She'd come over occasionally and…maybe it's stupid."

"What's stupid, Caleb?" Zoe asked.

"She told me that she felt like she could be herself," he said. "Like, she didn't have to perform for anyone if it was just the two of us."

Kidd eyed the boy carefully. "Did you like her?"

"She was my friend," Caleb said again.

"Did you like her more than a friend?"

"I don't know about you but not every single boy is after getting his end away," Caleb snapped. "She was just my friend."

Kidd sat back in his chair and took a breath, watching Caleb as his eyes darted from the cup to DS Sanchez, to DI Kidd, to the phone, and back again. He didn't know where to look, didn't really know what to do with himself. It had to be pretty intimidating being in a police station all by yourself at sixteen.

"Caleb," Kidd said. "Would you mind taking us through everything that happened with you and Sarah since last Friday?"

"All of it?"

Kidd nodded. "Every last bit."

CHAPTER THIRTY-SEVEN

Caleb was very thorough. He took them through everything that had happened since he met Sarah on Friday afternoon after school. They had gone back to his house—his mother had been working late—and spent the afternoon and evening together. The later it got, the more confused Caleb got about her going home. She told him that she didn't want to, so he let her stay. It wasn't the first time it had happened.

She stayed with him until Monday. When reports went around at school about her having gone missing, about the parents phoning the police and actually reporting it, Caleb got scared and told her all about it. He was meant to be seeing his grandparents that evening because his mum was working late, so he packed up and headed off to see them, thinking that she would go back home now that things had gotten serious. That she'd wait for his mum to vanish off to work and she would go back to her house.

He went to school from his grandparents' house on Tuesday, and when he found out she was missing, he thought that maybe she was still going to be at his when he got home. But she wasn't.

"Hold on," DS Sanchez said. "So when did you last see her?"

'The last time I saw her was around six o'clock on Monday night," he said. "When I got home from school, I had to go to my grandparents' house because both my parents work late. Mum is a little bit cagey about me being home alone. I assumed she'd go home and I'd wake up the following day to news that she'd been found or whatever."

"So she was with you for the whole weekend and your mother didn't notice?" Kidd asked.

"She works pretty odd hours most of the time," he said. "She works at Kingston hospital and was on early shifts so she worked for most of the day and then would be so exhausted she would go to bed quite early. She thought I was doing homework. But I didn't think it would be that long. After Friday night she went home and —"

DS Sanchez sat up a little straighter. "Sarah went home?"

Caleb nodded. "She went back to her house on Saturday morning after my mum had gone to work, but then showed up to see me a few hours later and was so upset, told me she didn't want to go back there. I told her we could ask my mum if she could stay at our house but she was having none of it because our parents are friends, they've been friends for years. She asked me to keep it a secret so I did." He sniffed. "I just didn't think it would end up like this."

DI Kidd looked across at DS Sanchez. He didn't know how well it all checked out. And it still meant that there was an entire day that was unaccounted. And her going home and coming back upset meant that somebody in that house had seen her. Kidd shook his head. It was hard enough to get things out of the parents before, but having to do it now that Sarah had died was going to be twice as difficult. They likely blamed him for not finding her sooner. Truth be told he was starting to blame himself for not acting quicker.

"Do you know who she spoke to when she went home?" Kidd asked.

Caleb shook his head. "She was just really upset. She was crying and, I mean, I could barely get a word out of her. I didn't know what to do so I chose not to talk about it. I'm sorry. That's really all I've got. I've told you everything."

DI Kidd took a breath and looked across at Caleb. DCI Weaver would put his head in the smasher for letting the lad go home, but it was late. It was late for both of them and DI Kidd knew that he wasn't going to get any further with this right now.

"Thank you, Caleb," DI Kidd said. "You've been very helpful. Just one more thing."

"What's that?"

"Can you tell us a little bit about your dad?"

Caleb froze. That wasn't good. That wasn't good at all.

"What about him?" Caleb asked.

"I want to know what he's like," Kidd said, trying to act casual. "There was an incident at the school reunion the other night. He attacked Sarah's dad."

"Oh, Jesus."

"Exactly," Kidd said. "Would you say your father is a violent man?"

"Not really," Caleb said. "He…he has a temper. But he's working on it."

"A temper?" DS Sanchez said.

"Yeah, but he's working on it," Caleb said, with a little more urgency.

"Why would you say he has a temper?" DS Sanchez asked. "Did he get angry a lot before he and your mother broke up?"

"They fought a lot," Caleb said. "There was always a lot of yelling, a lot of…I don't know… plates smashing and stuff. They didn't fit. That's what Dad said."

"But you say he's working on it?" DI Kidd asked.

"He's started doing yoga," Caleb said, a little bit of pink colouring his cheeks. "He really likes it. And he runs now. Apparently, he goes out for long runs to clear his head. Any time he gets frustrated he does that to get it out of his system, so he's getting better."

A chill covered Kidd's body. He knew that Caleb hadn't meant to say anything incriminating about his father, but all of a sudden he was worried about Norman Kaye's whereabouts. He didn't want to show any of that to Caleb though. It was pretty clear from where Kidd was sitting, that Caleb was loyal to his father. The last thing he would want to happen would be for Caleb to tip him off that they were going to be looking into him again.

So DI Kidd fixed a smile on his face, offering it to Caleb. "Thank you for all of your help this evening," he said. "Honestly, you're helping us build a better picture of Sarah's final movements. You've been great."

"Thank you," he said. "Can I...can I go now? My grandparents are expecting me and if I don't show up soon they're going to be calling my mum all worried and I don't want to do that to her."

"Sure," DS Sanchez said. "You've given us everything we need."

They left the interview room, Caleb heading down the corridor to use the bathroom before they left. Zoe turned to Kidd immediately.

"You buy it?"

"The kid seems upset," he replied. "I buy every word. We need to talk to his father."

"And Sarah's parents," Zoe added. "We need to find out who she spoke to before she went back to his all upset. I'd put serious money on it being her sleaze bag of a dad."

"You really don't like him, do you?"

"He's a twat."

Kidd choked on a laugh. "Concise."

"I'll put it in the report."

The door down the corridor opened and swung closed behind Caleb Kaye as he walked down the corridor towards them.

"I'll get him signed out," she said quietly. "Tell John I said hello."

"How did you—?"

"You were staring all lovesick at your phone, I'm not blind," she said with a wink. "Have a good night."

He smiled. "You too."

❖ ❖ ❖

DI Kidd left the station and messaged John to say that he was on his way. John quickly replied asking him to meet him at the riverside. DI Kidd turned around and headed there, waiting under a streetlamp and staring out of the water, unable to keep thoughts of the case out of his mind.

One of Sarah's parents had lied about the

last time they saw her. Whatever happened when they saw her on Saturday felt important. That was what had driven her to not go home, to think that anywhere but home was safe. And what of Norman Kaye? They'd already gotten the impression from Alexandra Kaye that he was pretty unhinged, but hearing from the son that he had a temper didn't sit right with Kidd either. Tomorrow was going to be a busy day, he could already feel it.

"Even from behind you look defeated," John said as he stepped up next to Kidd.

Involuntarily, Kidd leaned over and kissed John quickly on the lips before going back to staring out at the water, staring over at the spot where Sarah had been found that morning. It had been quite a day. All he wanted to do right now was forget about it.

"Hello to you too," he said, leaning on the railing next to him and stepping a little closer. Kidd could feel his body heat radiating and breathed in the calming scent of John McAdams. "You okay?"

Benjamin Kidd turned to John and took him in—his gorgeous open face, the little smile tugging at the corners of his mouth—and instantly felt a little calmer just because he was here. He didn't want to rehash the details of his day right now, he just wanted to spend time with John. So he pushed it from his head as best he could and smiled.

"Better now you're here," he said. "Shall we?"

CHAPTER THIRTY-EIGHT

He didn't know how much longer he could go on like this.

It hadn't meant to go this far, he knew that from the start. Once she was in the house, he just wanted to scare her. He hadn't expected her to run. He certainly hadn't expected to have to run after her.

He still ached from it, not that he would say that to anyone. He wouldn't want anyone getting suspicious. The only hope he had is that he wasn't seen. So long as he wasn't seen, everything would go to plan and everything would be alright.

He lay back in bed and stared at the ceiling, the white paint swirls overhead that were a little bit hypnotising in the streetlight pouring in through the crack in the curtain. He was tired, exhausted even, and no amount of counting sheep was going to help him drop off with all the things he had on his mind.

How much longer will it be? *he thought.*

He debated going out for a run just to ease his

mind but thought better of it. It was cold out.

He picked up his phone, tapping out a message that he quickly deleted instead of sending.

His mind was all over the place.

She was dead.

It was a thought that made him sit up so sharply in bed that his head swam. She was dead. He'd seen it on the news, not that he'd needed to. He'd been there as the life had drained out of her body, drip drip dripping into the river, and floating off down the Thames.

Maybe I shouldn't have left her there, *he thought.* All it would take was someone snooping around, a little bit of DNA left on her and they'd have me.

He had so much to lose.

His phone buzzed on the nightstand and his eyes widened as he saw the message. It hadn't been what he wanted to see, it was the last thing he wanted to see. His pulse quickened, his breathing coming in ragged, quick.

Now he really was in trouble.

Without thinking, he got out of bed and pulled on his tracksuit, flicking the hood up over his head before he walked out of the house. The blood was rushing in his ears, rushing so much he wasn't sure if anyone heard him leaving, if anyone saw him.

Sarah's death had been an accident.

This one wouldn't be.

CHAPTER THIRTY-NINE

After an evening of taking his mind off things with John, Kidd came into the office the following morning ready to tackle the day. When he made it into the Incident Room, he grabbed Sarah's phone and unlocked it using the code that Sarah's mother had provided.

"Check the messages," DI Kidd said handing it to DC Ravel. "She had loads coming through last night while we were talking to Caleb, a never-ending stream, there has to be something in there."

DC Ravel scrolled through, as Kidd watched over her shoulder, past the names that he recognised—Dexter, Taylor, Caleb, Jonno—and past a few more he didn't, until she reached one marked Mum.

"Try those," Kidd said.

DC Ravel clicked in and opened the messages. It was a stream of emotional messages asking her where she was. If you scrolled back far enough, you could see where they had started out as just asking when she was going to be home. It was on Sunday they went into full-blown panic.

Sarah. Please, just tell me you're okay.

Sarah, I'm starting to get worried.

ANSWER YOUR PHONE!

Please? Sarah?

There weren't too many more after she was reported missing. Once the report had been put on file and Laura had started posting things on social media with reckless abandon, Kidd imagined she'd given up on trying to reach her daughter by text.

The next ones down were the ones from her dad. And it was a different sight entirely.

"Bloody hell," Janya said.

"What?" Kidd asked, leaning in a little bit closer.

She handed him the phone and Kidd read the messages her dad been sending her.

Don't you say a bloody word.

You need to get home now. Stop attention seeking, your mum is worried sick.

Don't you breathe one word of this to anyone.

Sarah!

Answer me!

DI Kidd handed the phone back to DC Ravel. "Could you download all the messages, get them all put together as part of the file?" he asked before turning to Zoe. "I think we need to get Norman Kaye and Chris Harper back in. Letting them go the other night was premature."

"I'll say," Zoe said, looking over Janya's shoulder at the messages on the phone screen. "Do you reckon Sarah found out he was fucking the headteacher?"

"That seems likely," Kidd said. "Just in case we needed any more things happening in this case, we've now got a dad threatening his child. It's all looking a little bit—"

The door to the Incident Room swung open, clattering into the coat stand and announcing the arrival of DCI Weaver. DI Kidd did his best not to sigh too obviously. He was trying to get this done, the last thing he needed was DCI Weaver breathing down his neck every step of the way. It was always a heck of a lot easier when he cleared off to his office and let Kidd get on with things.

"Where the bloody hell is my arrest?"

he asked. Well, asked was definitely putting it mildly. It was more of a demand.

"We're working on it," Kidd replied flatly. He didn't need this right now. "And a good morning to you too, sir," he added, smiling at the beast of a man as he strode into the room. DCI Weaver didn't budge, his face fixed in a grimace like the wind had changed and left him that way...since birth.

"Not what I wanted to hear, Kidd," Weaver replied. "I've got the Superintendent wanting me to make an arrest and announce it to the public. I've got Laura Harper talking about us online and making us...you...me...look bad. Get someone in here and get them charged. Where are we on that?"

"We had Dexter Black yesterday," Kidd said. "We had his story corroborated by Nicholas and the fact that his parents kept him locked up in his house," Kidd continued. "They weren't too happy with some of the websites he'd been looking at, so they decided the right thing to do was act as prison officers and stop their son from leaving the house."

"And he found the body how?"

"An unfortunate coincidence."

"I fucking hate coincidences," Weaver growled.

"I've got the statements," Kidd replied. "Dexter Black hadn't been out of his house all weekend. He didn't even go to school. He's off the hook. We're working on the other leads and we're working as quickly as we can. Right now you've just wasted five minutes that could have been better spent trying to find the fucker who has done this. Any further questions?"

Weaver grumbled and was about to turn out of the room when he caught sight of the evidence board. He strode over to it, Kidd walking from around the computer and joining him, staring at the pictures that had been plaguing them for the past few days.

Their suspect list had gotten a heck of a lot shorter, only pictures of Norman Kaye and Chris Harper remained, but neither one of them really sat right with DI Kidd. There was something he was missing, something that he couldn't quite put his finger on. He didn't have the proof he needed for either of them to wrap up the case. Even if he got them in for a little chat, he didn't have the grounds for an arrest.

Not yet anyway.

"How are we getting on?" DCI Weaver said quietly. "I don't like this, Kidd. I don't like that we don't seem to be getting anywhere."

"We're getting somewhere, boss," Kidd replied. "It's taking a little longer than I would like, but we're crossing people off the list. We've got it narrowed down."

"And where's your money?"

Kidd stared at the board one more time. "My money is in a safe place, boss," he replied.

"I'm not a gambling man."

"Odds not good enough for you?"

"Not quite yet, sir," he replied. "But I'll get there.

DCI Weaver let out a heavy sigh. "You better," he said. "And fast. Mrs Harper has been posting again."

"You're joking," Kidd said. "What now?"

"She went live last night, after everything that had happened, doesn't think we're doing enough, doesn't think she's being kept in the loop with the investigation," Weaver said. "She's got a bloody FLO there for crying out loud. Caitlyn is rushed off her feet, always feeding her information when she can, trying to calm her down but it's not enough. The socials have gone insane, Diane has been fielding calls from the media all bloody morning."

"Right, sir, I'll get on it," Kidd replied. "We'll…we'll figure something out."

DC Simon Powell stood up from his desk at that moment, knocking a mug of tea and sending it flying across the room, cold tea covering the floor. DI Kidd was about to bark at him to get it cleaned up when he saw the look on the lad's face. He looked panicked. And while that might have been his default state most of the time, Kidd didn't like it one bit.

"What is it, Simon?" Kidd asked, moving towards his desk. "What have you got?"

"CCTV, sir," he said. "From the night that

Sarah died."

He beckoned them closer, pulling a video up and setting it at full screen. There were a few clips, stitched together from the various CCTV points around Kingston town. It followed Sarah as she ran through town, past the Bentall Centre, and towards the river. And there was the person who was following her.

Kidd immediately assumed it was a man, it certainly looked that way anyway. He was wearing a hood, probably because it had been raining, and the CCTV had him running after her. The lights were shit so they couldn't make out the face, but he was wearing black, head to toe, he was pretty well built and Christ, could he run.

Somehow Sarah was faster, but Kidd knew how this story ended. He looked from the screen to the notice board and back again. They needed to get these men in, and they needed to get them in now.

CHAPTER FORTY

DC Owen Campbell pretty much ran from the office the second DI Kidd had exploded at him, telling him to head to Norman Kaye's property and bring him in for questioning again. He'd grabbed DC Powell, his keys, and his coat and bolted out the door before he got himself in even more trouble.

To say that DI Kidd was on edge would be something of an understatement. He bundled Powell out of the building and into the unmarked Corsa in the car park and they started their drive out of Kingston.

Simon Powell was a quiet one, that's what Campbell had discovered in his time there. Even when they'd gone out for drinks after work, Simon was never one to be loud and have one too many and maybe fall over on the way home. That was Campbell's role. He didn't mind it. He was fine playing the clown.

"Do you think he did it then?" Owen asked

as they pulled onto the Kingston one-way system and headed out towards Norman Kaye's flat. They'd checked the location and the location that Sarah had been running from and gathered that she almost certainly came from this direction. Kidd was probably kicking himself that he hadn't kept Norman in for longer. Not that he could have done. He had nothing then. And Sarah had still been alive.

"I dunno," Simon said. "It all happened the same night that they brought them in for questioning. So maybe. Kidd said he seemed pretty pissed off with Chris Harper at the school reunion."

"Family drama gone a bit too far, innit?" Owen said, pulling up towards the flat. It wasn't a block of flats, but a small collection of houses that had been converted. One up, one down. It looked pretty deserted, at least from the outside.

There were no cars out front, no lights on in any of the windows. Owen didn't like the look of it. It seemed creepy somehow. And the last thing he wanted to do was walk into someone's flat unannounced and get a clobbering. He'd heard that had happened to people on the force before and, after what happened with the Warrington boy a month or so back, he wasn't keen on it happening again.

He rubbed the back of his head at the memory of it.

They walked up to the front door and knocked. He rang the doorbell too for good measure, a mechanical buzzing sound ringing through the hallway of the empty flat.

It was definitely empty.

He took a breath, bent down, and opened the letterbox, taking a peek inside.

No movement.

No sound.

No nothing.

"Anything?" Powell asked.

"Empty," Campbell replied, stepping back to look at the windows, half expecting to see a curtain twitch, somebody hiding inside. But nothing.

"Maybe he's at work," Simon said.

Campbell wasn't so sure. "Maybe," he replied. "Leave that for Kidd to decide. Come on."

◆ ◆ ◆

DC Ravel was quickly escorted through the reception by Ms Lu and into the office of Ms Chowdhury. The receptionist had tried to convince her that Ms Chowdhury would be too busy for visitors but she wasn't having any of that. She may not have been the prime suspect but there was a chance, however remote, that she would have something that would be able to help them.

"Another police officer," Ms Chowdhury said as DC Ravel was escorted inside. "I'll have met the whole team at this rate, do I win a prize?"

"I don't think it's a prize worth winning," DC Ravel said with a smirk. "It's lovely to meet you. I'm Detective Constable Janya Ravel, we just had a few follow-up questions for our investigation, it shouldn't take all that long."

"Lovely to meet you too," Ms Chowdhury said, a smile snaking its way across her face. "Have a seat, I can imagine what this is about."

"Then you won't mind if I get straight to it then," DC Ravel said, taking a seat across from her. She perched on the edge of the seat, remembering DI Kidd ranting about how much he'd sunk into it, and locked eyes with Ms Chowdhury. "I'm sure you've guessed that this is about your relationship with Mr Harper."

Ms Chowdhury laughed. DC Ravel burned.

"I don't think it's a laughing matter, Ms Chowdhury."

"Well I don't think it's a relationship," she replied. "It's two grown adults having sex."

DC Ravel winced. "One of them is married," she said, looking down at Ms Chowdhury's hands and not seeing a ring. "Also it is the parent of one of your students. Is that not unethical?"

"It's two consenting adults, what's unethical about it?" Ms Chowdhury said, sitting up a little straighter. That had gotten her attention.

"If that's all you have to speak to me about—"

"I'd like to know more," DC Ravel said, cutting her off. "How long has it gone on? When did you meet? Where?"

Ms Chowdhury sighed and rubbed at her temples. "Is it really necessary to go through all of this?" she asked.

"One of your students has turned up dead, Ms Chowdhury," Janya snapped. "She was murdered. I would like to think that you would care a little more about that. Or maybe if not about Sarah, perhaps you'd care about the daughter of the man you are currently sleeping with."

Ms Chowdhury locked eyes with DC Ravel, the two of them sat across from each other in a standoff. Janya knew she was going to be difficult to talk to, Kidd had made that abundantly clear, but this was something else.

Ms Chowdhury eventually backed down. "It's been on and off for the past couple of years," she said. "He was going through a hard time and I comforted him when he came to a Parents' Evening without Lau—Mrs Harper," she quickly corrected. "We met here, we met at his house, or... anywhere quiet, really."

"At his house?"

"No," she said. "At the unfinished ones. He has them all over town."

DC Ravel noted it down, it felt relevant. She remembered Kidd saying something about all of the houses Chris Harper had left unfinished. It made her shudder to think that he was using them to hook up with women who weren't his wife. There was something in that. She could feel it.

CHAPTER FORTY-ONE

Chris Harper had been surprisingly amiable when they'd finally managed to get through to him on the phone. Given the way that he'd spoken to DI Kidd at the school reunion and then afterwards at the station just a few nights ago, letting him know how bloody busy he was all the time, he half expected to get given the cold shoulder and have to pull rank. But it was like he'd had a change of heart. Chris Harper was suddenly more than willing to help. As they spoke on the phone, asking him to come in, he was already on his way from the office, wandering through town to come and see them.

"I don't like it," DS Sanchez said. "He's a fucking slime ball."

"I'm not denying that," Kidd replied. "But we obviously put the wind up him last time he was here, so let's use that to our advantage. Remember, Sarah wasn't dead last time. The guilt must be eating him up."

"He doesn't know we have the phone," Zoe added.

"Right," Kidd said. "We have all the cards. We just need to play them carefully."

Diane popped down the corridor to tell them when he had arrived, and they took him through to the nicer of the interview rooms. He wasn't under arrest, not yet anyway, so they needed to play this as carefully as possible. As far as he knew, they were just clearing a few things up.

Once they'd exchanged pleasantries and sat him down, DS Sanchez fixed him with an eagle-eyed stare that suggested to Kidd that it was her turn to play bad cop, he began.

"We just had more information come to light and we wanted to know if you could clear a few things up for us?" Kidd asked as calmly as he could, when all he really wanted to do was slam the printed messages on the table and demand answers.

"Of course," Chris said. "Anything I can do to help, I'll do it. I know I was cagey when we first started speaking but..." His voice cracked as he trailed off and DI Kidd watched as his mouth moved, no sound coming out. His eyes suddenly watery. He looked away from them for a moment, then back at them, taking a deep, heaving breath before he carried on. "I'm sorry. That was before Sarah was found and I...I didn't think that would be how things...happened."

"Okay," DI Kidd said, still watching the man carefully. He really was quite different to how he had been just a couple of days ago. Kidd had seen death affect people in a lot of different ways but it was surprising to see the way it had affected Chris Harper. He'd expected anger, that same frustration that his wife had been sharing on social media, but this was a man who had been broken by it. It was surprising to say the least. "We just have a few questions," DI Kidd continued, pulling the printouts of the messages from the file and sliding them across the table towards Chris. He went a little paler as he realised what they were. "These were messages that were found on Sarah's phone—"

"You found her phone?" he asked. "When did you find—?"

"The same day we found her body," DI Kidd said. It wasn't a lie, but he wasn't going to tell him the entire story about what happened with Caleb, not until they had the facts from Chris. He didn't want to put the kid in danger, after all. "I just want you to explain them to me if you can. Take your time. Read them."

Chris Harper picked up the pieces of paper and read them carefully. His eyes widened as he read them. He even looked a little bit confused at times, like they were things that he didn't remember saying. Kidd could already feel the lie coming from a mile off and he sincerely hoped he wasn't about to try it.

"I—" Chris started. "I—I don't—"

"If you can't explain the messages," DS Sanchez said. "Then perhaps it would be a good time for you to explain what happened between you and Sarah on Saturday morning."

Chris Harper looked up sharply. He swallowed, his eyes wide, his face ghostly pale. He'd been well and truly caught out. This was not what he'd been prepared for, not by a long way and he was very much on the back foot. DS Sanchez was enjoying herself.

"Take your time," DI Kidd said sitting back in his chair. "We've got plenty."

"But not too much time," DS Sanchez interjected. "You take too much time we're going to know that you're cooking up a story and that's the last thing you want us to think, Mr Harper."

DI Kidd looked across at her. She wasn't just playing bad cop. She was playing demon nightmare cop, and Chris Harper was very much on the receiving end of it.

Chris looked agitated. Kidd half expected him to stop their interview and call for legal representation.

"She came back to the house on Saturday morning," Chris said quickly. "I didn't know where she'd been, I didn't even ask. She went out a lot. I think Laura told you that, she just went places, didn't tell us where she was, and would show up sometimes days later and everything would go back to normal." He shook his head, nervous, sweating. "You didn't ask that."

"It's all helpful," Kidd said. "Keep going."

"Well…Sarah knew about my…infidelities," he said. "And she was threatening me, threatening to tell Laura all about them, and…I flipped out at her."

"Did you flip out at her often?"

"No, I didn't," he said quickly.

A little too quickly, Kidd thought.

"But I flipped out at her, I warned her about telling Laura, and it escalated into a big fight and she left again."

"Why didn't you tell us?" DI Kidd asked. "We've been working on the assumption that Sarah went missing on Friday and you've been keeping this from us? That's dangerous, Mr Harper."

"No, you see, this, THIS is why I didn't tell you," he said, pointing at DI Kidd across the table. "Because I knew if you'd known we'd fought, that I'd yelled at her, you would twist it into something ugly and sordid. You would make it seem like I was the one who took her." He took a few deep breaths. "And now you think I'm the one who killed her, don't you? That's why you've got me here."

"You're not under arrest, Mr Harper," DI Kidd said calmly, resisting the urge to tell Chris that if he pointed at him again he would probably snap his finger in two. "We had a few things we needed clearing up. The whereabouts of Sarah on that Saturday being one of them. These messages for another. What were you hoping to achieve with them?" he asked. "Was it a scare tactic?"

"Something like that," he replied.

"Was she scared of you, Mr Harper?" DS Sanchez asked. "Did you like that she was scared of you?"

Chris Harper laughed. "She wasn't scared of me at all," he said. "Sarah Harper wasn't scared of anyone. We made her that way and it was probably our biggest mistake."

They let that sit in the room for a moment longer. Chris sat back in his chair, still looking through the messages he'd sent to his now-deceased daughter. He looked upset, distraught, a shadow of the confident man who had sat in front of them two days prior. He looked like he would shatter at any moment.

"I can't believe these were the last things I said to her," he said. "And now she's gone and..." He trailed off, turning his gaze back to Kidd and Sanchez. "My wife is going out of her mind with all this. She's posting about it all day every day. She just wants justice. I want justice."

"We're doing our best, Mr Harper," DI Kidd said. "But withholding information from us wasn't the way to go about it. We were trying to create a picture of her final movements. Keeping things from us slowed that down."

"I know," he said, wrestling with something in his head. Kidd could see words dancing on the tip of his tongue.

"Mr Harper?" DS Sanchez said. "Whatever you need to say, you need to tell us. Everything helps at this point."

He sighed. "I don't want to be disloyal to a friend," he said. "But given everything that's happened. I...I've discussed it with Laura enough."

"What?" Kidd asked.

"Norman," he said. "I think...I'm wondering if...?" He trailed off and Kidd found himself holding his breath. They were done with him. It was Norman they needed to find now.

CHAPTER FORTY-TWO

"What do you mean he's not there?" DI Kidd barked down the phone. DC Campbell had been trying to get through to him for the past half an hour, his phone buzzing on his desk and annoying DC Ravel like you wouldn't believe. She pretty much threw the phone at him when he walked in.

"I mean he's not here, sir," Owen said down the phone, audibly wincing. Which Kidd sort of enjoyed. "We knocked, we checked next door, he's not in."

"Let me get you the address of where he works, he might be there," Kidd said, heading over to his desk and shuffling through his notes.

"That's what Powell said, sir," Owen replied.

"Well, he's got a brain, Campbell, I'd expect him to say something like that," Kidd snapped. He found the address and read it out, Owen repeating it to DC Powell who Kid hoped against hope was writing it all down.

"Thanks, boss. We'll report back!" DC Campbell hung up the phone and Kidd found himself staring at his handset.

He'll just be at work, Kidd thought. *He'll be at work, and then they'll bring him in here, and it will be fine. Nothing else is happening here.*

But he couldn't shake the feeling that it was. His instincts were telling him that there was something else going on here, something that he couldn't nail down and it was irritating him. He started reading through the notes DC Ravel had gotten from her interview with Ms Chowdhury. It was what he'd been expecting really—all of it a secret, no one allowed to know, sneaking around between houses but nothing incriminating. What was he missing?

DS Sanchez appeared at the door balancing three cups of tea on one hand. She delivered one to DC Ravel and then one to him. She sat on the couch between the two of them.

"Anything?" she asked.

Kidd shook his head.

"Kidd practically strangled Campbell down the phone," DC Ravel said, taking a sip of her tea and raising a careful eyebrow at Kidd. "I honestly thought you were going to reach through the phone and punch him, sir."

"If the technology were available, I would upgrade immediately," he said. "He's not home though. Norman Kaye, he's not at his flat."

"Maybe he's at work."

"S'what I'm hoping," he said.

Zoe watched him as he took a sip of his tea. "You don't think he is though, do you?" she asked. "You think he's done a runner?"

"If he's guilty, then maybe he knew we were onto him or something," he said. "Or maybe he just thought it'd be better to get away from here before we did end up getting onto him."

"You think the anger is enough of a motive?" Zoe asked.

Kidd shrugged. "It might be," he said. "You saw how quickly he saw red at the school reunion the other night. And everything that Alexandra Kaye said, how much of a maniac he was from Chris Harper. So maybe…"

But maybe not, he thought. He couldn't stand the waiting around. He walked over to the Evidence Board and dialled Caleb's number. The phone was switched off. That was the last thing he needed. He tapped in Alexandra Kaye's number and dialled that instead.

It only managed to ring for a second or two before Alexandra picked up.

"Hello? Caleb?" she squeaked down the phone.

"No, it's DI Benjamin Kidd," Kidd replied. "I tried phoning Caleb but his phone was switched off. I take it he isn't home?"

"No, he isn't," she replied. Her voice was so

high pitched, it ripped right through Kidd. "He hasn't been home since yesterday."

"Yesterday?"

"Yes," she said, frustrated now, angry even that he wasn't hearing what she was saying. "He was supposed to be at his grandparents' house but he never got there."

"We spoke to him last night," DI Kidd said. "He came to the station, gave us some information, then DS Sanchez dropped him home."

"His stuff isn't here," she said. "I looked in his room, he's taken his bag, he's taken everything. But he didn't make it to my parents' house last night."

"Have you already reported him missing?"

"No, I've been working!" she snapped. "I didn't know. I had no idea. I think…" She trailed off, her voice catching on a sob.

Kidd looked up to see Zoe staring at him.

"What?" she mouthed at him.

He grabbed a Post-it Note from her desk and wrote down CALEB MISSING in block capitals. She hurried to the other side of the room and grabbed the phone.

"Owen? It's Zoe," she said into the receiver. "No, wait, shut up. Shut up a second." He obviously did. "Caleb is missing. Norman Kaye's son is missing. We need to…" She looked up at Kidd. He nodded. "We need to treat Norman Kaye as a suspect in this. Go back to the house, we'll get a warrant, break the fucking door down, and see if he's in there."

She hung up the phone and walked out of the room. Seconds later DCI Weaver was in the room with them. He looked confused. He also had a napkin stuffed into the top of his shirt, probably from where he'd been recently eating his lunch. When he realised, he tore it out and threw it in the bin.

"What on earth is—?"

Kidd shushed him. "Ms Kaye, I need you to calm down," he said. "What are you trying to tell me here?"

"I think it's Norman," she said. "I've got messages from him."

"Is he saying he has Caleb?"

"No, nothing like that," she said. "When your DS was here the other day, the woman." DS Sanchez would love that. "She asked if I wanted to report him for what he was saying, the threats he was making, and I said no, and now...now I don't know if...if I've..." She trailed off. DI Kidd knew what she was getting at. She didn't know if her not wanting to cause problems with her ex-husband had ended up costing her son his life. He didn't want that to be the case either.

"We'll get on it, Ms Kaye," he said, turning back to the Evidence Board, to the mugshot of Norman Kaye staring back at him. Could they really have read him so wrong?

CHAPTER FORTY-THREE

There were few things DI Kidd hated more than waiting around. He liked to be out there, doing things, finding the bad guys, picking up the evidence, solving cases, but right now he was at a loss. DC Campbell and DC Powell were heading back to Norman's flat to find out if he was keeping Caleb there after all. DS Sanchez had gone to his place of work to see if he had shown up there. DC Ravel was tracking every credit card number that Alexandra Kaye could give them, trying to get a signal on his phone which was, like Caleb's, switched off.

None of it looked good. And DCI Weaver wasn't impressed.

"We bloody had him!" he barked. His breath stank of the curry ready-meal he'd had for lunch, the stench enough to make Kidd want to hold his breath. "We bloody had him and you let him go!"

"We had him, yes, but he'd not done anything yet."

"He had the girl, if we'd kept him here—"

"We had no reason to suspect him," Kidd barked. "He'd gotten into a fight with Chris Harper who had pretty much given us no reason to think it was him."

"Well, how about you look at this then?" DCI Weaver grabbed his computer screen and swivelled it around so violently he nearly threw the thing off the desk. It was the Laura's Facebook page. She was talking about something, nearly two hundred thousand people watching her.

The title of the video was chilling: Another child missing. Are the police doing anything?

The comments that were flying in below the video all agreed with her, condemning the police, people saying that something must be done.

"After what happened with Sarah, I feel the need to speak up for parents whose children are missing," she said. "Alexandra Kaye is a dear friend of mine and after everything that's happened to me, it only seems right that I use my platform for good and get the word out that her poor son Caleb is missing."

She picked up her iPad, a picture from Caleb's Instagram on it. The heart button went crazy, hundreds of people had to be pressing it at once, filling up the side of the screen.

"We'd not informed the press," DCI Weaver said gravely, switching off the video. "Alexandra Kaye told us less than an hour ago, and Laura Harper is acting like she's BBC News 24 all over Facebook, spreading it, making us look like idiots. She's been making us look like idiots the whole time," he added. "No wonder the Super is breathing down my neck about it. He just wants an arrest to be made. He wants to be able to tell the press something."

"Right."

"She's still calling for Dexter to go down for Sarah," he said. "I know you've told me he's innocent, told me that the parents locked him away all weekend, but she doesn't know that. She's got her followers out for blood and I don't know what she's going to do if she doesn't get her own way."

"Then we need to get Norman for it," Kidd said flatly. "That's the only thing we can do. We need to get Norman arrested for it, charged with it, and announced so that this vitriol will end." He looked back at the screen that was now facing away from him. "There's no way we can stop her?"

"Caitlyn asked the same thing," he said. "She's been in the house with her the whole time, having to listen to it all, watch all the bullshit."

"But it's her free speech," Kidd said.

"Fuck her free speech."

"Dangerous road to go down, boss," Kidd replied.

"But she's—"

"Saying stuff we don't agree with, but it's what she believes," Kidd finished for him. "I don't think it's about all that anyway."

Weaver knew where he was going with this, Kidd didn't need to go over it again. It was the same theory he'd had about her from the start. So much of this was to do with getting attention. That's what it had all been about really. Whether the attention was positive or negative, her number of followers was going up and that seemed to be all she cared about. But it was dangerous. Kidd hoped that DS Sanchez was having more luck than he was.

◆ ◆ ◆

DS Sanchez went with uniformed officers in tow to Norman Kaye's place of work. He worked in the ASDA just outside of Kingston town, a stone's throw away from the flat that DC Campbell and DC Powell were currently busting into, hopefully, to find Caleb. Based on what Alexandra Kaye had said about him, the last thing she wanted to do was deal with Norman on her own.

They pulled up.

"Do you want us to come in with you?" PC Eve was pretty new to the force. He had a baby face and the keen attitude of somebody who was fresh out of the academy and he wanted to impress.

"Might scare him off if he's in there," she said flatly. "But thank you. I'll keep you on radio. If he's in here, we just need him arrested as cleanly as possible. Don't want to alarm him."

"You think he's dangerous?" PC Grant had been in the force for longer than DS Sanchez, his grey beard a little bit wispy around the edges. One year away from retirement, as he liked to keep reminding her. He also liked to remind her that he would miss her every day once he was retired, which was a sentiment that Zoe didn't share.

"He might be," she said. Though what she really wanted to say was more than likely. Given what Alexandra Kaye had said to them, they needed to proceed with caution. And based on what she'd seen of him at the school reunion, she would. "Like I said, I'll radio."

"You be careful now," PC Grant said. She resisted the urge to tell him to go fuck himself, reminded herself he was old and from a different time, but it was a few shades too condescending for her to take lying down. She shot him a look that would make Medusa quake and opened the car door.

She felt in her back pocket for her handcuffs, just in case. Beneath her shirt was a stab vest—you could never be too careful with things like this. She didn't know what he would try.

The ASDA was bright white, an assault on the eyes when you walked in from the semi-dark of the outside. There were a lot of people milling around, baskets in hand, focussing on their shopping, no one paying attention to her. Which was, of course, what she wanted. If she'd have walked in there flanked by two police officers, then she wouldn't have had any chance of catching Norman Kaye by surprise.

She walked the aisles slowly at first, checking the bakery counter, the rotisserie, the fish, he was nowhere to be seen. All she knew of him was that he worked there. What his actual job could be anything, which meant he could be anywhere.

She looked down every aisle and couldn't see him, making her way to the freezers at the end of the store and down towards the checkout. If he was here, that was likely where she'd find him.

And she was right.

He was stood by the self-checkouts, a look on his face that told her he was bored, that he was barely paying attention, which was exactly what she needed. If she could catch him by surprise maybe—

No.

He looked up. He caught sight of her. That flicker of recognition flashing across his face before he realised that she was here for him.

And the panic.

The panic that, in her eyes, told her that he was guilty.

Without a second thought, he dropped everything and bolted for the door.

"Fuck's sake!" she growled, grabbing the radio from her pocket. "We've got a runner," she said. "I'm going after him. Coming out of the exit now."

CHAPTER FORTY-FOUR

"Nothing?" DI Kidd said down the phone. "There's nothing?"

DC Campbell made a noncommittal noise down the phone. It was enough to make Kidd want to throttle him.

"Going to need a little more than that, Owen," he grumbled.

"There's not a lot of anything here, sir," he replied. "There's a little bit of furniture, a bed in the bedroom, another in the spare, which I guess must be Caleb's when he comes here, but there's nothing of note."

"You've searched the whole place?"

"Forensics have just shown up, sir, they're looking for anything that might point to Sarah Harper having been here," DC Campbell said.

DI Kidd nodded. There was no point looking for Caleb's DNA, it would be all over it. But if they could find any trace of Sarah, that would be enough to convict, that would be enough to get this finished.

"Right, thank you, Campbell, good work. Get back here as soon as you can," he said before hanging up the phone.

DI Kidd turned back to the paperwork he'd been looking at, the interviews he'd already conducted, trying to figure out what it was he had missed. There had to be something. If there was nothing in Norman Kaye's apartment, where on earth could Caleb be? Where could Sarah have been kept the night before she ran off?

It was all coming from that same direction, the direction of Norman's flat. There was something obvious staring him in the face and he just couldn't get a handle on it. It was maddening. He opened Sarah's website and started looking again, scrolling through the posts, through the abbreviations. It was staring him in the face. He knew it. It was here somewhere. It had to be.

D is on my last nerve.

What if…?

There are too many lies, too many fights, and I don't think I can take it anymore.

Could it be that…?

D needs to change and he needs to change now.

Kidd could feel it coming to him when his phone started ringing.

◆ ◆ ◆

DS Sanchez bolted out of the ASDA and down London Road as fast as her feet would carry her. There was no way on this planet she was going to let him get away. She could see him up ahead, his high-vis jacket he'd been wearing in the store giving him away from a good distance.

He was quick, really bloody quick, which definitely matched up with the guy that they'd seen running in the CCTV chasing Sarah.

"Norman!" she shouted as she ran. "Stop. Don't make this more difficult than it has to be!"

He wasn't listening, or he couldn't hear her, because he kept running.

There was a set of footsteps coming up behind her. She turned in time to see that it was PC Eve joining her in her chase. She imagined that PC Grant would be staying in the car, or attempting to follow them in that.

She was catching up to him, and he could see that. He was pumping his arms as hard as he could, but the closer he got to town, he was running out of steam. She took her opportunity, putting on a turn of speed so she could catch up to him.

She jumped at him, tackling him to the ground which they both met with a thud. He grunted, he cried out, apparently she was hurting him, but she didn't have time for his belly-aching.

She grabbed his arms and pulled them out from underneath him, PC Eve showing up beside her and putting a hand on his back to keep him down. She put the cuffs over his wrists.

"Norman Kaye, I am arresting you on suspicion of the abduction and murder of Sarah Harper," she said. "You do not have to say anything, but it may harm your defence if you do not mention when questioned something which you later rely on in court. Anything you do say may be given in evidence."

He grunted and struggled beneath her, trying to get away, but she was having none of it.

"Thanks for the assist," she said to PC Eve, who blushed a little as she locked eyes with him. She shook her head. These young boys.

PC Grant pulled up in the squad car, the blue lights on, ready to take them back to the station. DS Sanchez let out a breath because they finally had their man.

CHAPTER FORTY-FIVE

DI Kidd demanded the most uncomfortable interview room possible when DS Sanchez returned with Norman Kaye in tow. While he was being booked in with the PCs, they got together their game plan. What they needed from him was a confession, and DI Kidd was pissed off enough that he was going to push him hard to get it. They'd been wrong-footed by him once before, Kidd would be damned if they were going to be wrong-footed by him again.

They had him deposited in the room where they left him to sweat for a little longer with his legal representation.

"Who have we got?" DI Kidd asked.

"Mr Ward from Shire & Ward," she said. "You heard of them?"

"No, you?"

"No," she replied. "But if they're representing him, I'd put my money on them being a bastard."

DI Kidd laughed. "A fairly safe bet given the job title," he replied. "Let's get in there then."

They stepped into the interview room and DI Kidd was presented with a Norman Kaye who looked a heck of a lot worse for wear than he had done the last time they'd interviewed him. This was a man who was at the end of his rope, and DI Kidd was determined to get him to tell all. He wanted this done as much as the gaffer did. He wondered how long it would take for him to break.

He got the pleasantries with the legal representative out of the way. He was a slimy-looking man with a green tone to his skin, though that could have been the lights, and way too little hair trying to cover up way too big of a bald patch. He smiled at Kidd as they shook hands, his lips thin, his eyes dark and snake-like. Kidd didn't like him. Though to find a solicitor that he did like would be pretty rare indeed.

He pressed record on the tape and started talking.

"So, Mr Kaye, it's lovely to have you back here," he said. "Bet you were clicking your heels all the way home when we let you go on Tuesday."

"No comment," Norman Kaye grumbled. DI Kidd rolled his eyes.

"How wonderful, your fine legal counsel has briefed you on all the evidence we have and told you the best course of action is to say fuck all."

"No comment."

"Fucks sake, Norman, I thought this was going to be fun," Kidd said, leaning back in his chair. "The least you could bloody do is defend yourself." He turned to the legal representative who was staring at Kidd with a downturned mouth. "You really think this is the right thing for him to be doing? You are joking, aren't you?"

"I don't think you should be pressing my client quite so heavily, Detective Inspector," Mr Ward mumbled. "He has every right to stay quiet if he wants to. If you really think you have the evidence to charge him, charge him."

"Oh, Mr Ward, you'd best believe that I intend to," Kidd said. "But perhaps a few questions first. Let's see if we can jog Mr Kaye's memory." He turned his attention back to Norman. He looked shaken, his eyes trained on his hands that were handcuffed. He looked like he was about to throw up. He certainly didn't look like someone keen on giving a no comment interview, but maybe Mr Ward thought that was his best chance at getting off with it. He would bet money on Mr Ward of Shire & Ward having a long history of defending scumbags.

But still, something didn't sit right with Kidd. He wanted Norman to talk to him.

"Mr Kaye, we brought you in on suspicion of the murder of Sarah Harper." Norman flinched at that, Kidd narrowed his eyes. "But while we have you, we also wanted to discuss the recent disappearance of your son."

Norman Kaye looked up sharply.

"Got your attention, have I, Mr Kaye?"

"What about Caleb?" he mumbled. "What's happened to him?"

"We'll come to that," Kidd said. Norman seemed genuinely shocked to hear it. How good of an actor was he? "First I want you to answer a few questions for me, would that be alright?"

Norman Kaye turned to Mr Ward who shook his head ever so slightly. Mr Kaye seemed torn, torn between doing what he wanted to do and what he was told would save his skin. DI Kidd decided to wade in.

"Ignore that fucker," Kidd said. "This is about you, this is about your life. He's going to get paid either way, you need to think about you right now."

Norman still didn't look sure. Kidd proceeded anyway.

"I want to know more about your relationship with the Harpers," Kidd said. "It must have pissed you off something rotten when you found out about Alexandra and Chris."

Norman Kaye shrugged. "They can do what they want, they're adults."

"Now, you say that, Mr Kaye, but the way you reacted at the school reunion just a few nights ago suggests otherwise," Kidd said. "The anger that you showed when you saw the two of them talking to one another might be enough to, I don't know, take drastic action against the person you held captive."

"That's bullshit."

"Norman," Mr Wade reprimanded, but his client ignored him.

"Is it, Mr Kaye?" Kidd replied, happy to have gotten a rise out of him. Now maybe they could get him to talk. "Tell me more about their one-night stand, tell me how it made you feel."

Norman Kaye scoffed. "One-night stand."

"Something to say about it, Mr Kaye?" Kidd asked, leaning back in his chair and gesturing to the tape recorder between them. "The floor is all yours."

"You called it a one-night stand," Norman said. "That's what they said to me too. I imagine it's what Chris said to Laura as well." Norman shook his head. "They're not just lying to themselves, they're lying to me, they're lying to Laura, it's disgusting."

"How do you mean?" Kidd asked.

"Their story is that it was a one-night stand," Norman said. "But they never stopped. Once they got going, it just kept on happening. I don't know how the fuck he managed to get away with it, to be honest." He added. "After everything that happened the first time they got found out, you'd think the smart thing to do would be to shut it down. But neither one of them wanted that. If Laura asked, you can bet your life that Chris would claim Alex dug her claws in, but they both wanted it, even if they couldn't admit it."

"So they've been sleeping together since...?" DS Sanchez asked.

"Since we split up," Norman spat. "And it never stopped, they just kept going, sneaking around like they had this big old secret, but it doesn't take an idiot to figure it out. I knew that Alex didn't work that much, all it took was a phone call to the hospital one night when Caleb was with me to find out that she wasn't there."

"Where was she?"

Norman shook his head. "Right under everyone's noses," he whispered. "That's the thing about Chris and his career. He started to build all of these houses and then suddenly ran out of money, suddenly couldn't pay me, couldn't pay anybody so let us all go. He's still got access to all these half-finished properties."

Kidd stared at Norman, the pieces falling into place in his head. Right under their noses the entire time. The houses.

"They sneak off to these secret houses, have their fun, no one is any the wiser. He's the only one who has access to them."

But that wasn't correct either. Sarah Harper had access to them too, she'd let Dexter use one to meet up with Nicholas. The one that was right next to Alexandra Kaye's house.

"I swear he has one for every woman that

he's slept with. You'd be naive to think it was just Alexandra." Norman tutted. "He's a disgrace."

Kidd shook his head. How had he missed it when it had been staring him right in the face?

He stood up abruptly, his chair falling onto the floor behind him. DS Sanchez jumped, so did Norman Kaye.

"Interview terminated," DI Kidd barked, punching the stop button on the tape recorder. He turned to DS Sanchez. "We need to go and we need to go now."

CHAPTER FORTY-SIX

They didn't waste any time, leaving the on-duty PCs to deal with Norman Kaye. They would keep him, in case they were wrong, but DI Kidd was pretty certain at this point that he wasn't wrong.

He explained his theory to Zoe as she floored it to get them over to the property quicker. They'd been played. He could see it now. And he wanted answers.

They got out of the car, DS Sanchez immediately heading towards the Kayes' house but Kidd shook his head.

"What?"

He pointed to the house next door, the one that had been in plain sight the entire time, the seemingly empty house that had probably had Sarah in it the whole time they were searching for her. He looked down the street, seeing a clear route past Fairfield Park, towards the centre of town. He'd been stupid, so blind.

They started towards the house, Kidd trying to keep his cool when he felt like he was about to explode. He sort of knew what to expect, he just hoped against hope that he wasn't too late to save Caleb. He didn't want to have another dead teenager on his hands just because he hadn't been looking in the right places.

It had been right in front of him, but he hadn't looked past the evidence they'd collected, hadn't looked into what people had been telling him, the things he'd seen. Stupid.

"Stop it," Zoe said as they stepped up to the front door.

"What?"

"You're beating yourself up," she said. "We're here, don't freak out on me now."

Zoe was right. Kidd pushed it out of his head, trying to focus on what was happening in the moment, needing to be present right now so nothing went wrong. He knew the cavalry was incoming, that they would follow them here, but he was determined to get Caleb out of there before the blue lights arrived. Their perp was cunning enough to do this in the first place. If they saw something wasn't going their way there was no telling what they'd would do.

Kidd pushed down on the door handle, hearing the locks turn inside, as they slid out of place and the door opened.

The house was deadly silent.

If they were here, they'd know about it,

there was no way to hide it.

Night had fallen, there were no lights on, just the moonlight shining in on a clear night. If they were hiding in the dark, they'd be able to catch them out. The chance of a surprise attack was enough to keep Kidd on edge.

"Watch your back," he whispered to Sanchez, who nodded in return. He could just about make out her silhouette as his eyes adjusted.

They walked through the hallway and towards the stairs. The second Kidd put his boot on it, the floorboard underneath creaked.

Jesus Christ, he thought. He wasn't built for this kind of sneaking around.

Carefully, he made his way up the stairs, trying his hardest not to draw attention, but it was a heavy footfall on bare wood. Anyone upstairs would hear him.

And they did.

There was a whimper. It started quietly at first but only proceeded to get louder. Without thinking, Kidd took the last couple of steps two at a time, dashing across the landing to a door that was closed, locked. He jiggled the handle but it wouldn't budge, not even a little bit. DS Sanchez appeared behind him.

"What are you—?"

She didn't get a chance to finish her sentence. DI Kidd had already taken a step back and kicked the door off its hinges, the wood cracking around the lock as it swung in.

It was the stench that hit him first. Piss. Shit. Sweat. The three mixing in the air to create such a noxious gas it about knocked him off his feet. But he stepped inside.

Across the room, huddled in the dark, was Caleb. His hands and feet were tied, a gag placed across his mouth, and he was sluggish in his movements. The whimpering seemed like it might have been involuntary. Maybe he'd heard them coming and started making noise, somewhere in his subconscious he was fighting for survival.

"He's been drugged," Kidd growled. "He's barely conscious."

He ripped the restraints from his wrists and ankles, a little more careful with the one that was around his face. Caleb took a deep, heaving breath as the one around his mouth came off. It was soaking wet with his saliva, his face was damp, his eyes flickering like he was about to fall asleep.

Kidd cradled him and slapped at his face. "Caleb, Caleb, you've got to wake up, okay?" he said. "Stay awake for me. Where is she? Where's your mum?"

"She's...she's here," he managed to slur through dry lips

"Kidd!" DS Sanchez shouted as a scream came from the door. Alexandra Kaye barrelled towards him with a plank of wood in her hands. She swung it hard, cracking it across Kidd's upper arm and almost knocking him sideways. He stumbled, leaning on the wall for support. He saw that she was heading for Caleb, but DS Sanchez reacted quicker than he did.

As Alexandra swung the piece of wood back, Zoe grabbed it and yanked it from her hands, pulling her off balance as she stumbled towards her. Zoe brought an elbow to her face, knocking her to the floor. Without a second's hesitation, she cuffed her, just as the blue lights appeared outside.

❖ ❖ ❖

The response team was pretty swift once they got inside the house. They grabbed Alexandra Kaye and dragged her outside, kicking and screaming, protesting her innocence, but it was all stacked against her. Anyone could see that.

An ambulance came to collect Caleb. He was in a pretty bad way. He'd been heavily sedated, unable to move or really do anything for himself. They would get answers from his mother as to why, once they got her to calm down, once they got her in interview. But Kidd could take a wild guess.

"Well done, Kidd." DCI Weaver had arrived on the scene with the response team. He hadn't expected him to show up, but given how high profile it was, he could hardly blame the old fella for wanting to be involved. He wanted to be able to report back to the Super as fast as possible, to give him the lowdown on what had happened, to finally tell him that it was over.

DI Kidd knew better.

"Never would have suspected her," Weaver said in his Scottish growl. "If I'd had my way—"

"The young lad would have been in the docks by now," Kidd interrupted.

"Yes," he said. "Thank you for finding the right man. Woman. Person."

Kidd shrugged. "It's the job, isn't it?" he said. "But this isn't over," he added.

DCI Weaver looked at him and blinked. "How so?"

"There's still one part that isn't closed," he said. "If you'll excuse me." DI Kidd pulled his coat tightly around himself and walked away.

"Detective Inspector," DCI Weaver barked. "Where the fuck do you think you're going?"

"To close the case, sir," he barked back. "Don't you worry, I won't be long."

DI Kidd stopped by one of the PCs and borrowed their handcuffs before he carried on walking. He rounded the corner, away from the secret house, away from Alexandra Kaye's residence, and walked up the imposing driveway to the Harper residence.

There were lights on inside, one upstairs in the bedroom, one down the hall in what he assumed would be the kitchen. His phone buzzed in his pocket. A text from DS Sanchez.

ZOE: Where the bloody hell have you got to? I thought you'd want to question her, wrap all this up?

He pocketed the phone. She could handle that. Now was the time for him to finish this off.
 He knocked on the door, unphased when Laura answered fully made up.

CHAPTER FORTY-SEVEN

"So that's what it was?" Laura Harper sat her breakfast bar, tears brimming in her eyes. She looked like she was about to breakdown, but she was holding herself together. This wasn't an act, wasn't a performance like the ones she'd conducted on her Instagram and Facebook posts. This was the most real he'd seen her and it was heartbreaking. "They were sleeping together the entire time? And she...she did this?"

DI Kidd nodded. "It wasn't a one-time thing, no," Kidd said. "And as or what happened to Sarah, that's not quite closed yet."

"I'm not surprised," she said, walking over to the fridge and pulling out a half-drunk bottle of wine. She offered some to Kidd but he raised his hand to decline. She poured it into a mug. She was coming undone right in front of his eyes. "He was never able to keep it in his pants." She took a heavy gulp. "You sure you don't want any?"

"No," Kidd said. "I'm fine, thank you."

"As for Alexandra, she can go fuck herself, we were supposed to be friends," she said. "And it turns out she was the one who…the one who…" She couldn't finish her sentence, replacing it with a heavy gulp of wine. "She's been arrested?"

"Yes."

"Charged?"

"Not yet," Kidd said. "But she's been arrested for," he checked his watch, "about fifteen minutes, so give it time. But I wanted to come round here straight away and tell you. Didn't want to leave you without all the information you needed and wanted."

"And deserved," she added. "You've been terrible, the lot of you. Can't get any updates. Can't get you to arrest the right person. Useless."

Kidd knew she was grieving but her comments stung a little bit. He hadn't worked quickly enough, she was right. If he'd been focused, maybe they would have caught Alexandra faster, maybe Sarah would still be alive, but to dwell on things like that would drive him insane. There were a lot of mistakes Kidd had made over the years, decisions that he regretted. This was no different. It was another in a long list. He didn't know how many more of them he could take.

She took another swig from her wine. "Is that what you came here for? To tell me that?"

DI Kidd shrugged. "I thought you'd want to know sooner rather than later," he replied. "Is Mr

Harper here? I'd love to be able to tell him too."

"No," she replied. "He said something about working—"

There was a noise upstairs.

"Is there someone else here, Mrs Harper?"

"No," she replied, looking to the ceiling. "Something must have fallen off the—"

"Kidd!"

Caitlyn!

There was a clatter down the stairs, the sound of someone running. DI Kidd moved as quickly as he could, watching Chris Harper bolt out the front door.

Jesus fucking Christ! he thought, turning his back on Mrs Harper and heading for the door. He didn't want to leave Caitlyn here, not if she was in some kind of trouble but he couldn't let Chris Harper get away. Not again.

He hurried up the stairs where he saw Caitlyn on the floor. Her face was bleeding, he'd hit her before he ran. There were marks around her neck.

"Are you alright?" he asked.

"Fine," she breathed, her pale face looking all the paler. "What are you still doing here? Go and get him."

"Caitlyn—"

"I'll call somebody, you need to go."

He pulled his phone out of his pocket and called DS Sanchez.

"Kidd? Where are you?"

"Have you left the house yet?" He hurried down the stairs and practically leapt through the open door and out onto the street. He could see Chris Harper off in the distance, running towards town.

"What are you talking about?"

"You need to come to the Harper residence now," he snapped. "Caitlyn, the FLO, she's been hurt. And bring some cuffs, we're bringing in Laura Harper."

He hung up and started running after Chris Harper. He was pretty far ahead now, but Kidd could still see him in the distance and he was determined not to lose him. He pumped his arms as hard as he could, his boots feeling like the wrong choice for a foot chase.

Chris sprinted across the road, cars skidding to a stop just long enough that Kidd could follow, waving an arm in apology as he went. The ground was still slippery from where it had been raining, but he wasn't about to let it slow him down.

There were people out, Chris having to dodge them as he ran, Kidd having to follow suit, yelling at people to move out of the way as he barrelling through the centre of town.

"Get out of the fucking way!" Kidd shouted at a group of school children who cackled at him as he ran past.

He hurried past the Bentall Centre, watching Chris make his way towards Kingston Bridge.

And Kidd knew where he was heading. He was going to try and hide and Kidd wasn't going to let that stand. No chance.

He sprinted after him, out of breath for sure, all the running that he'd been doing over the past six or seven months feeling like it had prepared him for absolutely nothing. He'd be able to pass the fitness test but it hadn't prepared him for sprinting after this fucker, that much was for sure.

He stopped in the middle of the bridge, watched as Chris Harper made his way down to the riverside. The same place that his daughter had been found. The same place he'd chased her to just a couple of days ago.

If he thinks he can hide from me, he's got another thing coming, Kidd thought as he jogged down towards the riverside. He picked up his phone and sent a quick text to Zoe so she knew where he was, so she could send some backup. He couldn't imagine this ending with Chris coming quietly. Given the fact that he'd done a runner, he pictured this ending with a bang rather than a whimper.

Taking a deep breath, DI Kidd turned down the road towards the riverside. The trees were encroaching from either side of the pathway, leaving space for the lights of the streetlamps to creep through. Even though they were right near town, just across the river, everything here was bathed in darkness, like someone had switched off the light in Kingston. It was enough to have DI Kidd on his toes, waiting for Chris to jump out at him.

He decided to get on the front foot.

"I know you're down here, Chris," DI Kidd yelled, making sure his voice was loud enough to carry through the trees, into the darkened corners where Chris could have been hiding. "I saw you come down here. There are police on the way. You can't keep running from this one."

There was no response. A breeze blew by, sending leaves and litter flying into the air, obstructing any sounds of movement. He looked around. He could be behind a tree, he could be down by the water, he could be anywhere.

"Don't make this any worse for yourself!" he shouted.

There was the sound of a horn honking on the bridge, enough to pull DI Kidd's focus away from the riverside. And that was all the opportunity that Chris Harper needed.

He bolted from behind a nearby tree, knocking into Ben and sending him sprawling across the ground, skidding into the mud. Without hesitation, Chris rushed him again, but Kidd could see him now, see where he was coming from, and countered. He rugby tackled the man, grabbing him around the waist so he hit the ground on his back, the wind knocked out of him.

He swung for Kidd, connecting with his

jaw, knocking him sideways. He hit him again, in the stomach this time and it was enough to get Kidd off of him. He rolled back, rolled away, putting some distance between them. Getting to his feet, his hand immediately found its way to his jaw. Fuck that had hurt.

Chris was panting, out of breath, his black jacket covered in mud, his face glistening with sweat. His eyebrows were knitted together in fury, in anger. At this point, he'd given up any hope of being innocent, of getting away with what had happened. At this point, he was willing to take DI Kidd down for finding him out. A last punishment.

"Why'd you do it?" Kidd asked across the space between them as Chris sat up. "What did you do it all for?"

"Fuck off!"

"I'm serious!" Kidd panted. "I didn't think it was you. You got me. You got me good. Why? That's all I want to know."

"It was Alexandra," he replied, climbing to his feet. "Sarah had been hiding at her house. She panicked, when she said she would tell everyone, thought the best thing to do would be to keep her there."

"Why?"

Chris shrugged. "Because Sarah knew about us. She'd seen pictures on my phone, she knew that we were seeing one another, she just didn't know who'd kidnapped her."

"So you drugged her?"

"Alex drugged her," he said, determined to not be blamed for everything. To show that getting rid of Sarah was a team effort. "She showed me after the school reunion, showed me that she had Sarah. Sarah woke up, got loose, and came downstairs. She saw us together and ran. When she fell I—"

"You could have called an ambulance," Kidd said.

"She was already—"

"She bled out, Chris," Kidd shouted. "But that wasn't enough for you. You needed to make sure the job was done right."

"Shut up!"

"You needed to cover your tracks, so you strangled her," he said. "You wrapped your hands around your own daughter's neck and you forced the life out of her. You didn't just let her die. You killed her."

"I didn't know what to do!" he yelled. "I panicked. I wanted to talk to her, to reason with her. But she ran away. If she'd have gotten away, then I would have gone down for her kidnapping."

"Instead, you're going to go down for her murder," Kidd said. "Well done. It's a much longer sentence. Will really give you some time to think about what you've done."

Chris didn't hesitate a second longer, launching himself at Kidd. Ben dodged the first swing, managing to punch Chris square on the nose, but it wasn't enough to deter him. Chris countered, punching Kidd hard across the face, hard enough that Ben stumbled over his own feet and onto the ground by the water.

Chris kicked Kidd's stomach, once, twice, a third time.

Kidd coughed, blood splattering the rocks.

Chris straddled Kidd, punching him in the face over and over and over until the world started to swim in front of Kidd's eyes. He could see blue lights flashing in his periphery. He just needed to hold on long enough for them to get here, for them to realise where he was.

The punching was relentless, Kidd unable to block every single one, unable to stop his face from being battered. And then there was a hand around his neck. Squeezing.

The world was already fading away, and Kidd knew he wouldn't have long to do something. He swung an arm wildly, hitting Chris in the side of the head, once, twice, a third time. Refusing to let go of him, but Chris' grip was loosening. Enough that Kidd could get a breath full of air into his lungs.

With what strength he had left, DI Kidd ripped Chris' hands from his throat and smacked him hard across the face. It was enough. Kidd knew it would be his only opportunity.

With great effort, he pushed Chris Harper

off of him and punched him once more, sending him tumbling onto the mud. A police car on blues drove down the road towards the riverside, headlights blazing, lighting up the area. In its light, Kidd could see that Chris Harper was in no fit state to get up.

A couple of uniformed officers got out of the car, quickly followed by DS Sanchez, concern painting her face when she caught sight of Kidd. The uniformed officers cuffed Chris Harper, dragging him over to the car as DI Kidd fell to his knees and the world faded to black.

CHAPTER FORTY-EIGHT

There was a nearby beeping sound as Benjamin Kidd awoke, the sound of air being pumped, of light footsteps click-clacking across the floor, of voices that he didn't recognise breaking through the quiet. He came around slowly, the brightness of the lights on the ward assaulting his eyes as he opened them.

The smell of the place was all too familiar. He'd spent one too many nights in hospital wards, whether that had been with a colleague, a victim, or even a suspect. But today it was his turn to be checked out, to be fixed up, and he felt like a wreck.

"Well, well, well." Zoe's voice was a welcome one. She appeared by his bedside as if by magic with a steaming Styrofoam cup, tea so weak it wouldn't be able to defend itself, nearly overflowing the rim. "Sleeping Beauty has finally awoken from her slumber." She took a quick sip of the drink and winced. "Want one?"

"Fuck no," Kidd said, though his throat hurt. He needed something. He was about to reach for the water on the bedside table when Zoe made a noise that stopped him. "What?"

"You probably shouldn't be moving about like that," she said, putting her tea down and marching around to the other side of the bed to pour him a glass. "You've almost had your fucking head caved in, reaching for a glass of water is probably enough to send you unconscious again."

"How long was I out?" Kidd asked, aware of how much of a cliché it was.

She rolled her eyes. "Drama queen, it is literally the next day," she replied. "You collapsed at the side of the river, I panicked, so did the PCs who picked up Harper, we called an ambulance and got you here. They said you were concussed. It's a fucking miracle you've even woken up." She handed him the glass of water.

"Did we—?"

"Get him?" she interrupted. "Yes, could you stop working for a second?"

"No," he snapped. "Tell me what happened. I need to know."

"You're going to kill yourself working all the time, you know?"

He was very much aware. But it was not working all the time that had cost him Sarah Harper's life, stopped him from managing to figure it all out a little bit quicker. It wasn't a thought he wanted to dwell on, but it was one he was having.

Zoe sighed and returned to the other side of the bed, sitting in the chair where Kidd assumed she'd spent her time waiting for him to wake up. She was his friend, he had expected her to be here when he woke up, but he hoped she wasn't keeping vigil at his bedside.

"We got Alexandra Kaye, got a full confession out of her actually," Zoe said. "The guilt got the better of her I think. And the sudden realisation that she was about to kill her own son, or at least have Chris kill him. The details of that are still a little fuzzy."

"Are they blaming each other?"

"Absolutely," she said. "One says the other was going to do it, trying to get away with a shorter sentence probably."

"Sounds about right."

"They were trying to frame Norman, it turns out," Zoe said. "The death of Sarah Harper, while tragic, was an accident. He chased her through town and she fell."

"He strangled her."

"She might have already been dead."

"But we'll never know," Kidd said, taking another sip of water. He moved to sit up in bed and Zoe made another noise. "Stop it, Sanchez, I've got to sit up or I'll spill my water."

"Be careful."

"If he hadn't have strangled her and called

an ambulance maybe she'd be okay," he said. "He killed her for the sake of his secret. To keep everything quiet about his relationship. He chose Alexandra Kaye over his daughter and I want him to rot for it."

DS Sanchez shrugged. "Fair enough."

"Carry on," he said, already sick of the mollycoddling. It really wasn't Zoe's usual style. Maybe the state of him at the riverside had scared her, it was hard to say.

"They tried to frame him because they thought it was the only way they could get out of it," Zoe said eventually. "But Caleb figured it out. He didn't go to his grandparents' house after he left us, he came here. And when he got here he realised his mum wasn't working. When he got home, there she was with Chris and he put two and two together I think. Or they thought he did. It gets a little fuzzy around that point."

"So they locked him up in that house?"

Zoe nodded. "That's where they'd kept Sarah. She'd been there the whole time and we had no idea. They sedated her, tied her up, just like they'd done with Caleb." She shook her head. "When we search Alex's house we'll probably find receipts for some kind of heavy sedative."

"Or evidence she stole it from here."

"Possibly," Zoe said. "What got you there?"

"Huh?"

"We were in the interview with Norman and suddenly it clicked in your head," she said. "What happened?"

"I finally put it together," Kidd said. "The 'D' that Sarah had been talking about on her website was her dad. It was his secrets she was sick of keeping, not Dexter's, his yelling that was frustrating her. And it was the mention of the houses. Suddenly, it all fell into place. I just wish I'd gotten there sooner."

Zoe nodded. "It makes it hard to have faith in humanity when you do this job, doesn't it?"

"How so?"

"You constantly see the worst of people," she said, taking a sip of her tea, wincing again, and putting it down. It really must have been as awful as it looked. "And even when you think you've seen people being utterly despicable, someone else comes along and is like, 'I can do worse than that, watch me lock up my own daughter and then strangle her at a riverside.'" She took another sip. "Fucking hell, this is dire."

"The tea or the world?"

"Horrible combination," she said with a wink. "I don't know if I want to live in a world this bad, with tea this bad."

"There will always be bad tea, Zoe," Kidd said. "We just have to find the better cups."

"You really did get your head hit quite hard, didn't you?" she said with a smile, which made Kidd laugh. He winced a little at the pain as he did but it was worth it.

"What about Laura?" he asked.

"That's a little more complicated," Zoe said.

"How so?"

Zoe looked down at her cup of tea and shook her head. "She got off."

"What?"

Zoe shrugged. "She claimed not to know anything about it," Zoe said. "Didn't know that he was in the house, or that he had Caitlyn upstairs, didn't know that he had anything to do with what happened with Sarah, didn't know a damn thing."

"And they bought it?"

Zoe shook her head. "Weaver didn't. I didn't. Caitlyn definitely fucking didn't. The team didn't, based on what you told them. DC Powell was livid. Never seen him show any emotion apart from panic so to have him actually react to something was exciting."

"How is Caitlyn?"

"Shaken, but okay," Zoe replied. "But she thinks that Laura was in on it too. We've got all the phones for evidence, going to download the messages and see what we can come up with but —"

"She's smarter than that," Kidd said. "If she wants to get away with it, she'll get away with it. Everything will have been done verbally if at all." He sighed and took another sip of water.

Never in his life had he enjoyed a glass of water so much. He downed the rest of it and leaned over to pour another. His body ached, but it was his face that hurt more than anything else. Chris Harper had really done a number on him.

"Anything else to report?" Kidd asked as the door to the ward opened. He looked to see John McAdams walking in, looking a little bit lost. He was carrying a bunch of flowers and had a little brown paper bag in his other hand. He scanned the room, looking from bed to bed until he clocked Benjamin, a smile spreading across his face.

"Just this guy," she said.

"What about him?"

"He called the station this morning because he'd shown up at your house, apparently you were meant to have a date—"

"Shit."

"He got worried something had happened and when you weren't answering your phone, he spoke to Diane."

"Diane!"

"She's a very lovely woman," John said as he got to the foot of Ben's bed. He smiled at him, his eyebrows knitted together in concern. Kidd didn't want to know how banged up his face looked, but based on the way that John was looking at him, all puppy dog eyes and worry, he imagined it didn't look good. Hey, at least he still wanted to look at him. "She told me that you'd been taken into hospital. I didn't know if I should come."

"I told him it was the right thing to do," Zoe said. "Which it was, right?"

"Oh God, absolutely," Kidd said. He smiled at John. "Are those for me?"

"I know we've not done gifts or anything like that yet, but flowers felt like the right thing," he said seeming so unsure of himself. It wasn't exactly a romantic milestone that he was coming to visit Ben in hospital after he'd had his head kicked in, but there was something romantic in the fact that he was there at all.

"No, it's great," Kidd said. "I'm sure the nurse can get a vase or—"

"I'll go check," Zoe said.

"Zoe, you don't have to—" John began.

"No, no, you two talk," she said, a knowing smile on her face. "I'll find a vase and then head back to the station. There's paperwork to do, all sorts. I can keep myself plenty busy, I'm sure."

She hopped up from her chair and walked towards the door, making suggestive faces at Kidd as she left. They were enough to bring some colour to his cheeks, colour that he hoped John wouldn't notice being surrounded by all the cuts and bruises.

John put the flowers down on the end of the bed and sat down in the chair Zoe had been sitting in. He didn't take his eyes off Kidd once he sat down.

"You're out of your mind in this job, you know that?" John said.

"Oh, I know," he replied. "This is an occupational hazard."

"Christ, the worst that could happen to me is getting a fucking paper cut, you had someone punching you," John said. "I've not taken a punch since high school."

"Count yourself lucky," Kidd said. "I don't recommend it."

John reached over and took hold of Ben's hand as it rested on top of the blanket. Kidd flinched at first. He wasn't used to it, the affection, at least not so publicly. He looked at the other beds, wondering if anyone was watching, but they weren't. They were focused on their own lives. So he relaxed into it, squeezing John's hand a little tighter and let out a heavy breath.

"You must be exhausted," John said. "I can go if you want. I don't want to disturb you."

"You're not disturbing me," Kidd said with a lazy smile. "I don't want you to go anywhere at all."

CHAPTER FORTY-NINE

Once the Doctors had established that Kidd hadn't suffered any major head trauma—something that Zoe disputed, albeit jokingly—he was discharged and sent home with strict orders from DCI Weaver not to come to work until he was a hundred percent better. He'd barely set foot in the door of his house before Zoe texted him to say there was a pool on how long it would take for him to come back, and she had six days, so if he could wait that long, she could really use the money.

John stayed over for a couple of days, making sure that Kidd was alright and not overexerting himself. On the second day, he'd tried to go for a run, and John had all but barricaded the door to stop him from going.

"If you hurt yourself, it's on my watch, and I don't think Zoe will be all that forgiving," he had said as he put his body between Kidd and the door. It was sweet that he was looking after him like that, not that it was really needed. He'd suffered worse in his life. It was some cuts and bruises to his face, and they were fading pretty quickly.

His arm still ached a little from where Alexandra Kaye had whacked him with that wooden board, and if he moved wrong the bruise on his stomach where Chris Harper had hit him sent a shock of pain through him, but he was getting better, steadily. As the days passed, he felt more like himself and looked less like Quasimodo when he looked in the mirror.

He was going to head back into work tomorrow, making it a full six days since he'd last been in the office, earning Zoe her sweepstakes money and possibly him a pint, if he played his cards right. John had spent a lot of time at Kidd's house over the past few days, working from his kitchen table or heading home in the afternoons to have zoom meetings, but it wasn't necessary.

"You can go home," Kidd said on Wednesday morning. "I know you have work to do, I won't be offended. All I'm going to be doing is watching TV and reading."

"You're not going to go running?"

"I'm not going to go running," he said with a laugh. "I might take a walk, but it will be a slow walk, glacial. So slow the old guy from next door could beat me."

John smiled and left Kidd to his own devices for the day.

He sat down with some scrambled eggs on toast and switched on some morning TV. He'd gotten into something of a routine, one he really hoped he'd easily lose once it came time to go back to work. It was surprisingly addictive once you got used to the fact that everything after BBC Breakfast was pretty much garbage.

But he hadn't been expecting the next guest. He stopped eating mid-mouthful.

Laura Harper walked out onto the set, all smiles, her hair freshly coiffed, her smile as pearly white as it had been in all of those Instagram and Facebook videos he'd been subjected to. She took a seat with the hosts and Kidd could hardly believe what he was hearing.

"It's been a tough time, yeah," she said, brushing her hair out of her face. "But I'm starting afresh, starting anew without my husband. My followers know I've been on such a journey through all this. It has changed me. I lost my...I lost my daughter," she wiped her eyes, her voice cracking a little, but Kidd could see there wasn't a tear in sight. "And I thought it would break me. But I galvanised myself. I got myself back out there, I used my following to help find her, and even though it ended tragically, with my fans by my side, I know I'll be okay."

The hosts praised her, talking about what an inspiration she was and taking it all in like she really truly believed it. Kidd felt sick as he watched Laura smiling away on morning television. He was sure that she was only smiling because she'd gotten away with it.

She started talking about how her followers had helped her reach new heights and she was working on a book about her life and freeing herself from the toxicity of her soon-to-be ex-husband, which was enough to make Kidd change the channel.

He picked up his phone with the intention of messaging Zoe about what he'd seen but saw there was already a message there waiting for him. From Andrea Peyton.

His breath caught in his chest. It had only been a week or so ago that he'd decided to let it all go, to put his past behind him, and leave Craig Peyton in it. He could see there was an attachment to the message. Surely she'd not found something else.

His curiosity got the better of him and he opened the message.

Hello Ben,

I hope you're doing well. I'm sure you weren't expecting to hear from me so soon, but I have developments and I couldn't wait to share them with you. The attached photo is from two months ago. You might recognise the place. You holidayed there together I think. Southeast coast I believe.

Anyway, he's looking well, isn't he?

Speak soon.

Andrea

And there he was. He really did look well, exactly the same as Ben remembered him. Maybe a few more creases on the forehead, a crinkle or two more around the eyes, but it was definitely him. It was another CCTV shot, but it must have been a good system because the quality was impeccable.

He was sitting in a cafe that Kidd recognised, one that was in Essex, one they had been to together when they'd stayed in a caravan by the sea early on in their relationship. He didn't know what to do, but his heart was afire as he looked at the photo, and the certainty that he was still out there.

Craig might not want to be found but Kidd could feel himself making a silent vow that he would find him, and he would find out what happened to him. He had to. Now that he'd seen him again, now that he knew where he'd been, he needed to.

He fired a reply to Andrea, one with his phone number in it so they could chat properly, maybe get together and make a plan. He was going to find Craig. He was going to find out why he'd left. And if he was in trouble, even if it killed him, Benjamin Kidd would save him.

DI BENJAMIN KIDD
WILL RETURN IN

YOUR BEST SHOT

Coming June 2021

ACKNOWLEDGEMENTS

It feels very strange to be doing this again so soon after having written the acknowledgements for book one, but here we are. Once again I need to thank the people in the group who have helped to make this possible. The advice, the insight, these books would not exist without you.

Thank you to my wonderful editor Hanna for all of your edits and insight on this one. So many very good spots that I didn't find myself and so many great suggestions on how to fix the issues. You are brilliant. And thanks again goes to Meg for this stunning cover!

To my marvellous partner who has listened to me bellyache about this one more than its predecessor. You are a gem. Truly.

And to all of you who have read and enjoyed the first book, and who have joined me and Benjamin Kidd for another adventure, I appreciate you so much. If you enjoyed it, feel free to leave a review, it really helps me out. Hopefully I will see you for the next one. Until then...

GS

ABOUT THE AUTHOR

GS Rhodes has been writing for as long as he can remember, scribbling stories on spare bits of paper and hoping to one day share those stories with the world. The DI Benjamin Kidd series is GS Rhodes first foray into crime writing, combining a love of where he has lived for a lot of his life with his love of a good mystery. For more information and updates on GS Rhodes, you can follow him on Twitter and Instagram @GS_Rhodes or on Facebook @GSRhodesAuthor. Or, to stay updated with blog posts and more, visit www.gsrhodes.co.uk

Printed in Great Britain
by Amazon